Dutch justice

This is a true story: one of the last great spy stories to come out of the Second World War. The dramatic adventures in this book have been lightly fictionalized and the names of certain people changed to avoid embarrassment to them, but the adventures themselves are true, and happened to a young man called Richard Sanders, son of an English father and a Dutch mother, who arrived in Amsterdam from Java not long before the outbreak of War.

The bizarre and tragic first part of the story all happened to young Sanders – called Alex in the book – before his eighteenth birthday: his recruitment in a lowly capacity into the ranks of the British Secret Service operating in pre-War Holland, his first rapturous encounter with love, and terrifying experience of murder and imprisonment.

In such English expressions as 'Dutch courage' and 'Dutch treat', the word 'Dutch' has a derogatory meaning. So it is with the title of this book, where 'Dutch' signifies not only the country involved, but also implies that there was something very wrong with the 'justice' meted out to Alex.

The gripping second part of the story sees Alex back in Nazi-occupied Amsterdam on an undercover mission that has only the remotest chance of succeeding – and bent on administering some justice of his own . . . It is as breathtaking and extraordinary a tale as any spy thriller, but with the added twist that, however unbelievable the events appear, *Dutch justice* tells nothing but those events exactly as they happened.

This is a true story. The events depicted in this book are true. However, it has been told in the form of a novel and the names of certain persons, places and dates have been changed to avoid identification of people still living.

1

Alex knew he was being watched. His desire to be inconspicuous had made him more conspicuous. He had isolated himself in a corner near an open window. He was British, in the British Legation, at the reception for the King's official birthday, yet he felt an outsider.

He knew no one and, although he spoke excellent English, it was evident that his mother tongue was Dutch. He had tried to mingle but failed. He had hovered and heard the conversations. Everywhere in the room the talk was the same, the imminence of war. To a seventeen-year-old, the talk of war both thrilled and chilled. He had wanted to burst into one of the conversations but hadn't the confidence. Now the tall, dark-haired man, with the military bearing, the thin moustache and face of a film star, was staring straight at him.

'You look lost. A young fellow like you shouldn't be lost.'

The man came towards Alex and thrust out a hand. 'Stevens. Major Stevens.' There was reassurance in the handshake, warmth in the dark eyes. Alex's sense of isolation melted. He forgot that a moment ago he had been hiding. Now all he wanted was to respond.

'Alex Richards.'

Stevens nodded. 'I know. You're the young fellow just back from Java. Your father died out there. He was English. Your mother's Dutch. She brought you back to Holland.'

Alex showed his surprise and concern. He was a private person. He had never liked people knowing much about him. Now he had just listened to a dossier on himself.

Stevens saw the look on Alex's face and laughed. 'Don't look so surprised. I'm the Passport Control Officer. Not one poor little English sparrow falls to earth here in Holland without the Passport Control Officer knowing.'

Alex found the words strange, almost ominous. He felt

7

disconcerted. It was as if the man was playing a game with him.

Stevens laughed a second time, rubbed his chin but never took his eyes off Alex. The tall, slim, good-looking young man, whose skin was still tanned from the tropical sun, looked older than seventeen. His features were already sharp, his blue eyes clear. Stevens liked what he saw.

'Where do you live?'

'In Amsterdam.'

'With your mother?'

Alex nodded.

'Are you at school? Have you a job?'

'I'm at the Technical High School at Delft.'

Stevens smiled. The information seemed of particular interest. 'So every day you take the train from Amsterdam to Delft.'

'It's not bad. It only takes an hour.'

Alex watched the older man. He had wanted to talk to someone from the moment he had entered the room. Now he wasn't at all sure that he was talking to the right person. The questions had not been mere pleasantries. Stevens' friendliness concealed something.

'There's someone I want you to meet,' said Stevens abruptly. 'Don't move. Don't move an inch. I'll be right back.'

Stevens disappeared. Alex was again on his own. He stared up at the ornate cornice. Stevens' knowledge, questioning and abrupt departure had upset him more than he would have expected. He felt a strange disquiet. Then he told himself that it was all his own imagination. Major Stevens was exactly what he appeared to be: a typical English officer who happened to have taken a liking to him. He should be flattered not worried. Alex told himself all that but he was not convinced.

Stevens reappeared with a heavily built, very English-looking man sporting a monocle. Stevens introduced the man as Captain Best. Alex shook hands and felt the blood squeezed from his fingers.

'You're not by any chance Henry Richards' son?' boomed Best.

Again Alex felt the sinking feeling. Too many knew too much about him. He could only nod and mutter, 'Henry Richards was my father . . .'

Best beamed. 'I knew your father before he went out east. Your mother too. I went to their wedding. How is your mother?'

'Considering everything, fine, sir. Fine.'

Best stroked his moustache. The muscles of his eyebrows and cheeks gripped his monocle tighter. His pink complexion turned ruddier. 'You've certainly picked a damned bad time to come back to Holland and study. Europe's not going to be the nicest place by the autumn.'

'If war does break out,' said Alex firmly, 'I shall go to England and join the RAF.'

'Ah, a young man eager to do his bit,' cried Best. 'A young man with no love of Hitler and the Nazis. That's what I like to see.'

Alex hadn't thought of Hitler or the Nazis. He had merely thought of England. England versus Germany. But Best was evidently pleased by the younger man's remark. He glanced at Stevens. There was a long silence. Although he was used to the heat, Alex found the room oppressive. He took out his handkerchief and dabbed his brow. It was Best who broke the silence.

'I'd like to meet your mother again. It would be nice to have a chat about old times. That is what we elderly people like. Talking about the past. I have your address in Amsterdam. Why don't I come and see you?' Best opened his diary and scanned the pages. 'Let me see . . . What about tomorrow at three?'

'Tomorrow?'

'Why not? The sooner the better. Make up for all those lost years.'

Alex half shook his head. He was amazed at the request. It was all happening so quickly. The two officers were taking him over. There was a moment of panic. He was in a dream, no longer in control of even himself. Best's self-invitation was not a social one. Alex's mother and the memory of a wedding twenty years ago were not the true reason for the visit. Then

Best was repeating his request: 'Tomorrow afternoon at three. And as it's Saturday you won't be at Delft.'

Against his will, Alex found himself nodding.

In the train home Alex brooded. He was excited but disturbed. It was disquieting to be the centre of attention and not know why. He sat looking out of the window at the flat, green fields, the clumps of trees that could hardly be called woods and the endless market gardens. He suddenly realized just how one-way the conversation with Stevens and Best had been. Everything had been *to* the Passport Control Officer and his colleague. That was, if Stevens really was the Passport Control Officer. Somehow Alex visualized that post being held by a lesser, less flamboyant character. Nevertheless, the mystery of the two men had aroused him. He was excited, sufficiently exhilarated that after he had reached Amsterdam and taken the tram to the Daniel Willinkplein, he leapt from the vehicle before it stopped, raced across the road and, without waiting for the lift, ran up the seven flights of stairs to his mother's flat.

'Captain Best, mother, *Captain Best!* A big man with a monocle and a long, brushed-up moustache. You *must* remember him. Once seen never forgotten.'

Alex's mother leaned back on the couch, held her forehead but could not remember a Captain Best. 'It was a long time ago. People change.'

'Your wedding photos! He was at your wedding!'

They went into the spare room and rummaged through an old trunk. In a faded, sepia photo Alex spotted Best. Twenty years ago Best had had no monocle, only a very small moustache and his build had been the slight build of a young man. But there was no doubt that the man in the photo was the man in the Legation.

Mrs Richards remembered. 'Best. Ah, Captain Best. Now I remember him. He had a very un-English Christian name. Sigismund. More German than English.' She sighed and added, 'But he was a handsome man. A most gallant figure.'

'But what was he? What do you know about him?'

Mrs Richards knew nothing about Captain Sigismund Best, only that he had been exceedingly popular with the brides-maids.

For Alex, three o'clock the next afternoon seemed an age away.

Best's flamboyancy was not confined to his person. He drove a large, deep-throated, white Buick. Alex saw it roar into the square. He went down in the lift and accompanied Best up to the flat. To Alex's mother, Best displayed all his old gallantry. It was as if time had not ravaged, nor waistbands expanded. Best joked about their joint indulgence in *rijsttafels* and talked about the old days in Holland. He learned of her husband's death from malaria. When the talk got thin he eulogized on the view from the window and glanced at Alex. When he tapped his fingers upon his knee, Mrs Richards got up and took out the tea things.

Best lit a cigar and went to the window. Beneath them the waters of the Amstel rippled in the afternoon sun. The leaves of the trees that lined the Amstellaan shimmered in the heat. A barge passed slowly under the Berlage Brug, its shadow dark and foreboding. Beyond the Amstel station were the fields, green all the way to Utrecht. In his years in Holland, Best had grown fond of the Dutch and their country. He had come to love the cities. When war came he prayed that this country would not be involved.

'So every weekday you go from Amsterdam to Delft by train. In doing so you pass through The Hague.'

'That is so, sir,' said Alex. 'I told Major Stevens.'

'There'll be war in three months,' said Best without turning his head. 'Wars always wait for the harvest.'

Alex felt his heartbeat quicken. 'You really believe there will be war?'

'No doubt, no doubt whatsoever. The Hun has been pre-paring for it for years.' Best turned his head and stared into Alex's face. 'You seem keen to do your bit. You talked about joining the RAF. At the moment, of course, you're too young.' He stopped and scratched the side of his face. After a while he said, 'You don't necessarily have to wait for the shooting war.'

Alex said nothing.

'In a way the war's already here. Like the poor, it's always with us.' Best was gazing out of the window again.

'I don't understand,' said Alex, shaking his head.

'It's all very simple really,' said Best quietly. 'There's no reason why you shouldn't start doing your bit right now.'

Alex looked puzzled but his heart was beating even faster. 'Do my bit now?'

Best nodded. 'If you remain in Holland you could be of considerable help to us here.'

Alex's mouth was dry, he was conscious of his own breathing. For a moment there was silence, then very quietly Best said, 'Wars aren't always won on the battlefield, you know. Nor on the playing fields of Eton.'

'Go on,' said Alex, struggling to control his excitement.

Best glanced towards the kitchen door. It was shut. When he spoke he addressed the glass of the window. 'We need a courier between Amsterdam and The Hague . . .'

'We?'

'Major Stevens and myself.'

'I thought Major Stevens was the Passport Control Officer?'

Best ignored the remark. 'Once a week an envelope has to be picked up from a house in Amsterdam and delivered to The Hague. Making the journey every day as a matter of course, you are in an ideal position to help us. Your movements would cause no concern.' He glanced at Alex. 'You simply collect the envelope on Thursday evenings and on Friday take it with you on the train. You open the window of your compartment at The Hague and hand the envelope to Major Stevens who will be on the platform waiting.'

Alex's surprise at the task was tempered with anger. Once again, so much of his future seemed to have been decided.

'You talk as if I'd agreed . . .'

Again Best ignored Alex's remark. 'Do you think you could do that?'

Best's way of talking down to him and the apparent meanness of the task upset Alex. 'Do it? Of course, anyone could do it. If that's all you want?'

The moment he had spoken Alex realized that his words had committed him. His anger at being frogmarched by the aristocratic-looking officer with the monocle had been overcome by his curiosity and desire to do what Best wanted. He had even sounded disappointed at the prospect of being a mere postman. He was sure he was now wearing a crestfallen rather than angry air.

'It isn't a matter of *anyone*. It isn't at all a matter of anyone. Far from it. We need a person of absolute integrity.'

'An envelope . . .' said Alex, almost contemptuously, while reconsidering the matter.

Best smiled. 'Yes, just a brown envelope. But you must know the old adage, "For the want of a nail the kingdom was lost"?'

Alex gave Best a glance. 'Are you saying . . . ?'

'Oh, yes. The contents of that weekly envelope are extremely important.'

'I just pick up the envelope and give it to Major Stevens . . .'

'You collect the envelope and you look after it. You must never ever lose an envelope. If one single envelope should fall into the wrong hands, the results could be devastating. Quite devastating. And you give the envelope only to Major Stevens and to no one else.'

As one mystery was revealed, another took its place. Alex knew that it was pointless to ask what was in the envelopes. He just accepted the excitement and felt none of the concern.

'Where do I pick up these envelopes?'

Best hesitated and again glanced towards the kitchen door. At last he said, 'You are to collect them from a young woman who lives in a part of Amsterdam which you are really too young to be visiting. And one that your mother would throw me out of the house for mentioning.'

'You mean the Red Light district? The Walletjes? The streets east of Dam Street?'

Best grunted, readjusted his monocle then carefully wrote a name and address on a piece of paper. 'Memorize this then destroy it.'

Alex took the paper and stared at the words 'R. Blum' and a number at the Achterburgwal. 'Is the woman a prostitute?'

13

Best shrugged. 'I'm saying no more. You will meet her next Thursday.'

Best made a note of the train that Alex caught every morning. He asked which coach he usually travelled in. Satisfied with the details, he put his hand on Alex's arm. 'Remember, I came here just to see your mother. To renew an old acquaintance-ship. What you will be doing you will tell no one.' Again Best glanced towards the kitchen door. 'Understand? *No one.*'

Alex ran his tongue over his lips. He had never had a secret from his mother in his life.

'You've grown up, Alex,' said Best quietly. 'You've grown up.'

Alex's mother made only superficial reference to Best's visit and asked no questions. She too knew that Best had not come to see her, but to see her son. She simply accepted that that afternoon, Alex had reached manhood. Alex was relieved that while knowing nothing, his mother had accepted everything.

'Captain Best could still charm bridesmaids,' said Mrs Richards, a little sadly.

Alex smiled. Best could do more than that.

It was early in the evening. But for two sailors standing on a bridge staring down into the water, the streets to the east of Dam Street were empty. It was Alex's first visit to the area. He found the Achterburgwal without difficulty. Two narrow, cobbled streets sandwiched a wide canal. The old houses on either side were like so many others in this part of the city: façades of small, dark bricks and large, white-painted, framed windows. Here, however, the houses had even larger windows. Posed in those windows on chairs, couches and *chaises-longues*, sometimes framed by flowers, were the women, of all ages and in various stages of undress.

They were like sculpture but their eyes were alive. The slightest sign of interest, a flicker of the eyebrow, a half-smile, and the door was opened and the price quoted. Alex was not shocked. He had lived in the Dutch East Indies where prostitution was a way out of starvation. This was just a different form of market-place.

Alex found the number. There were two doors. He saw 'R. Blum', the name he had memorized, and pressed the bell. The door to the ground-floor flat opened. A well-built woman wearing only her underclothes looked him up and down with a lewd smile.

'*Ben je niet een beetje te jong?*' The woman's voice was harsh and flat.

Alex blushed and quickly shook his head. He heard a buzz from the other door and pushed his way inside. He climbed three flights of narrow stairs and came to a small landing. The light was not good. It took Alex a moment to see the figure in front of him. He had expected another blowzy woman like the one in the ground-floor flat. The one standing on the landing was different. She was tall, thin and elegant and had long, black hair. She was wearing a white dress with a blue scarf knotted casually around her neck.

Alex stood with his mouth open. He was so bewildered that when he spoke he spoke in English. 'I'm looking for Miss Blum.'

'I am Rachel Blum.' The soft, cultured voice confused Alex even more.

'Are you sure?'

'Of course I'm sure. Who are you?'

'I'm Alex Richards.' Alex lowered his voice. 'I've been sent by Major Stevens to collect some envelopes.'

The woman waved him into a small living room, sparsely furnished. Although what furniture there was was bright and cheerful, there was a shortage of small items, personal things like photographs and ornaments. It seemed that the woman had moved in quite recently and had yet to make herself at home.

She told Alex to sit and he instantly sat. She sat opposite him. He found himself looking at her legs. They were long and slender. He raised his head and saw her dark eyes now full of worry, her long face with its smooth skin. She had a fine, noble face with a clear bone structure. She sat without speaking, never taking her eyes from Alex's face. They sat like that for several minutes. All Alex could see was her beauty.

'Please describe Major Stevens.'

Alex did his best but found it difficult. He had only seen Stevens once, and Stevens had that film-star handsomeness, a gentleness of features so hard to describe.

When Alex finished, Rachel was evidently satisfied. She got up, went into the next room and returned with a large envelope which she handed to Alex. There was neither a name nor an address upon the envelope. Alex sat with it on his lap. He wanted to ask a hundred questions but was too tongue-tied. When he had finished staring at the envelope he stared at Rachel.

Her coolness and grace amazed him. There was something almost statuesque about her. He was young and impressionable. He had come from the Colonies. Here was a woman of refinement and sophistication. He imagined her in what he thought a smart Parisian restaurant must be like. Or coming down the steps of the Ritz. Or upon a plinth. He could certainly not imagine her in the heat, dust and bustle of a Batavian street. He shifted his gaze from her face and hair back to her body and legs. He was suddenly conscious of his own staring and that it was rude, but excused himself. He was mesmerized.

'Is there anything else?'

Her voice came from far away. Alex looked at his watch. He wanted to stay, but realized that by just sitting and gazing he was making a fool of himself. He got up. As he was being shown out of the door he managed to say, 'I look forward to seeing you next week.'

He thought she was smiling as she shut the door, but he couldn't be sure.

Alex hurried home just as he had after meeting Stevens and Best. This time the excitement was different. It was warmer yet mixed with pain. He had already decided that, although she lived in the Red Light district, Rachel was not a prostitute. She could not possibly be one. She was Jewish, probably a refugee. Although she was in her late twenties, ten years older than himself, age was of no concern. Alex had no doubt he was in love. That thought and the memory of the day kept him awake all night.

The next day Alex caught his usual train to Delft. At The Hague, Stevens was waiting on the platform. Alex opened the window of the compartment. Stevens came casually towards him and took the envelope.

'Everything all right? No problems?'

'Everything was fine, sir.'

'See you next week.'

The Major gave a friendly wave and walked away. The next stop was Delft. At Delft Alex got out and walked slowly to the Technical School. He walked slowly to suppress his own excitement. Had he let himself go, he would have leapt into the air. He was a courier. Of what, he did not know, except that the contents of the envelope must be of profound importance. He supposed he was almost a spy, a secret agent. But it wasn't just the envelope that had made his new life so exciting. It was the tall, dark-haired Jewish woman. Rachel.

2

At his desk in the Gestapo building in the Prinz-Albrecht-Strasse, SS-Hauptsturmführer Joseph Schreieder loosened his tie, ran his thick fingers through his dark hair and sighed. The day was warm. Schreieder had a dozen more reports to get through before lunch. Not that Schreieder disliked reading reports. He enjoyed them immensely. His problem was that being the archetypal Gestapo policeman, hard-working, fiercely loyal to his organization, short on imagination but meticulous on detail, he never scanned a report but read every word. His toothcomb mind sought anomalies, inconsistencies, any event casually reported yet, to Schreieder's paranoiac brain, full of menace to the Third Reich. All that took time. And it seemed to Schreieder that in his office he never had time.

Automatically he opened the next report. It was from a factory near Dortmund. The report was full of minutiae which

Schreieder struggled conscientiously to absorb. One sentence, however, almost written as an afterthought, did catch his attention. He was so alerted, he read the sentence three times. A blueprint had disappeared from a safe one night and then been 'found'. No action had been taken by the two local Gestapo men at the factory, the matter had merely been reported.

Schreieder glanced at the heading of the report. It was from the Henschel factory. Henschel made armaments. Schreieder's suspicions deepened. How could a blueprint disappear and then be 'found'? Blueprints didn't naturally disappear, it wasn't their nature. In spite of the matter-of-fact tone of the report, Schreieder's interest grew. The more he thought about the event the more bizarre and promising it became. Schreieder grew excited. He shouted for the clerk, Unterscharführer Hausser. When Hausser entered the office, Schreieder waved the report.

'You read about the missing blueprints, Hausser?'

'Yes, Herr Hauptsturmführer. I read about them and knowing you would want more information I have made certain enquiries . . .'

The Unterscharführer stopped.

'Go on, man, go on!'

'The particular factory manufactures tanks. At the moment it is the Panzerkampfwagen Mark III. However, there is a small section devoted to future developments. It was from this section that the blueprint was lost and afterwards found.'

'What exactly is the nature of this particular future development?'

'A new tank, Herr Hauptsturmführer. The prototype has still to be tested. It will be the Mark IV and carry a new, long, 75 mm anti-tank gun.'

Schreieder looked thoughtful. After a moment he said, 'And with this gun the Mark IV will be the king of the battlefield?'

'Completely, Herr Hauptsturmführer. There is no British, French or Russian tank that it cannot destroy.'

'So it is a very important weapon. We might say a vital weapon.'

'One of the most important.'

'And what exactly do you know of the disappearance of this particular blueprint and the subsequent "finding"?'

'The night shift foreman had a problem. He needed a particular drawing. The blueprints are kept in the works manager's safe. Both the day shift foreman and the night shift foreman have access to them. When the night shift foreman couldn't find the particular blueprint he wanted, the following morning he reported the matter to the works manager.'

'How many blueprints are there for this tank?'

'Several hundreds, Herr Hauptsturmführer. What our local men call "a large stack".'

'And this particular blueprint, the missing one, was "found" the following morning,' said Schreieder contemptuously.

'The day shift foreman had forgotten to return it to the works manager and left it in his drawer. The next morning he found it and handed it back.'

'The name of the day shift foreman?' snapped Schreieder.

'Klisiak. Mark Klisiak.'

'Klisiak!' cried Schreider. 'Klisiak's a Polish name! The man's a foreigner! *A filthy Pole!*'

'The man is most respected at the factory, Herr Hauptsturmführer. He has lived and worked in Germany for the last thirty years. He is married to a German woman. His only son is serving in the Luftwaffe.'

Schreieder felt his excitement rising. He had followed his instinct and been rewarded. In that factory was a traitor. An enemy of the Reich. Schreider was short, thickset, with a swarthy complexion. The compactness of his body suggested a coiled spring. No part of his frame could be called languid. He survived by respecting his superiors and inducing fear into his subordinates. His pale blue eyes first instilled that fear then rejoiced at watching his orders carried out. Now he smiled a thin smile that scarcely moved his lips. 'I am glad you have been doing your homework, Hausser, but you have missed one very important point. The man Klisiak may be respected, he may have a German wife and his only son may well be in the Luftwaffe, *but he is still a Pole!*' His face darkened, a vein stood out on his temple. 'And no doubt he is also a Catholic!'

The Unterscharführer nodded.

'Details, Hausser, details! It is only by paying attention to the details that we come to the heart of the matter. Details are like signposts. Ignore them at your peril.' Schreieder glanced down at his desk. He hated being cooped up in the office. Now, with the discovery of a traitor in an armaments factory, was his moment to get out. Correctly handled, this could lead to promotion.

'I shall go to Dortmund on the next train. I shall go to the factory that has the Polish foreman and where blueprints disappear and reappear as if by magic.' Schreieder's voice changed to a snarl. 'I want a car to meet me and tell the local police that I want Klisiak's file in that car.'

The Unterscharführer jumped to attention. 'At once Herr Hauptsturmführer.'

The Unterscharführer hurried from the room.

The Gestapo office at Henschel Maschinenfabrik AG was a cell-like room at the end of the main administrative block. It had one high window, a rickety table, a hard chair and two old, stained easy chairs. From a small fireplace set deep in the wall, ash and burned papers spilled out on to filthy tiles. Two men sat in the room, one laboriously checking figures, the other staring up at the window. The one checking figures, as the jacket draped over the back of his chair indicated, was an SS-Scharführer, the other an SS-Oberschütze. Every factory of any importance in the Third Reich had its resident Gestapo team. For Henschel Maschinenfabrik AG, it was the Scharführer and the Oberschütze.

When Schreieder walked in, both men stared like a pair of rabbits surprised in their hole by a ferret. Then the paralysis faded. The men leapt to their feet, the Scharführer struggled into his tunic and simultaneously they gave the Nazi salute. Schreieder acknowledged the salute, then sat in one of the easy chairs.

'I am not here,' announced Schreider, and put his feet up on to the table. 'I am in Berlin. Understand? In Berlin enjoying myself.'

'Yes, Herr Hauptsturmführer.' Both men spoke as one.

Schreieder opened his briefcase and took out a thin, buff,

paper file. He opened the file and started reading. He read very slowly. The two Gestapo men watched the Hauptsturmführer's eyes move from line to line. Suddenly Schreieder closed the file and flung it on to the table.

'Nothing! Not a damned thing!' Schreieder stared at the Scharführer. 'What do you know about Klisiak?'

'The foreman . . . ?'

'Yes, the foreman! The Polish swine!'

'He's worked here for a long time, Herr Hauptsturmführer. He's thought a lot of. The works manager has the highest possible opinion of him.'

Schreieder frowned. 'Wherever I go it's the same. A gramophone record. Everyone, everywhere thinks highly of Klisiak. The man is a paragon!' He raised his voice. 'But the man is a *Pole! A Catholic! A foreigner!* He must have done something, sometime. We must have something on him!'

'We've nothing on him, Herr Hauptsturmführer,' said the Scharführer, sadly. 'Nothing.'

Schreieder got up and began striding about the tiny room. He kicked at the legs of the table and at the ash in the grate. Suddenly he stopped and glanced at his watch. 'What time does the shift change?'

'At 6 p.m., Herr Hauptsturmführer. In twenty minutes.'

Schreieder's face brightened. 'Ah, so I can see this Pole, Klisiak, *and* the night foreman!'

'Yes, Herr Hauptsturmführer.'

Schreieder threw open the door. The Scharführer led the way through the factory. They passed the lines of tank hulls, the last being slowly lowered on to its tracks. They climbed a steel ladder on to the catwalk that ran along the wall of a small workshop. In the far corner of the workshop a man in blue overalls was at work at a bench, measuring a metal shaft with a micrometer. Beside him on the bench lay a number of blueprints. The Scharführer pointed. Schreieder stared at the man. In his triumph he had a moment of acute disappointment. The man was tall with fair hair, more like a good German than a Pole. The man turned his head. The features were truly Nordic. Schreieder began to walk away, back the way they had come. The two Gestapo men followed.

'Deceptive,' muttered Schreieder, when they were out of the workshop, 'most deceptive. A man of an inferior race with the appearance of a Teutonic knight.' He glanced back at the Scharführer. 'That is what the Reichsführer-SS is always telling us to be on our guard against. And now you can see why.'

The Scharführer agreed.

In the office, Schreieder returned to his agitated pacing. After a while he beat his fist into the palm of his other hand. 'Tell me about the night shift foreman. Is he a good German?'

'Yes, Hauptsturmführer,' said the Scharführer, 'a very good German.'

'A member of the Party?'

'No, Herr Hauptsturmführer.'

'Is he married? Has he a wife and children?'

'He is married, Herr Hauptsturmführer, and he has three children.'

Schreieder gave his thin smile. 'Good. Excellent. Bring him to me the moment he comes on duty.'

The night shift foreman was no match for Schreieder. He merely wanted to keep his job and the peace. One warning about the possible fate of his wife and children should he fail to co-operate was sufficient. The same warning obtained his agreement to absolute silence. That evening, with the night shift foreman's help, the Gestapo checked the blueprints. One was missing. Schreieder told them to check again.

'141/27 is definitely not here, Herr Hauptsturmführer,' said the night shift foreman.

'Klisiak,' muttered the Scharführer, clenching his teeth. 'Shall I go and get the bugger now?'

Schreider shouted at the Scharfürer that he was an idiot. 'Use your head for once! This could be the beginning not the end!' Schreider picked up his briefcase and gave his orders loudly and precisely. 'I'm going back to Berlin. While I am away check the blueprints every night. No doubt you'll find one missing every time.'

In the train, Schreider mused on his good fortune and the glories of the Third Reich. A spy in a factory making a new, secret tank was a most serious matter. Serious enough to be brought to the attention of the very highest. First thing in the morning he would report his startling discovery to his chief, the head of the Sicherheitsdienst, Gruppenführer Heydrich. In making his report to Reichsführer Himmler, Heydrich would almost certainly mention Schreieder's name. It was not inconceivable that, within twenty-four hours, the Führer himself would know of Schreieder's exploits. The name Schreieder would be engraved upon the history of Germany for ever. Warmed by such thoughts, Schreieder leaned back in his seat and stared through the windows into the evening landscape. The factories were blazing with light, the chimneys were belching smoke. Unemployment and the bad, old days had gone, all thanks to Adolf Hitler. There were still one or two traitors to be weeded out, men like Klisiak, but thanks to his own organization, the SD, they were getting fewer each day. Germany today was certainly a wonderful country to live in.

Heydrich saw Schreieder at noon. Schreieder delivered his report in short, sharp sentences, no point of detail being omitted. Schreieder was delighted at Heydrich's evident interest, unaware that his chief saw far more in the event than even Schreieder had seen. Heydrich was building his empire. Amongst those standing in his way was the Abwehr, the Intelligence Bureau of the Oberkommando der Wehrmacht, headed by Germany's spymaster, Konteradmiral Wilhelm Canaris. Both Himmler and Heydrich dreamed of absorbing the Abwehr into the SS. Carefully handled, the Polish spy in the tank factory might be turned to their advantage. But the matter needed to be pursued by someone with brains and far more senior than a mere Hauptsturmführer.

'You have done very well, Schreieder, very well indeed,' said the Gruppenführer. 'I am glad you had the sense not to rush in and arrest this Pole. We must find out who he is working for, who are his accomplices. He is a man to be watched. Who knows where he may lead us. You will return to Dortmund and organize operations there. SS-Standartenführer Schellenberg will take over the case. In future you will take your orders from him.'

Schreieder cried, 'Heil Hitler!' and threw his arm up in the

Nazi salute. As he turned from Heydrich and left the room, he showed no sign of the feelings within him. Delight at the compliment he had received over the thoroughness of his investigations – the Gruppenführer seldom gave compliments to those below him – vied with bitterness that the case was to be taken from him and given to a higher-ranking officer who was, in fact, younger. By the time he took the train back to Dortmund the only feelings Schreieder had were a deep hatred for all foreigners, particularly Poles, and a burning resentment for all young, well-born SS-Standartenführers.

Alex raced up the three flights of stairs. He had counted the hours, even the minutes until his second meeting. He had hung about the entrance of the Achterburgwal waiting for the prescribed time; now he couldn't get to the landing fast enough. Rachel Blum was holding open the door to her flat. This time her long, black hair was loose over her shoulders. She wore a navy blue skirt and blouse and draped around her neck was a bright, floral scarf. Alex stopped and stared, even more spellbound than before.

They went into the sitting room. Alex sat. Rachel went into the other room and returned with four large envelopes.

'Four!' cried Alex in surprise.

'Four,' said Rachel and put the envelopes into Alex's hands.

Alex stared at the envelopes. After a while, he said, 'Must I leave right away?'

'You must stay half an hour. Didn't Major Stevens tell you that?'

Alex shook his head.

'Everyone who comes here stays half an hour.'

'Everyone?'

'Everyone.'

Alex understood the implication of the word. He felt a pang of despair and jealousy. 'Anyway, I want to stay,' he said firmly. 'I like being here. I'd like to stay longer than the wretched half an hour. Much longer.'

Rachel smiled. 'And what do you want to talk about?'

'You.'

Rachel laughed. It was a long time since she had laughed. Alex was ten years younger than herself, Major Stevens had told her. She had never thought that a mere boy could cheer her up and make her laugh. The idea embarrassed her and made her feel guilty. The age difference suggested that the boy could be her younger brother.

'You are very beautiful.'

The words had been in Alex's head a long time. Now he whispered them.

Rachel blushed. 'You mustn't say things like that.'

'Why not? It's true. You are beautiful. You're lovely, very lovely. I like being here with you. I want to talk to you, know much more about you.'

Rachel would have laughed again but for the great intensity with which the words were spoken, and the look upon Alex's face. The look was a mixture of extreme ingenuousness and youthful directness and honesty. Although she had tried to conceal it from herself, she too had waited with pleasant anticipation for Alex's next visit. Loneliness was a fearful, frightening condition.

'You are an extremely precocious young man. However, thank you for the compliments. All of them.'

Alex smiled. He was glad she hadn't called him a boy. 'You're German, aren't you?'

'I mustn't talk about myself. Major Stevens would not approve.'

Alex was not discouraged. 'Why do you live in this awful area?'

Rachel frowned. 'Do we have to go into details? I should have thought the answer was quite obvious.'

Alex shook his head. 'You don't have to live here. I'm sure you don't.'

'I do have to live here,' said Rachel quietly. 'You see, it's the way I make my living.' She looked down at the floor. 'If you must have it spelt out, then I am what men call a whore. A prostitute. I have to live here. We all live here.'

Alex blushed as Rachel spoke the word 'prostitute'. Immediately he blurted out: 'Don't be silly. You can't be a prostitute! I know you're not.'

For a long time Rachel said nothing. At last she raised her head and looked at Alex. There was a tear on her cheek. 'Thank you,' she said softly. 'Thank you for having faith in me. Now please, no more questions.'

'I knew you couldn't be a prostitute,' said Alex vehemently. 'It just wasn't possible.'

'No more questions.'

For a while they were silent then Alex said, 'It's camouflage, isn't it?'

'Camouflage?'

'You being here in this district. It's camouflage.'

Rachel smiled. It was an acknowledgement that Alex was right.

'Camouflage for what?' asked Alex.

Rachel got up. Her manner changed. The softness, the sadness vanished. 'Let's talk about you,' she said. 'While I make coffee you can tell me about Java. About Batavia.'

Rachel went into the kitchen. Alex followed, unable to bear being parted for one moment. While Rachel made the coffee, Alex talked. The words flooded out. He had been born in Java and brought up on a large rubber plantation where his father had been manager. When he was twelve he had been sent to Batavia to secondary school. Then his father had died and his mother had decided to return to Holland. Now he was at the Technical School at Delft studying to be an engineer.

'I should be a lawyer . . .' said Rachel softly.

'A lawyer?' cried Alex in surprise.

She nodded, but however much he pressed her she would say no more.

They went into the sitting room with the coffee. For a while they sat in silence. Suddenly Alex said: 'Do you ever go out?'

'Not really. Only to shop. Why?'

'You should go out. It would do you good. It must be terrible to be cooped up in this awful area all day. I really don't see why you can't . . .' Alex stopped.

Rachel shook her head. 'Remember what I said. No more about me. We are now talking about *you*.'

'You must go out! It's not human to stay in here all day.

You're like a wonderful, exotic bird held captive in a tiny cage. It's cruel. Wicked!'

Rachel smiled.

'I'll take you out! I'd love to do that. I'll take you to the pictures.'

'Young man,' exclaimed Rachel, 'don't you know that I'm much older than you?'

'You don't look it. You look young, very young. You will always be young. Perennially young.'

'I've had enough compliments from you for one day. There must be plenty of nice young girls of your own age you can take to the pictures.'

Alex persisted. Rachel demurred. But it was a long time since any man had wanted to take her out. It would be a pleasant change just to go to the pictures. It would be a few hours without the loneliness.

'When do you want to go? It will have to be at the weekend.'

'Saturday,' said Alex breathlessly. 'I'll be here at half past six.'

She smiled and when she opened the door and said, 'Goodnight,' she called him Alex.

3

In the dining room of the Adlon Hotel two very different men sat opposite one another. The one with his back to the door was Schreieder. The other, with his back to the glass panelling, facing the other diners, was SS-Standartenführer Walter Schellenberg. Where Schreieder was short and thickset with plebeian features, Schellenberg was tall and dark with a fine aristocratic face and delicate movements of both hands and body. Nor were these comrades of the SS alike in other, less apparent ways. Schreieder had languished in the lower officer ranks of the SS for nine years; Schellenberg's rise had been meteoric. Son of an old and much respected German family, a law graduate with an excellent brain, in as many years he had risen six ranks from Untersturmführer to Standartenführer. Where Schreieder was the typical SS thug, Schellenberg was the university-trained, intellectual gangster.

'So at this stage of the great spy hunt,' said Schellenberg, smiling and raising his glass, 'what exactly do we know?'

For the moment, Schreieder had forgotten his bitterness at being superseded by this younger man. He was flattered to be sharing a table with a Standartenführer at the best hotel in Berlin. All he wanted to do was to please, even though he was quite aware that it was Schellenberg who would report their progress to Heydrich and get all the compliments.

'Blueprints are missing for two, sometimes three nights . . .'

'Which means each one has to be carefully copied by the Pole,' said Schellenberg. 'He has no help and the work takes a considerable time.'

'Exactly, Herr Standartenführer. A watch on Klisiak's house showed a stranger, a man unknown to the neighbours, entering at 11 p.m. on Tuesday evening. When the stranger came out of the Pole's house he was carrying an envelope. Trailed, he proved to be a lorry driver who had parked near by. The lorry's number was taken and its journey checked. The lorry belonged to a Düsseldorf cheese and butter wholesaler. It was further discovered that once a week the lorry went to Holland.' Schreieder paused, then spat out the words: 'And the driver is a Catholic.'

Schellenberg smiled.

'The following Tuesday, the event was repeated,' said Schreieder.

'But this time, with the Reichsführer's permission, we follow the lorry into Holland.'

'From Dortmund the driver drove to Oberhausen and then headed for Emmerich. The border was crossed at the Emmerich–Arnhem crossing. After that the lorry proceeded to Amsterdam.'

'Where the driver parks near the Red Light district,' said Schellenberg, laughing, 'and goes with his envelope to a house in the Achterburgwal.'

'After half an hour he came out again *without* the envelope,' said Schreieder most seriously.

'And no doubt without a good few guilders!'

Schreieder permitted himself a laugh. It was time he showed how much he enjoyed his superior's jokes.

Schellenberg glanced at his watch. 'And now all we can do is wait. Who will remove the envelope from the whore's den and where will he take it?'

Two days later, Schreieder was able to complete the story. This time it was not in the splendour of the Adlon Hotel dining room, but over the telephone from the German Legation at The Hague to the Gestapo offices in Prinz-Albrecht-Strasse. Schreider was quite unable to conceal his excitement. His voice shook. But first came the details.

'We know the occupant of the whore house, Herr Standartenführer. A Jewish bitch, Rachel Blum. We first saw her at 10 a.m. yesterday morning. She was trailed but only went shopping. At three in the afternoon a man called at the flat. He was also carrying an envelope.'

'You followed him when he left?' asked Schellenberg.

'No, Herr Standartenführer. The observers' orders were quite precise. They were to follow the progress of *the envelope the lorry driver brought.*'

'Fool!' cried Schellenberg. 'You bloody idiot! God knows what you've missed by your damned stupidity!'

'Wait, Herr Standartenführer! Although our observers took no action over the afternoon visitor, at 7 p.m. a young man visited the flat. Later that evening he came out with *several* envelopes.'

'You followed him, I hope?' asked Schellenberg sarcastically.

'We did indeed, sir. We followed him to the Amsterdam Central Station where he boarded a tram. He got off at the Daniel Willinkplein and entered a block of flats. At 7 a.m. this morning he came out of the block of flats . . .'

'Don't tell me that everyone is just walking about carrying these envelopes as if they were love letters? They can't be that sure of themselves. It doesn't make sense.'

'No, sir. This morning the young man had nothing in his hands but carried a large school satchel over his shoulders. Our men reckoned that the envelopes must be in the satchel.

They trailed him back to the Central Station where he caught a train for Delft.'

'And then?' cried Schellenberg.

'When the train stopped at The Hague, the young man in question suddenly got up and handed the envelopes out of the window to a man waiting on the platform. Our man leapt from the train and trailed this other man. He went to the Visa Section of the British Legation.'

At the Hague end of the telephone, Schreieder visibly collapsed. He had delivered his astonishing information in a precise, meticulous way. He had done his duty swiftly and efficiently. Now it was up to the Standartenführer. He only hoped that in taking the matter further, Schellenberg would not forget to inform his superiors of the sterling work Schreieder had done.

At the Berlin end of the phone, Schellenberg nodded several times. The nods were of attainment and satisfaction. It was as he had expected, as he had hoped. By taking no precipitate action they had trailed the envelope from its source to its destination.

Heydrich listened attentively to Schellenberg's report. When Schellenberg finished, Heydrich got up from his desk.

'The British Legation at The Hague . . .' he said, almost to himself.

'That's the end of the trail.'

Heydrich shook his head. 'Anywhere but the British Legation.'

Schellenberg looked puzzled.

'If British Intelligence are involved, we are obliged to inform the Abwehr before going further. That means taking that old rogue Admiral Canaris into our confidence.'

Heydrich turned towards the window. The light fell on his face. Like Schellenberg he was tall and good-looking, but Heydrich's hair was blond, in striking contrast to his black SS-Gruppenführer's uniform. Slowly Heydrich's blue eyes closed, a flicker of annoyance crossed his long, classical face. He was back fifteen years on the training cruiser *Berlin*. Standing, uncertain, was the young cadet: lecturing him from behind the desk was the First Officer. Heydrich and Canaris. But that was before the scandal, the pregnant beauty and the director's daughter, the subsequent Court of Honour and the 'Dismissal for impropriety', and before Himmler had cast his spell.

'I fail to understand why the Führer still trusts that old devil, but his ruling is quite clear. In all matters relating to British Intelligence, we consult the Abwehr.' Heydrich turned his head. 'So you'd better go and talk to Canaris.' His voice rose. There was a cruel, uncompromising crispness about the next words. 'But remember, Schellenberg, any action to be taken in this matter will be taken by the Gestapo.'

Schellenberg understood.

Promptly at six-thirty Alex pressed the bell of Rachel's flat. As usual Rachel was waiting for him at the top of the stairs. This time she was dressed entirely in black. The dress being short-sleeved, her arms were left bare. There was a youthfulness about her Alex had not seen before. The lines of her body were more accentuated, the figure more evident. Alex was stunned. He stood with his mouth open, staring. Rachel handed him her coat. He helped her into it. As he did so he realized that she had deliberately kept her coat off, wanting him to see her in her dress. Her eyes still showed her pleasure at his admiration.

The film was *Robin Hood* with Errol Flynn and Olivia de Havilland. Half-way through, Alex took her hand. She made no effort to stop him. He laid his hand on her lap and she did not brush it away. As they walked back home along the canal she put her arm in his. Alex returned to his questioning. At first Rachel was reluctant to talk, but slowly, little by little, Alex pieced together an outline of her life. She was the daughter of a well-known Berlin surgeon. She had just completed her law studies when Hitler forbade Jews to practise certain professions. Her father was only allowed to treat other Jews. She was on her way to England and safety when she stopped in Amsterdam. At that point Rachel would say no more. Alex had to guess the rest. It seemed easy enough. Unable to become a practising lawyer she had become a secret agent.

Back in her flat, Alex was unusually quiet. He sat and stared at Rachel but said nothing. Suddenly she leaned forward and touched his arm. 'A penny for them . . .'

'I'm thinking about you. Or rather us.'

She raised her eyebrows.

'You know I'm in love with you, don't you?'

Her face darkened. She frowned. 'You're talking rubbish. Complete rubbish.' She was evidently upset. She looked to either side of her as if trying to escape. Alex was sad that he should have upset her, but such were his feelings he could not understand why he had. All he wanted to do was to love her and at that moment it seemed the most important thing in the world. And the simplest.

'I can't hide the fact that I love you. I can't hide it from you any more than I can stop breathing. It's there. It's there all the time.'

'You are much too young to think of love.'

'The other day I was too young to take you to the pictures.'

She shook her head and again looked to either side of her.

'There's no law that says you can't be in love at seventeen.' Alex remembered Best's words in his mother's flat: 'You've grown up, Alex. You've grown up.' 'Some men are still not mature at twenty-five. I happen to be mature at seventeen.'

Rachel's defence was to laugh. The young man was quite preposterous. But she saw the look of sincerity, almost fanatical earnestness on Alex's face. She reminded him yet again of the ten years between them. 'Maybe those ten years don't matter all that much now, but when you are forty, I shall be fifty, an old woman.'

'I shall still love you.'

'You've no idea what you're saying.'

'I know exactly what I'm saying. I love you now and I shall always love you. I have absolutely no doubt.'

Again she shook her head. Her long, dark hair streamed out and swept across her face. For an instant she looked mad. Wonderful, beautiful and mad.

'This is crazy! Absolutely crazy! I should never have allowed you to take me to the pictures.'

'You enjoyed it. You let me hold your hand. We walked back arm in arm.'

'You're only . . .' She stopped and bit her lip.

'In a few months I shall be eighteen. Old enough to join the RAF. Old enough to fly an aeroplane and fight in one. You could come with me to England and we could get married.'

Rachel said nothing. She had no idea what to say or do. She was frightened at the way the conversation was going, worried at Alex's intensity, but most disturbing of all was that something, somewhere inside her, was very receptive. Alex's words were disquieteningly warming. She wanted him to go on saying them for they helped her to live.

'I mean it,' said Alex strongly. 'I mean every word.'

He jumped up, lifted Rachel from her chair and carried her to the couch. All Rachel's instincts cried out for her to resist. To slap his face and push him away. She had no wish to get involved with a seventeen-year-old. At the moment, with her existence so insecure, she had no wish to get involved with any man. But she was paralysed. The lonely, miserable life she had lived for so long had left her yearning for affection and love. When his hands were on her body she managed to whisper, 'No. No, you must stop,' but she hadn't the will to do anything. As he cupped her breasts and kissed them, she had a fleeting, ironic thought. Up until this day she had lived in the Red Light district without a man touching her.

They lay quietly together, her head on his chest. Alex thought of manhood and love. A love full of chivalry, burning with protection and possession. He was the white knight upon the great charger, Rachel, the maiden he had just untied from the tree. Then the charger changed to a Spitfire and Rachel was in an English cottage waiting for his return. He dived through the clouds and waved to her in the garden. She waved back. Then he raised his head a little to see her black hair spread over his chest. Gently he ran the tips of his fingers through the dark strands.

For Rachel there was a kaleidoscope of memories, some sweet, many bitter. The happiness of childhood hadn't lasted long. She had been thirteen at the time of the Munich *putsch*. Since then she had seen many things: Röhm's brown-shirted SA, Himmler's black-shirted SS with their death's head and their runic double-S flash, singing as they tramped the cobbles:

> Clear the streets, the SS marches.
> The storm-columns stand at the ready.
> They will take the road
> From tyranny to freedom . . .

She had seen books hurled on to bonfires, shops looted and her fellow Jews paraded through the streets, placards about their bodies proclaiming them to be Jewish louts. She had seen on the news-stands Gauleiter Julius Streicher's weekly *Der Stürmer*, shrieking its anti-Semitism: 'The Jew is not a human being. He is a symptom of putrefaction.' She had been twenty-three when the word 'Dachau' crept into the language and Hitler had become Reich Chancellor. She had fled from Germany after the *Kristallnacht*, the anti-Jewish pogrom.

'You know I could go to jail for this.'

Alex moved his head. 'Why?'

'Because you are a minor and I am an adult. It is against the law for an adult to have carnal knowledge of a minor.'

'Stop being a lawyer.'

For a while they were silent. Rachel was only conscious of the beating of a heart. Then again she remembered the old men, women and children being beaten along the streets and the crowds laughing.

'You know that I'm Jewish, don't you?'

'Of course I know. I knew the moment I saw you.'

'And it doesn't worry you?'

'Why should it? I told you, I love you.'

She felt a great surge of warmth. It seemed then that she would never get used to the idea of a Jew being loved by a Gentile.

'How did you get out of Germany?'

'Major Stevens got me out.'

'Is that why you're working for him now?'

She shook her head. 'Not really. I was working for him before, in Germany.'

'That must have been very dangerous.'

She shrugged and said nothing.

'What about now?' asked Alex. 'Is the work you do now for the Major dangerous?'

She raised her head and smiled. 'Here in Holland I am safe.'

He asked about her family. Her parents, her brother and her younger sister had all been sent to Dachau. She had no idea whether they were alive or dead. She put her head on Alex's shoulder and cried. Alex's anguish knew no bounds. He was at his wits' end how to console her. He could think of only one way. It was midnight when he said goodbye.

The war that Best said would come with the autumn came on time. At 04.45 hours on 1 September, a few hours before the staged 'Polish attacks' on the German border radio station at Gleiwitz and the Hochlinden Customs Post, the Panzers rumbled over the Polish border. By noon of 3 September, Britain and France had joined the conflict. For the moment, Holland retained her neutrality.

4

Konteradmiral Wilhelm Canaris lifted his gaze from the mass of papers on his desk, rested his chin in the palm of his left hand and thought. He was tired and worried, and found it hard to concentrate. A month ago, when he knew that war was imminent, he had expressed the opinion that it meant the end of Germany. Nothing that had happened since had led him to change his mind. He was still deeply disturbed by the Gleiwitz incident – expressively code-named 'Operation Canned Goods' – the SS-staged attack on the border radio station that Hitler had used as his pretext for invading Poland. He was

35

thankful that it had not been his idea and that he had not been ordered to provide the 'bodies', but to his everlasting anger and shame, the Abwehr had been ordered to provide the one hundred and fifty Polish uniforms. Now he was getting sickening reports on the way the SS were treating the inhabitants of the newly conquered territories. They had let loose Einsatzgruppe extermination squads. The war was a disaster, but the actions of the SS were making it an even greater disaster.

In his moment of despair, Canaris stared at his dog, an animal that accompanied him everywhere, even here in his office in the Tirpitz Ufer. The sight of the dog sleeping in its usual place in the corner helped to soothe the Admiral, but nothing could remove his anxieties for the future or his loathing for Hitler and the death's head.

He was re-reading a report of events near Lwów, considering the realities of pits 'five metres by fifty metres . . . groups of one hundred at a time . . . each shot through the nape of the neck . . .', and a plea from the writer for the reader to spare a thought for the strain upon and exhaustion of the executioners, when a visitor was announced. It was SS-Standartenführer Schellenberg who strode into the room.

Schellenberg gave the Nazi salute. Tetchily Canaris waved the raised arm down, then he got up and held out his hand.

'My dear Schellenberg, how nice to see you.'

Canaris indicated the leather chair in front of his desk. Schellenberg sat. For a moment the two men stared at one another. However great his loathing of the SS, however deep his conspiratorial activities, Canaris had long ago learned not to make his feelings too evident. He had to work with the SS and he made the best of it. Besides, there were certain individuals in that organization that Canaris actually liked. Schellenberg was one. Even for Schellenberg's chief, Heydrich, Canaris still had a lingering, nostalgic regard.

'Spies, Herr Admiral,' said Schellenberg. 'British spies in the Ruhr. An espionage network in the heart of Germany draining it of its military secrets. Burrowing away under our very noses.'

Canaris puckered his lips. He didn't like being told his business by the SS.

36

'A chain that starts at the Henschel Maschinenfabrik AG at Dortmund and stretches right to The Hague.'

Schellenberg enjoyed making the most of his information and watching the discomfort of the Abwehr.

'It is easy to talk of espionage,' said Canaris gruffly. 'These days there are rumours of spies everywhere . . .'

'We have proof, absolute proof.'

Again the two men faced each other in silence: Canaris, a slight, dapper figure with silver-grey hair, more Latin in appearance than Teuton, dressed in the dark blue of the Kriegsmarine, wearing on his cuff the four gilt rings; Schellenberg, younger and taller, fine-looking in the black uniform of the SS.

'From The Hague the information goes to London . . .'

'You know a great deal.'

'We are efficient, Admiral. And patriotic.'

Canaris held up his hand. 'If it's about British Intelligence, let's get Giskes in. He's the expert.'

Canaris picked up the telephone and asked for the Head of Section III F to come to his office. Section III F of the Abwehr specialized in British Intelligence. With Hauptmann Giskes present, Schellenberg related the complete story from the Polish foreman and the tank blueprints to the envelopes disappearing into the Visa Section of the British Legation at The Hague. When Schellenberg finished, Canaris and Giskes glanced at one another.

'We know all about the Visa Section of the British Legation at The Hague,' said Canaris, blandly. 'It's the headquarters of the British Secret Intelligence Service in Europe. We've known about it for years. And kept an eye on it.'

'Run by Major Richard Henry Stevens ably assisted by Captain Sigismund Payne Best,' said Giskes, then with considerable satisfaction added, 'We caught one of their spies in Hamburg a couple of months ago.'

'But you don't know about Klisiak the Pole or the Panzer blueprints!' cried Schellenberg. 'You don't know a thing about them! So what you've been keeping an eye on I don't know.'

'We knew there were more agents,' said Giskes lamely.

'Two more at least,' said Schellenberg, then remembered

37

Heydrich's instructions. 'And those two are a Gestapo matter!' Schellenberg stared challengingly first at Canaris and then at Giskes. Neither argued. Canaris smiled.

'But to pick up the chain neatly and cleanly, you need our help. To be precise, you'd like to positively identify the man at The Hague who picked up the envelope from the courier on the train. All you know about British activity in Europe is what Giskes has just told you.'

Schellenberg remained silent. Canaris slid the telephone towards the Standartenführer. 'Get your man who saw what happened on the platform to come and see Giskes. Giskes will show him all the photos in his rogues' gallery.'

Schellenberg phoned the Gestapo man who'd seen the transfer of the envelopes. In Giskes' office the man was shown a number of large photos. He identified Major Stevens as the recipient of the envelopes. Schellenberg asked which was Captain Best. Giskes indicated a photo of a well-built man with a monocle. When Schellenberg left the Tirpitz Ufer he carried in his briefcase copies of both photos.

Back in his office in the Prinz-Albrecht-Strasse, Schellenberg propped up the photos of Stevens and Best, sat at his desk and stared at them. He looked at them on and off all afternoon. He would have liked to have had more photos, taken at different angles, but after a while the features were so imprinted upon his memory that had he passed either man in the street he would have recognized him. Study your enemy's face and eyes and you will know how he thinks. Schellenberg became quite sure he knew exactly how Stevens and Best thought. In spite of their position in British Intelligence, they were typical British army officers. They would 'play the game' in the only way they knew: as it had been played upon the playing fields of their public schools and upon the battlefields of the old Western Front. Compared with the Gestapo and its modern methods, they would be as lambs.

Late in the afternoon, Schellenberg's thoughts were sufficiently composed for him to see Heydrich. It wasn't just a matter of catching a Polish foreman and a traitorous German lorry driver. Schellenberg had thought bigger than that. Far bigger. The tail could be mopped up easily enough. His proposal was to destroy the organization by lopping off the head. Or, to be more precise, removing it, placing it in safe custody and, with the help of recognized Gestapo methods, prising out all the information and knowledge it contained.

Schellenberg's plan was so startling, so unorthodox that Heydrich did not feel able to give the go-ahead on his own. He would have to consult SS Reichführer Himmler. It was possible that Himmler would wish to consult the Führer himself.

Schellenberg had to wait.

The night air sharpened. The autumn mists rose from the canals. The shadows grew longer and thinner. Alex saw more and more of Rachel. They met at least twice a week. Every Thursday, the moment he got back to Amsterdam from Delft, he went to her flat. Every Saturday they went to the cinema. Rachel enjoyed cooking dinner and when they were together it was like the heady days of early marriage.

Alex came to love the flat in the Achterburgwal as much as his own home. He forgot the unsavoury nature of the area and even began waving at some of the women in the windows. He delighted in buying flowers in the flower market or at the station and arranging them in the sitting room and bedroom. With each visit they seemed to grow closer. Alex could no longer remember a time when there had been no Rachel. She seemed to fill his life. After each visit Alex waited impatiently for the next. Rachel knew that she was living in a make-believe world, but was grateful for the happiness. Loneliness was no longer the terror it had once been. She could survive the blank days. But in her heart Rachel wondered how long it would last. One evening, when the darkness of approaching winter made them put on the lights early, she thought aloud.

'Of course it will go on,' said Alex with all the enthusiasm of his age. 'Why shouldn't it go on? You said yourself that you were safe in Holland. Anyway, Major Stevens will look after you.' He added with a laugh, 'That is, when I'm not looking after you.'

Rachel was not reassured. She was in a negative mood. 'The war could spread. The Germans could invade Holland.'

'They didn't last time, why should they this time?'

Rachel shrugged. 'It's a different sort of war. You've no idea how horrific it could be. How horrific it already is.'

'You mean in Germany . . .?'

'I've seen the Nazis at work. I know how they think, what they will do. There are some terrible stories about what they are already doing in Poland.'

'They might not be true . . .'

Rachel looked at him. Her dark eyes were full of sadness. Recently she had talked a lot about life in Germany and the treatment of the Jews. He knew exactly what was in her mind.

'You're crossing your bridges . . .' he cried angrily.

'You've never seen them,' she said quietly. 'You've never seen the hatred in their eyes. The fanaticism in their faces.'

For a while they were silent. Suddenly Alex said, 'I don't know what you're worried about. I'm here with you, aren't I?'

'You're not always here. Anyway, you know that one day you want to go to England and join up.'

'We've been through all that! If I do go to England, you can come with me.' Alex had said the words quickly, before he had remembered Best telling him how useful he would be in Holland. Indeed, how useful he now was in Holland. 'Anyway,' he said quietly, 'I don't see Captain Best letting me go to England. Not for a long time.' He held out his hand and grasped Rachel's hand. 'Don't be so miserable. There's nothing to be miserable about. We're in the same team, you and me.'

'You have a wonderful, seductive way, Alex, of hiding from reality.'

Alex shook his head with exasperation. 'We are reality, you and me. The reality is here in this flat. Now. At this moment.'

'And we ignore everything else going on in the world outside these four walls? Is that what you're saying?'

'There are times when one has to . . . Otherwise . . .'

'Otherwise life is impossible.'

Alex started to laugh. Suddenly he stopped and, putting his

arms around Rachel, looked into her face. 'I want to enjoy life,' he said with great intensity. 'Now that I've found you, war or no war, I want to enjoy life.'

There was no reaction on her face. She was looking away into the distance. Alex suddenly had a stab of fear. 'You do love me, don't you?' he asked quickly.

Rachel laughed and kissed him on the cheek. 'That has nothing whatsoever to do with it.'

Alex looked relieved. Rachel was smiling. A faint, wan smile. She still wondered how long it would last. In his youthfulness, Alex believed that it would last forever.

Himmler saw Heydrich and Schellenberg together and told them of the Führer's agreement. However, Himmler could trust no one, so he added one proviso. Schellenberg could not undertake his plan on his own. He must be accompanied. Himmler wanted Schellenberg to take Schreieder, but Schellenberg considered Schreieder eminently unsuitable. Schreieder looked and acted like a policeman, and the last thing he wanted was a man with him who looked like a policeman. If he had to take anyone, Schellenberg preferred to take Giskes, who knew and understood the British.

Himmler's reaction was predictable. No officer of the Abwehr could be trusted. They were all Canaris's poodles. Schellenberg persisted and Himmler gave way. It would be Schellenberg and Giskes who would bait the trap.

Schellenberg went back with Heydrich to the Gruppen-führer's office. As they discussed the details of Schellenberg's plan, Heydrich picked up a report from his desk. It was Schreieder's report, full of the usual minutiae.

'Schreieder mentions a Jewish womam, Rachel Blum, as the letter-box in Amsterdam. The woman was born in Germany and escaped a year ago.' Heydrich glanced up from the report and looked into Schellenberg's eyes. 'I don't want her to escape again.'

'Shall we pick her up and bring her back?'

Heydrich shook his head. 'Too risky. Much too risky. We're sticking our necks out as it is. Picking her up and bringing her back could easily spark off something nasty. We don't want an international incident over her, she's not worth it. Just have the bitch eliminated at the same time as you deal with the Englishmen.'

In spite of his position in the SS, Schellenberg had no stomach for arranging the death of an individual young woman, Jewish or otherwise. He would delegate the job to Schreieder. No doubt Schreieder would get a kick out of it.

5

Best was in high spirits. He rapped on Stevens' door and didn't wait for an answer. Stevens looked up from his desk and frowned. Best sat down, stuck out his long legs and adjusted his monocle.

'Guess what? A couple of German officers would like to talk to us.'

Stevens raised his eyebrows.

'Do you know a German called Dr Franz?'

'I know of him, I've never met him.'

'He came to see me early this morning. It appears that he's been contacted by two Wehrmacht officers. Part of an anti-Hitler conspiracy. They want to get rid of their beloved Führer and need our help.'

'Stories, fairy tales . . .' muttered Stevens.

'Not this time,' said Best firmly. 'This one smells better than the others. I got the distinct impression that there are some pretty high-ranking generals involved.'

'General Beck?' asked Stevens quickly.

'No names were mentioned.'

'And I suppose they hope to form a new German government and make a peace treaty with the Allies?'

Best nodded. 'But before going ahead they want to make sure the British government will be prepared to talk to them once Hitler is out of the way. In view of their problems it's not an unreasonable query.'

Stevens thought for a while then said, 'You really felt that Franz was genuine?'

'I got a sense that it was all very real, that it was coming from high quarters. That over there in Berlin, in OKW, a volcano is waiting to blow.'

It was a beautiful October day. Stevens looked up at the window. Rumours of plots against Hitler had been rife for a long time. The recently dismissed Chief of the Army General Staff, General Beck, was thought to be the centre of discontent, but there were others. Stevens trusted Best's judgement; he was also infected with his enthusiasm. In spite of his own innate doubts about the genuineness of any conspiracy within Germany, this might just be the beginning of the end of the war. He certainly could not ignore it. Stevens' excitement began to mount.

'What did you tell Dr Franz?'

'That we would check with London.'

'How do you suppose Dr Franz knew you were the man to approach?'

'The Wehrmacht officers told him,' said Best, blandly. 'And you can guess where they got that from, can't you?'

Stevens looked thoughtful. Gently he rubbed his hand over his chin, then he got up and stood facing the window. 'I've always believed that the Abwehr knew all about us. And that means one thing. K knows all about us.' Canaris was often referred to as K in British Intelligence circles. 'If there is a genuine plot against Hitler, you would expect K to be involved or at least know about it.'

'Up to his neck in it,' said Best, affably.

'Was any reference made to K?' asked Stevens.

'Not explicitly . . . but he must be there somewhere.'

Stevens was satisfied. He was certain Canaris was involved somewhere along the line and it gave him confidence that whoever they were dealing with were likely to be genuine.

Stevens called in the communications officer and dictated a message to Colonel Menzies in London. Menzies was Head of SIS. An hour later they had their reply. They were to proceed with caution and beware of a trap.

Ten days later, in Best's magnificent house at 19 Nieuwe

Uitweg on the outskirts of The Hague, Stevens and Best were hosts to a Major Schaemmel and Hauptmann Hartmann of the Wehrmacht. Dr Franz, who had brought the German officers, was also present. The Germans had the advantage from the start. Both had seen photos of Stevens and Best. Stevens and Best had never seen photos of Schellenberg and Giskes. Ignorant of the true identity of their visitors, the two Britons took them at their face value: two anti-Nazi Wehrmacht officers willing to put their lives at risk in the cause of removing Hitler.

Major Schaemmel, alias Schellenberg, did most of the talking. The conspiracy had wide support in the Wehrmacht and to a lesser extent in the Luftwaffe and Kriegsmarine. The conspirators also had contacts in the German Foreign Office. The plan was to assassinate Hitler, arrest all prominent Nazis and take control of government. However, the generals involved wanted some assurance that Britain would be prepared to negotiate an honourable peace treaty with a new German regime.

Stevens withdrew and phoned London. He returned to inform the Germans that, while his superiors couldn't speak for the British government, they were quite sure that once Hitler had been removed the path to negotiations would be open. A toast was drunk to the early end of the war. Captain Best's Dutch wife prepared an excellent dinner, the Germans accepted the offer of beds for the night. In the morning a second meeting was agreed to. The Germans had two requests. They needed British explosives to help them in their endeavours and, as it was difficult for them to come all the way to The Hague without making themselves conspicuous, they asked that the next meeting should be held nearer to the border. Stevens and Best agreed.

The second meeting, at a hotel near Arnhem, went off equally well. The generals seemed to be reassured. The most important thing now was to get rid of Hitler. Stevens handed Schellenberg the parcel of explosives and a small radio. After an excellent lunch the Germans departed, promising to keep in touch through Dr Franz.

*   *   *

Schellenberg had had his reminder from Heydrich, Schreieder had had his orders from Schellenberg. Rachel Blum was to be 'eliminated' and the job could best be entrusted to 'Dutch friends'. Schreieder had therefore travelled to Utrecht, the headquarters of the Dutch Nazi Party. He had seen the Party secretary and now he was to meet one of the most influential members of the National Socialist Party in Holland, Mr Fatesma, the Public Prosecutor at the District Court of Amsterdam. As the secretary had so succinctly put it, 'Fatesma will be able to help you.'

Schreieder took the train to Amsterdam and booked in at a hotel near the Central Station. The National Socialist Movement in Holland was an official political party of some importance. Of the one hundred seats in the Dutch Parliament, the Dutch Nazis held fourteen. To curb their corrupting influence, the government had passed a law forbidding civil servants from membership. The result was that civil servants, whilst resigning from the Party officially, became secret members. Fatesma came into this category. As his Nazi activities had to be clandestine, Schreieder could not visit his house until after dark. The appointment was for 8 p.m. and he had time to kill. He knew Rachel Blum's address and he knew what she looked like from her photo in the Gestapo files. He decided to take a walk into the Red Light district.

Schreieder stood outside the house and watched. He caught no sight of Rachel but he did catch the welcoming eye of one of the women in the downstairs flat. He went into the woman's flat, spent his guilders and came out at a few minutes to six. A young man was standing in front of the door that gave access to the upstairs flats. For a moment the young man's eyes met Schreieder's. Then the door opened and Alex entered and went up the stairs. Schreieder went off to his dinner and appointment.

Fatesma opened the door himself. He showed his visitor into a study where the walls were lined with books. Schreieder had never seen so many. Most were Dutch law books, but Schreieder spotted several German publications on National Socialism. There was Hitler's *Mein Kampf* and Himmler's *Die Schutzstaffel als antibolschewistische Kampf-organisation*. The

45

German was delighted. He was evidently in the presence of a like mind.

Politely Fatesma pointed to a chair. Schreieder sat. At once he began outlining the purpose of his visit. He wanted a German Jewish girl now living in Holland eliminated on the same day that her British spymasters were to be taken care of. It had to be the same day and about the same time, otherwise the British might get suspicious.

'Have you set a date for getting rid of the British?' asked Fatesma.

'The ninth of November. However, that date is flexible, depending upon events in the meantime.' Schreieder began to laugh. 'After all, we have to have the co-operation of the British.'

Fatesma was in his early fifties. He was a lumbering, lugubrious-looking man with thinning hair and a sallow complexion. Now his dolefulness increased. He shook his head as if the whole request was impossible. But that was not what he meant. He was merely worried. 'That leaves me just two weeks to make all the arrangements. Two weeks is not very long.'

'It's urgent,' said Schreieder, accusingly. 'I was assured that you would help.'

'Of course I'll help,' said Fatesma quickly. 'I'm only too delighted to be able to help. Have no doubt whatsoever, Herr Hauptsturmführer, that I will see that the Jewish woman is dealt with. It is simply a matter of the available time. It is a little short.'

'We can't put the date back,' said Schreieder firmly. 'It's not in my hands.' The inference was evident and not lost upon Fatesma. The event was in higher hands. Far higher hands. 'The Führer himself is interested.'

Fatesma nodded. He was not unflattered to have the Führer interested in something in which he was to be involved.

'And what about the young man who collects the envelopes from the woman? Surely we can't let him run free? When the woman is killed he might talk.'

'True,' said Schreieder, a little doubtfully, for he had had no orders upon the subject. 'Perhaps it's just as well that he's killed at the same time as the woman. He should be there

46

visiting her on the ninth. That's the day he collects the envelopes.'

For a moment they were silent then Fatesma shook his head. 'No, it won't do. It won't do at all. It would leave me with two unsolved murders on my hands. One is bad enough. Two, and the Press will be asking questions. Murders are rare in Amsterdam. They always cause a stir.'

For a moment it seemed that Alex would go free. But now that his future had been brought up, neither Schreieder nor Fatesma liked the idea of freedom.

'If the Press get hold of even a whisper that this woman was connected with British Intelligence,' said Fatesma, 'they will most certainly connect her death with whatever you have in mind for the British officers. Then it will be us, the Dutch National Socialist Party, who will get all the blame.' He paused, then added, 'There is only one way. All mouths *must* be silenced.'

Schreieder could think of nothing more helpful than murder. He was used to murder. It was simple and thorough. But Fatesma remained opposed to the idea so they sat silent, Fatesma at his desk, Schreieder lounging in the chair. Fatesma ran his hands through his thinning hair. Suddenly he sat upright, his massive shoulders back, his mournful look gone.

'That's it! I've got it, the perfect solution.'

Schreieder looked expectantly at the Public Prosecutor.

'Whyever didn't I think of it before? It's so obvious, so neat. It was staring me in the face and I never saw it.' Fatesma jumped to his feet. 'Have no more worries, Herr Hauptsturmführer, everything will be taken care of. *Everything*. This calls for a little celebration.'

Fatesma opened a cabinet full of bottles. He poured two large gins and handed one glass to Schreieder. The other he raised in a toast: 'To the Führer and the success of our enterprise!'

Schreieder jumped to his feet. 'Heil Hitler!'

They touched glasses and drank.

'Tell me, Herr Prosecutor, what will happen to the young man, the courier?' asked Schreieder anxiously.

Fatesma's normally joyless face broke into a full smile. 'What am I going to do with him?'

Schreieder nodded.

'Leave it to me, Herr Hauptsturmführer. Leave it to me. You have enough to think about. We are strong and better organized than you imagine. There are Party members in the police force who will do exactly what I want. Men who are absolutely reliable. I can think of two detectives now, devoted Party members who are only awaiting the opportunity to strike a blow against the enemies of National Socialism. We shall not let you down, that I can assure you.'

In spite of the Prosecutor's confidence, Schreieder's anxieties were only partly allayed. Tomorrow he would have to report to Schellenberg. He was perfectly aware that Schellenberg, the university-trained law graduate, thought of him as a dull-witted policeman, not far off a fool. Schellenberg would probe him with questions. If he didn't know exactly what the 'Dutch friends' were going to do, Schellenberg would have every cause to dub him an idiot.

The room was warm. Schreieder's glass had been refilled. He drained it a second time, then took out his handkerchief and mopped his brow.

'Herr Prosecutor . . .' he began a second time when again Fatesma refilled the glass. Schreieder drank. The strong liquid burned his throat and warmed his stomach. With the gin, his dinner and his visit to the woman in the Achterburgwal, he was feeling sleepy. He had a struggle to keep his eyes open. Through half-closed lids he saw that Fatesma was standing over him.

'Allow me to tell you, Herr Hauptsturmführer, how proud I am to be doing something of such importance to our comrades in the Reich National Socialist Movement. It is a great honour for me, one that I shall never forget. And it will be a great honour for those others in our Party who will be assisting . . .'

Fatesma droned on. Schreieder didn't realize that both of them were slightly drunk. He still had no idea of the Prosecutor's plans but he was now quite certain that Rachel Blum's elimination was in the most capable hands. He could return to Berlin and face Schellenberg with confidence. Not only had he arranged for their 'Dutch friends' to kill the Jewish woman, but the young courier would also be looked after by the very man appointed to uphold the law and prosecute criminals. Even in his present state Schreieder could see the irony and it appealed to him. He congratulated himself upon an excellent day's work.

The ninth dawned cold and overcast. Although he was tired, Best awoke early. As he shaved he thought of the day's events. After four meetings the excitement of dealing with the German dissidents had worn off. Best wished he had some excuse to avoid going to what he now considered a beastly little frontier café. Yesterday's visit had made him feel extremely uncomfortable. Cooped up in that little side room with the Germans he had felt cut off from the outside world. He had hated the big glass window, the dark, dense undergrowth just outside and the close proximity of the frontier barriers.

Only a fortnight ago he had told Stevens that they were going up in the world. At last they were to meet a Wehrmacht General, a leading member of the conspiracy. The meeting, the fifth, was to have taken place on 8 November at the Café Backus just inside the Dutch border at Venlo. The last few meetings had all been near the border for the Germans felt too conspicuous venturing far into Holland. In particular, the General claimed he was well known and might be recognized.

Stevens had checked with Menzies at SIS and been told that the meeting could go ahead. Stevens could tell the General he would be received in London. Stevens and Best had driven the hundred and twelve miles to Venlo only to be told by Major Schaemmel that the General had been held up in Munich and could not reach Holland before 4 p.m. the next day. The Britons had no option but to go home and return the following afternoon.

Best got to his office early, did a little routine work, but could not settle. Soon after ten, he went to Stevens' house. The moment Stevens saw Best, he waved a newspaper. 'Read this?'

Best shook his head.

'Last night Hitler gave his annual speech to the old Party cronies of the '23 Putsch. Unfortunately he left the Munich Buergerbraükeller early. It says here that he rushed away. Twelve minutes later there was a pretty massive explosion. It's all in here.'

The paper was that morning's *Voelkischer Beobachter*. Best took the paper and started reading.

'You'll see that we get the blame,' said Stevens cheerfully, then lapsed into mock German. 'The attempted assassination of the beloved Führer is entirely the foul work of the British Secret Service and the wicked Neville Chamberlain.'

Carefully Best read the article. The assassination attempt at that moment was unexpected. He wondered if it was the work of the people they had been dealing with or another group. If it was their people, how would they act today? Since the attempt upon Hitler's life had been unsuccessful, ten to one they wouldn't even be at Venlo. Suddenly his doubts as to who they were were resolved.

'They say here that the explosives and detonating devices were British!' cried Best excitedly. 'They may have missed Hitler, but at least it proves one thing. Our people are quite serious about getting rid of him.'

Best was relieved on another count. The seemingly endless series of meetings had made him even begin to doubt the genuineness of the conspirators. That too had now been cleared.

'Better luck next time,' said Stevens drily, 'and let's hope he doesn't make a habit of leaving places early.'

Best put the paper down and glanced at his watch. 'If we're going to get to that wretched little café by four, we'd better think about going.'

'I'm getting to hate that bloody journey,' said Stevens.

'With luck it's the last time. After this, London can take over.'

Stevens opened a drawer and took out two Browning automatics. He gave one to Best. They loaded the automatics and pocketed them. Then they went outside and got into Best's white Buick.

6

They had with them in the Buick a lieutenant from Dutch Intelligence. His name was Klop. There were rumours that the Germans might march into Holland at any time. Klop did not believe the rumours, but he was useful in getting them through the roadblocks. They stopped for a quick lunch at a little roadside café near s'Hertogenbosch. Between Venlo and the Café Backus they were halted twice. The last sentry was stationed near the bend in the road just before the straight with its view of the border. Best's apprehensions of the morning returned. He noticed that the German barrier across the road, normally closed, was now lifted. He felt a strong sense of impending danger, yet the scene was still peaceful. The only people in sight were a uniformed German customs officer and a little girl playing ball with a big, black dog.

Best slowed the Buick. Klop called out: 'Go ahead, everything is all right.' Best stopped in front of the café, then backed into the car-park beside the building. Major Schaemmel was standing on the veranda. When he saw the Britons he made a sign indicating that the General was within the café. Best stopped the engine and Stevens got out. Best was just getting out when there was shouting and shooting. A large, open car raced across the frontier shattering the wooden barrier on the Dutch side, roared into the café car-park and stopped with its bumper against the bumper of the Buick. The open car was packed with a dozen SD thugs. Some were shooting, all were shouting.

As the car stopped, four men leapt from it and rushed towards Stevens and Best shouting at them to put their hands up. Best scrambled out of the Buick and found himself next to Stevens.

'Our number's up, Best,' muttered Stevens.

Best felt for his Browning but it was too late. They were seized by rough hands, dragged apart and handcuffed.

Best heard shots to his right. He saw Klop creep out from behind the cover of the open car door and run diagonally away towards the road. As Klop ran, he zigzagged, firing at the Germans. After a moment of surprise, the Germans returned the fire. A few more steps and Klop crumpled and collapsed, a dark heap of clothes upon the grass.

'March!' shouted the Germans. Stevens and Best felt the muzzles of the pistols in their backs. 'Hup! Hup! Hup!' cried their captors and they were hurried along the road to the frontier. Then they were across the border and the black and white barrier, whose near-vertical position had so worried Best when he had first seen it, closed behind them.

In Nazi Germany they were tossed into the SD car like bundles of hay. Schellenberg watched with grim satisfaction. This part of the enterprise had gone perfectly. He had the spymasters. He hoped the lesser fry were being dealt with equally successfully.

Alex had had one of his loveliest, most cherishable evenings. He had called on Rachel at his usual time of six. They had had dinner together and later made love. Alex was certain that they had never been closer. He was astonished how his love continued to grow with every visit. He was delighted that Rachel had been so happy. There had been no trace of the doom and gloom that sometimes encompassed her. In fact she had been particularly light-hearted and laughed a great deal. They had even talked about the future with hope. The war seemed to be static and there were rumours of peace moves on both sides. Alex really did feel that such happiness could have no ending. Had there been a moon he would have jumped over it.

It was eleven when he said goodnight, walked jauntily down the stairs from the flat and strode quickly towards the Central Station to get the last tram. In his hand he carried a single envelope.

He was in the square, moving to board the tram, when he was suddenly grabbed from behind. He swung his head and saw a well-dressed, good-looking man of about thirty, wearing a trilby hat and grey mackintosh. As Alex struggled to extricate himself, the man displayed a police warrant card. 'I am Detective Sergeant Bearends of the Amsterdam police and I am arresting you.'

For a moment Alex couldn't speak. He was too surprised, too shocked. It might have been a bad dream, it might have been happening to someone else. It was impossible that it was happening to him.

'Arresting *me?*' he muttered stupidly.

'You heard. Arresting you.'

Alex took in the words. Suddenly he understood their meaning. In a wild gesture of despair he shook his head and tried to push the man away. 'What for? *What the hell for?*'

'You ought to know.'

His hands were wrenched behind him, the envelope was whisked from his grasp and he felt the cold steel of handcuffs clasping his wrists. It had all happened quickly and expertly before he could act. For an instant he was more concerned for the envelope than for himself.

'You can't take that! It's private!'

Bearends laughed. 'I bet it is. Anyway, you don't have to worry. I'll take good care of it.' He put the envelope in his pocket and patted his jacket. 'It's safe enough where it is.' He gave Alex a push. 'Now we're taking a little walk together.'

In spite of the lateness of the hour, a small crowd had gathered. Bearends took Alex's arm and tried to push their way through. Blocked, he produced a revolver. The crowd parted. Alex saw the faces looking at him and became even more confused.

'Where are we going?'

'You'll soon see.'

Bearends was steering Alex back the way he had come, towards the Red Light district, towards the Walletjes. Alex could make no sense of the move. In his mind he was still catching the last tram home.

'You're making a mistake . . .' he began, when Bearends gave him a shove.

'Keep walking. And there's no mistake. None at all. I know exactly what I'm doing. So do you.'

53

They walked along the cobbles beside the canal. Suddenly the Achterburgwal was in front of them. Alex was surprised to see the door to the flats open. The door was never open. A chill sense of unease, almost divorced from the policeman walking beside him, overcame him. For the first time since being seized outside the Central Station, he had the feeling that whatever had happened, whatever was wrong, Rachel was in some way involved.

A big, thickset man, middle-aged, with a pug-like face, was standing at the bottom of the stairs. He watched Bearends and Alex walking towards him, then with considerable satisfaction muttered: 'Good, you got him then.'

'Running off,' said Bearends, indicating Alex. 'Trying to get away on a tram.'

Pushed by Bearends and the new man, Alex was forced up the stairs. On the landing he was even more surprised to see that the door to Rachel's flat was also open. Again he demanded to know what was happening. 'Come and see,' said the new man and, pushing Alex into the flat, threw open the bedroom door.

Rachel lay motionless on the bed. She was dressed in her black dress exactly as Alex had left her. She had her face away from him and her hair lay across the pillows. Alex thought she must be asleep, but could not understand why. He called her name and tried to reach the bed, but strong arms held him back.

'What is it? What's wrong?'

'Come off it, you know what's wrong,' said Bearends.

Alex looked at both men and shook his head in bewilderment.

'You killed her,' said Bearends as if explaining something to a child. 'Strangled her by the look of it.'

The blood drained from Alex's face. He felt faint and found it hard to keep his balance. The bad dream at the Central Station was now a nightmare. He drew in his breath, ducked under the restraining arm and rushed to the bed. With his hands still handcuffed behind him, he sank to his knees and put his head on the woman's breast. There was no heartbeat. Already the body was chill.

54

'A pretty scene, I must say,' said the new man and smiled at Bearends. 'I've seen some villains in my time playing the innocent but this one takes the biscuit.'

Alex tried to speak but the words choked in his throat. He was crying, shaking his head as he managed to mutter: 'She was all right . . . Just now she was all right . . .' Then he screamed the same words: '*She was all right!*'

'We saw you run out of the house,' said the new man. 'You must have fairly raced down those stairs.'

'We came in here immediately after you left and found her just like that.' Bearends indicated, then added coldly, 'Dead. As dead as a dodo.'

'As if you didn't know,' said the new man sarcastically, scoffing at the perplexity on Alex's face.

Alex looked again at Rachel. He saw the red weals around her neck, the blue tinge to her lips. He could make no sense of anything he saw. He wanted to pick her up and hold her in his arms and press her to his chest, but his arms were firmly pinioned behind him. He tried to move; the handcuffs dug into his wrists. Then he was seized by the neck and lifted to his feet. He was still looking at Rachel lying sprawled on the bed when the two men thrust him out of the room. At the bottom of the stairs was a police car.

At police headquarters he was handed a piece of paper signed by an assistant commissioner stating that he was suspected of the wilful murder of a female known as Rachel Blum. He would therefore be detained for two days pending further investigations. He was not cautioned. The Dutch police did not believe in putting a suspect on his guard. His handcuffs were removed, his fingerprints taken, then he was locked in a small cell that contained an iron cot, a wash-basin and a lavatory. He sank down on the cot and put his head in his hands.

It was well after midnight, but there was no welcome sleep. Alex's dulled mind had started working in the police car. He had noticed none of the journey. All he could think of, all he could see, was Rachel lying dead on her bed. Without forgetting her or the vision of her dead, he now had other thoughts. He was vaguely aware that he had been accused of killing her.

55

It was such a ludicrous accusation it hardly registered and certainly didn't worry him. Even in his bemused state he was sure he would soon be cleared. All that concerned him was that Rachel was dead. Killed.

He began to differentiate between dead and killed and wondered who had killed her. Someone must have entered the flat after he left. The police said they had gone in immediately after he had come out of the door, but in spite of his dislike of them and the way they had manhandled him, he did not give the police a second thought. The police were the good guys. They protected people. A man looking for a prostitute might somehow have gained entry then, finding himself thwarted, turned nasty. The Germans might have caught up with her. Alex dismissed that possibility too. The Germans would never dare to do anything in Holland, a neutral country. But the vision of Rachel lying dead never left him.

His skin was dry with tiredness, his eyes wet, his body racked with sobs and he had a splitting headache. He went to the wash-basin and doused his face with cold water. He lay down on his cot and pressed his eyes shut but still there was no sleep. Only Rachel lying still in her black dress.

In the early hours he began to think of other things. He thought of his mother anxiously waiting for him to return home. She might even have phoned the police and been told of his arrest. He thought of missing the University tomorrow. It was then, with a pang of horror, he remembered the envelope. In the morning he should be passing it through the train window to Major Stevens. But they had taken the envelope. The envelope he had sworn never to let out of his sight. The loss of which Captain Best had said would be a catastrophe. He had let the two British officers down. Failed them, and failed his country. Then he saw Rachel again lying sprawled on that bed. At six in the morning, physically and emotionally exhausted, he fell asleep.

7

This time it was a nightmare. It was a girl doll. The head kept falling forwards on to the chest or lolling grotesquely back on to the shoulders. It was as if the neck was double-jointed. The face he knew well. He knew every curve of the flesh, every rise of the bones. He was crying out at the feeble, broken thing when he was shaken awake. A uniformed policeman with a mug of coffee and a metal plate on which were three slices of bread was shouting at him to get up. Reality was back. There was nothing but the policeman and the grey cell walls. Alex had left one nightmare for another.

At nine, Bearends' colleague, the big, ugly policeman, unlocked the cell door. 'Sleep well?' he asked, with an unpleasant, supercilious grin.

Alex shook his head.

'Ah, that's the trouble with having a guilty conscience. A guilty conscience can keep you awake all night. You see it a lot here.' The man's smile had gone. 'My name's Deepground, Detective Constable Deepground. If you're a good lad and co-operate then we shouldn't get on too badly.'

Alex said nothing. Although he found the man deeply offensive and remembered his actions in the flat, he made no grimace and showed no emotion. Then he noticed the size of the man's hands. They were massive. They seemed to hang from his arms like pendulums. Alex was still staring at them, fascinated, when Deepground grabbed his shoulder and pushed him out into the corridor.

He was taken to an interrogation room. Bearends was seated behind a desk, a dozen sheets of blank paper in front of him.

'Name?'

'Alex Richards. Alexander Richards.'

'Address?'

Alex gave his mother's flat in the Daniel Willinkplein.

'Age?'

57

'Seventeen and a half.'

'Nationality?'

'British.'

'I'm going to ask you a few questions,' said Bearends, glancing up at Alex for the first time. 'I advise you to answer truthfully. If you answer truthfully and don't waste our time, the judge will take that into consideration. What were you doing in Rachel Blum's flat last night?'

'I had dinner with her.'

'How long have you known her?'

'Three months.'

'What was your relationship with her?'

'We were friends.'

The questioning was slow. Bearends wrote everything down in longhand. He looked up, leered and said: 'Close friends?'

'Very close.'

'Then why did you kill her?' The words were spoken flatly, almost automatically.

'I didn't kill her!' shouted Alex.

'If you didn't kill her, tell me who did.'

'How should I know who killed her? She was alive when I left.'

'No, she was not!' Bearends shouted. 'You are lying! But it won't help you. We saw you running out of the house. We went straight upstairs, found the flat door open and the woman lying there dead. There was no one else in the flat.' He paused, his pale blue eyes narrowed and he added very slowly, 'So it must have been you that killed her. It couldn't have been anyone else. There isn't anyone else.'

The questioning went on in the same vein. Alex shouted that it was the detective who was lying. Deepground, who had been standing behind him, swung his fist. Alex felt the flash of pain as he was struck on the cheek. He was told to respect police officers. Suddenly he was conscious that Bearends was questioning him again.

'Are you in the habit of visiting whores?'

'No. Of course not.'

'Then why visit this Blum woman?'

Alex felt trapped. He wanted to shout out that Rachel hadn't been a prostitute, but remembered that that was her cover. Even now Major Stevens would not want her cover broken.

'Come on!' shouted Bearends. 'Why did you visit a whore?'

At that moment Alex hated the two detectives with all the hatred he was capable of. 'We were friends. She was different,' he muttered.

'I bet she was different,' said Deepground, sniggering.

'Did you have sexual intercourse with her?' asked Bearends.

Alex felt sick. He shook his head.

'Did you quarrel with the woman last night?'

'No, we parted friends.'

'*Then why kill her?*' shouted Deepground in Alex's ear.

The questioning and the accusations went relentlessly on. Alex denied everything. They tried to persuade him to confess, saying it would help his case. 'Judges consider persons who stubbornly deny their guilt hardened criminals,' said Bearends. It made no difference. Alex maintained his innocence. Deepground suggested a little rough stuff but Bearends wasn't ready for that yet. So Alex stood exhausted and the two detectives sat. At one o'clock he was returned to his cell.

In the afternoon the torment continued. Alex asked to see a lawyer.

'You can't see a lawyer as long as you are in police custody,' said Bearends. 'We are investigating a crime we have every reason to believe that you committed. When our investigations are complete, we shall hand you over to the Public Prosecutor. If he decides that there is enough evidence he will put you in front of a Judge of Instruction, who will decide whether to commit you for trial at the District Court of Amsterdam. Only then will you be allowed to consult a lawyer.'

The wearisome questioning went on for another two hours. Alex denied everything. Finally Bearends decided to give up for the day and told Deepground to take Alex back to his cell. Back in the cell Deepground did what he had wanted to do all day. 'This will teach you to keep lying to us,' he shouted and swung his great fists into Alex's face, chest and stomach. 'Confess tomorrow, or you'll get another dose!' Too exhausted to resist the big man, Alex passed out. Deepground picked him up and threw him on to the cot.

The next day they left him alone. His only visitor was the policeman who brought his food and a note from the assistant commissioner telling him that his forty-eight hours' detention had been extended for another forty-eight hours. Left alone, Alex brooded and puzzled. For the first time he began to see his own danger. It was evident that the detectives believed him guilty. He began to go over the questioning. One thing he failed to understand was why they insisted that he had come running out of Rachel's house without closing the door. He always closed the door and he never ran out of the house. He sometimes came down the stairs two or three steps at a time, but he never ran. Then, alone in the cell, his body aching, his mind dulled, he had doubts. Maybe he had run and left the door open. Maybe they were right.

On the morning of the third day he was taken back to the interrogation room and questioned for six hours. He had eaten nothing, just drunk the coffee. By three in the afternoon he could hardly stand. It was then that Bearends offered to change the charge of murder to one of manslaughter provided Alex admitted to having killed Rachel Blum in a quarrel. Alex refused. Under a barrage of accusations and blows from Deepground, he collapsed. When he came to he was in his cell. That evening he drank the coffee and ate the dry bread and for the first time slept soundly. The following morning he was taken out of his cell and the property taken from him after his arrest was returned. For a moment, Alex's hopes were high. At last the detectives had come to realize he was innocent. He was about to be released. Then he noticed two things. He was still being closely guarded and the brown envelope picked up from Rachel Blum and due to be handed to Major Stevens was not with his watch, wallet, fountain pen, belt and tie. He asked for the envelope but everyone denied knowledge of it. He was however told that enquiries would be made. He was still sufficiently naïve to believe it.

Fatesma, the Public Prosecutor of the Amsterdam District Court, sat behind his desk and for a long time took no notice of the young man standing in front of him. Then he raised his joyless face, glanced at Alex and addressed him, reading from the file open upon his desk.

'You are Alexander Richards, aged seventeen, a British subject, residing in Amsterdam?'

'Yes, sir.'

'On the evening of the ninth of November a woman by the name of Rachel Blum was murdered in her flat in this city. There is evidence to suggest . . .'

'I did not kill her, sir!'

The Prosecutor took off his glasses. Without the glasses his eyes seemed smaller, sunk deep into his face. Although trying to keep calm he was evidently agitated. His hands were clenched. The muscles on his face were knotted. 'Young man, it is only fair that I should tell you that there is ample evidence to prove that you killed the woman. Denying it is not going to help. You are young and if you make a frank confession, the court might be lenient with you.'

To Alex's surprise and dismay it was the interrogation room all over again, only this time there was one Prosecutor instead of two detectives. In spite of the Prosecutor's massive, hunched, almost ominous appearance behind his desk and the bad beginning to the interview, Alex was not frightened by him, nor was he without hope. The Prosecutor was a lawyer, a man of learning, a man with an important position in society. A representative of justice and the authorities. He was far above a mere policeman, certainly far above thugs like Bearends and Deepground. Alex believed that he must be able to reason with him, make him see the truth.

'You haven't let me speak. You haven't let me say a word. You're just condemning me out of hand. That's not justice.'

The Prosecutor was surprised. It took him a moment to gather himself, then he indicated the file. 'It's all here. The police officers have questioned you; that is their job, not mine. It is their job to obtain all the evidence and that is exactly what they have done. It is my job to study that evidence and decide whether there is a case against you.' He glanced down at the file. 'In the matter of the murder of Rachel Blum the case against you is absolutely clear. There can be no doubt whatso-

61

ever. So, I repeat, if you make a frank confession, there is every chance the court will be lenient with you.'

'You are asking me to do what the others did. You're trying to force me to admit that I killed my best friend.'

The Prosecutor raised his eyebrows. 'Your best friend a whore?'

'She wasn't a . . .' Alex began and stopped.

'She wasn't a whore? Is that what you're saying? In which case why did she live in the Walletjes?'

Alex bit his lip. After a while he said, 'She was a very nice person.'

'Did your mother know about her?'

'She knew I went to see someone . . .'

Fatesma nodded. 'Just as I thought. You're not the first young man from a good family to get himself entangled with a woman of ill repute. Nor the first to have a quarrel with one.'

'I didn't have a quarrel with her. We loved each other!'

Fatesma had a quizzical look. There was a hint of exasperation in his voice but he had stopped clenching his hands and his face was more relaxed. 'Don't you realize that I'm trying to help you? You are young. It is still not too late. Just tell me, in your own words, exactly how you came to kill the poor, wretched woman, and when we get to court, the judges will no doubt take your co-operation into consideration.'

'I did *not* kill Rachel Blum!'

'Of course you did. Now don't be stupid. Tell me in your own words just what happened.'

'I tell you, Mr Prosecutor, as I've told the others, Rachel Blum was my friend, I loved her.'

'We've had all that,' said Fatesma impatiently, and sat back in his chair quite evidently waiting. When Alex remained silent, Fatesma smiled and said, 'I'm trying to help. Make things easier for you. If you won't think of yourself and your own conscience, then think of your poor mother. To have a son a murderer is terrible enough. To know that son is also a liar, a perjurer . . .' He stopped and shook his head with an air of infinite sadness.

Alex wanted to scream out that the man was more devious than Satan but restrained himself. Instead, he stuck to the

62

words that were going round and round in his head, all that was keeping him sane. 'I did *not* kill Rachel Blum!'

Fatesma began to shake. His face darkened. He pushed on his glasses and stared up at Alex. 'You don't know what you're saying,' he spluttered, and indicated the file in front of him. 'It's here, the most damning evidence I have ever seen. The police caught you virtually red-handed.'

Alex took a deep breath. He began to feel that he was slipping into an abyss, that this man was no different from the others. He might look different, he might hold an important position, he might be intelligent, but for some reason that Alex could not understand, the Prosecutor had a mind as blocked and dangerous as the rest of them.

Fatesma was smiling again. 'Now, I'll give you one more chance. For your own sake you must make a clean breast of it. It'll make all the difference in court.'

Alex leaned forward and said, 'I did *not* kill Rachel Blum and I won't admit it just to please the court!'

For a moment there was silence. Then all Fatesma's pretence at friendliness vanished. 'You fool! You foolish, stupid fool!'

The heavy face that had professed the wish to help was transformed. Alex was shocked at the anger and hatred. There was a greater depth of evil emotion in the Prosecutor's face than either of the detectives had displayed. Alex remembered Rachel's words about the hatred in the eyes of the Nazis and the fanaticism upon their faces. Then he put the thought from him. In Holland the Nazis were not allowed to hold offices in the civil service and the Public Prosecutor couldn't possibly be a Nazi.

'Don't you dare to speak to me like that, you insolent scoundrel! Remember who you are talking to. You are a criminal and a foreigner. A foreigner who has abused our hospitality.' Fatesma's fury was such that he found it difficult to speak. His voice rose to a hysterical pitch. 'I've done all I can to help, but I shall help you no longer. Murder is a most heinous crime but I swear you will not get away with it. Not in my country, Holland! *I shall see to that!*'

Alex was only vaguely conscious of Fatesma's words. He was mesmerized by the face. The wild, burning hatred in a man in this position horrified him. It seemed that the face grew

63

bigger and ruddier as he watched. Yet one word in all those Fatesma had spat out shocked him more than the others. The word 'hospitality' in this man's mouth was too much. Alex lost the last vestiges of his self-control. All the rage and resentment he had felt at his treatment since his arrest welled up. 'Hospitality! You call being beaten up, kept standing for six hours without even a drink of water, hospitality!'

For the moment, astonishment quelled Fatesma's anger. Prisoners didn't argue with him, they trembled before him. He was particularly galled at such a young one behaving in such a manner. He snapped shut the file and pushed it away with a gesture of great finality.

'You are a most depraved youth,' he said coldly, struggling to control his resurgent fury. 'If the others in charge of your investigation found it necessary to chastise you, then you must have deserved it. When you have committed murder, are being questioned and stubbornly cling to lies, you can hardly expect to be served tea and biscuits. However, I am not going to waste my time with you any longer. I shall ask the Judge of Instruction to commit you for trial at the District Court on a charge of wilful murder.' He paused for a moment, then added in an icy voice, 'When you come to trial I shall make quite sure you are sentenced to life imprisonment.'

With a flick of his hand, as if removing an annoying fly, Fatesma dismissed Alex. Before his arm was seized and he was marched out of the room, Alex had one more look at the massive face above the desk. There was now a slumbering malevolence. It was the face of a shaggy he-devil, a cross between a giant and a toad, who had just crushed its prey but would soon be hungry again. Alex prayed that he would never see the face a second time but he also knew that as long as he lived he would never forget it nor the heavy, hunched shoulders that seemed to be part of it.

In the afternoon, Alex was brought before the Judge of Instruction who committed him for trial at the District Court and ordered that he remain in custody for six days. He was allowed a lawyer.

*　　*　　*

In the quiet of his study, in the silence of the evening, Fatesma sat and considered events. He had got over his anger and was well satisfied with the ways things had gone. Bearends and Deepground had done their part well. He trusted both implicitly. That is, he trusted both as honest, devoted members of the Party. Neither would ever knowingly let him or the Party down. However, Deepground always gave him some concern, for he invariably put action before thought. Where Bearends used his brain, such as it was, Deepground used his brawn. Fatesma was pleased and relieved that this time the combination had worked so perfectly. He was not particularly interested in the sequence of events in the flat in the Achterburgwal, only that the job had been well done. Bearends would have worked out the final details, Deepground would have done the actual killing. Certainly Deepground had the right-sized hands for the task. In spite of the precocity of the young Englishman, the trial should not prove difficult.

Fatesma poured himself a drink. On his desk was a photo in a silver frame. The photo was of his wife. From where he was sitting, with the angle of the light, the glass was acting as a reflector. He saw no sign of his wife's face, only the image of his own. He was in a particularly pensive mood. The sight of his own face merely heightened that mood.

He had done well at University but remained something of a loner. Although many respected him, he had few friends, only acquaintances. Most of the time he put this down to his position. It might be thought difficult to be a close friend of the Public Prosecutor. But when he sat alone, as he was sitting this evening, he knew that it was more than that. There was something within him that in personal contacts made him draw back. Even as a boy he had been frightened of being taken over. He always had to be in control of himself and, as far as possible, those around him. He supposed it was this natural desire for isolation, this sense of never fitting in – particularly strong when he saw people enjoying themselves – that had led him to join the Party.

Fatesma had never met Hitler nor seen him in person, yet he admired him as he might have admired a great painter or musician. Where the painter transformed a palette of individual colours into a sensible, coherent, sometimes majestic, often wonderful creation and the musician transformed marks upon paper into spell-binding sound, so Hitler had picked up the shattered remains of the decadent Weimar Republic, the Germany defeated and ruined in 1918, and transformed it into a strong, efficient, modern state. Fatesma admired the strong and despised the weak. The world belonged to the strong. In the nineteenth century it had been Darwin who was right – in the twentieth century, Hitler.

There was a lot in his country that Fatesma would have liked to have changed. Holland should model itself upon Germany. When he thought of the pathetic antics of the government in The Hague, he wished he had the power to trample them underfoot or cast them into the sea. A country needed a strong leader backed by a united people. One day Holland would understand. In the meantime, the Party gave Fatesma something he had not had before: a feeling of comradeship he would never have thought possible. With Holland's destiny linked to that of its great and powerful neighbour, the Führer's Third Reich, Fatesma could see nothing but hope.

He got up and poured himself another drink. He stood and smiled into the shelves of books. He was like no other lawyer in Holland. He was a lawyer with a mission. One day, in the not-too-distant future, the shambles he saw every day upon the streets of Amsterdam would be swept away by the New Order. People would look smart, be proud of themselves and feel important. There would be no more woolly thinking, the road ahead would be clear-cut. The Jews could no longer control the country nor run the economy. They wouldn't simply be driven underground to burrow like rats, they would be eliminated. The Blackshirts of Holland would come into their own and the nation would be clean again. For the present they must do their duty. The trial of the young man would be no problem: merely one more link in the chain that bound the great European National Socialist family.

8

'Your clothes,' said the warder, indicating a bundle of what looked like rags. 'You might as well get used to them.'

Alex stared at the prison clothes: underwear, socks, a pair of baggy trousers, a rough woollen jacket dyed dark brown and a pair of soiled clogs. Alex had never worn clogs. He looked at them in dismay. 'I don't know whether I'll be able to walk . . .' he muttered.

The warder laughed. 'You'll learn soon enough.'

Then came the real shock. The shock that reminded Alex where he was and so sickened him. He was handed his 'cap'. It was more like a beret and made of the same rough material as the jacket. Attached to the beret was a mask of stiffer material. There were slits for the eyes but no opening for either the nose or mouth.

'Put this on,' said the warder harshly, and thrust the object into Alex's hands.

Alex fingered the mask. It was alien and horrific, redolent of obliteration – of a lost soul. He remembered the story of the Man in the Iron Mask, incarcerated and locked away from the world for ever. Then the warder grabbed the beret and thrust it on Alex's head, pulling the mask down over his face and completely covering it. Alex felt the coarse material on his cheeks and smelt the stale, fetid smell. The tender areas of his nose and mouth became irritated and he had a sense of overwhelming nausea. He felt shame and degradation as he had never felt it before. He fought back the tears.

'That's better,' said the warder, almost cheerfully. 'You wear this cap every time you leave your cell. Understand?'

Unable to speak for the material hanging over his mouth, Alex nodded. Then he raised the mask and asked why he had to wear it.

'Because prisoners are not allowed to see each other's faces and are also strictly forbidden to talk to one another,' said the warder blandly, then opened a large ledger and ran his finger down the entries. 'Your number is A3-10. In the House of Custody you have no name, only a number. So you can forget your name. Just remember A3-10. That's you from now on.' He rummaged through a drawer of his desk, and produced a metal disc on which the code A3-10 was printed. Carefully, almost lovingly, he pinned the disc on Alex's jacket.

'There you are, all dressed up, ready for your new home.'

Walking with difficulty, often stumbling, Alex was taken through an iron gate then through a heavy wooden door to the centre of the building. In front of him and to his left and right were long corridors, A Wing, B Wing and C Wing, each three storeys high. Along the corridors were rows of heavy cell doors. Several warders and prisoners were visible. Every warder had a truncheon hanging from a leather strap around his wrist. Every prisoner, whether scrubbing the floor or merely being escorted from one place to another, wore a cap with a mask. No prisoner showed his face. The only thing to indicate humanity behind those coarse woollen masks was the shaded eyes.

Alex was taken in front of the Chief Warder, whose place of authority was the very centre of the building, the hub of the wings.

'Who are you?' shouted the Chief Warder.

'Alexander Richards . . .'

'No, you're not! You are A3-10! Haven't you been told that you're no longer a person, *just a number*?'

This was a time-honoured trap for new prisoners and most fell into it. It was guaranteed to degrade and frighten. His joke over, his position established, the Chief Warder took Alex to the third floor of A Wing. With a truncheon, Alex was motioned into cell number 10.

'Now you can take your cap off.'

Alex took the cap off. Even in this dismal place it was wonderful to breathe freely again. He was handed a piece of cardboard that hung from a nail in the wall and told to read the rules and regulations of the House. The Chief Warder left, banging the cell door shut.

Alex was not actually in prison although he could be forgiven for thinking he was. Under Dutch law there was no provision for bail. People suspected of having committed a felony were to be kept in custody. So the Dutch authorities euphemistically created 'Houses of Custody'. Left alone, free of the fearful cap, Alex considered his 'new home' within the House of Custody. He paced the cell and found it eight feet by sixteen. On one side was an iron cot anchored and hinged to the wall. It was held in the 'up' position by an iron hook. Inside the bed was the mattress, a large sack filled with straw. There was a pillow, also filled with straw, and two horse blankets. High up in the end wall was a barred window through which was visible a fragment of sky. In the corner near the window was a small metal drum with a lid. This was the lavatory. In the other corner were two triangular shelves. On the top shelf was a metal plate, a metal jug and a spoon. On the bottom shelf was a metal wash-basin and water jug. There was a three-legged stool anchored to the floor. It was upon this that Alex sat, read the House Regulations and thought.

He was allowed to write one letter a week to his nearest relative, but not to mention anything about the House of Custody or the staff. He noted his rigid routine and was horrified that he would be allowed only one bath every two weeks. He realized that the moment of peace, if there could be such a time here, was between six-thirty and nine. This was when he would have his supper and be allowed to read his book. Unfortunately he had no book. A warder brought him a sheet of paper, an envelope, pen and ink, and he wrote his first letter to his mother. Writing the letter released all his emotions. He struggled not to weep and not to remember too much. On a positive note he asked her to get him a lawyer. In the evening he learned how his food arrived. When a little flap in his door opened, he put first his plate upon it, then his mug. He was the recipient of the usual coffee and three pieces of dry bread. At nine the House of Custody thumped with the dull thuds of the cots being lowered. Alex undressed and lay on the bag of straw. He had no pyjamas and slept in the prison underwear. The sacking that covered the mattress and pillow, combined with the straw inside, made him itch all over.

He slept badly and was awake long before the morning bell sounded.

On his first full day, after slopping out and breakfast of the usual coffee and three slices of bread, he learned the nature of his work. A warder brought him three large sacks of strangely shaped paper. The paper meant nothing to Alex until the warder showed him how, with the help of a template, each piece of paper could be folded into an envelope. He was expected to make a thousand envelopes a day. Mid-morning he was taken to see the Governor of the House of Custody. It was not an auspicious meeting. As he stood in front of the desk he had his hands behind his back, a stance that infuriated the Governor.

'Stand to attention when you are before a white man.'

The man was a half-caste of mixed Dutch and Indonesian extraction. Used to telling his Indonesian subordinates to stand to attention when speaking to him, now that he was Governor of a prison in Holland where all the inmates were white he was still using the same insulting expression. The irony that he was not pure white, but that the inmates were, was no doubt lost upon him.

'Remove your cap!'

Alex took his cap off. The Governor peered at Alex's face. 'I see that you were born in the Dutch East Indies and I know that people from there are not used to discipline.'

'Both my parents were Europeans,' said Alex quietly.

The Governor's face grew ruddy; for a moment he was speechless. Then he pointed towards the door. 'You're an insolent young bastard! I will keep my eyes on you, so watch yourself. Now get out!'

Alex was thankful to go. He had hated the man from the moment he had set eyes on him.

Just before the midday meal, Alex was taken for what was known as 'airing out'. In the prison garden were ten large cages, each separated by a brick wall. A prisoner was put in each cage and once inside was permitted to take off his mask. For half an hour he was allowed to pace about like an animal in a zoo. The procedure was repeated in the afternoon. No talking or communication was allowed between the cages. By the time he lowered his cot on the second evening, Alex realized that he would be spending twenty-three hours of each day locked in his cell.

On the fourth day of his confinement he was visited by the lawyer his mother had engaged. The interview took place in a small room with a warder watching through a glass panel in the door. The sight of the lawyer sitting waiting at the little table was like stumbling upon an oasis after months in the wilderness.

'Leon Jacobs,' said the lawyer, introducing himself. 'I have been retained by your mother to defend you.'

The man was smiling. It was the first friendly smile Alex had seen since his arrest.

'How is my mother?' asked Alex eagerly.

Jacobs shrugged. 'Being brave, as you'd expect. It hasn't been easy for her.'

'Tell her not to worry,' cried Alex, then with great confidence and ingenuousness added, 'I didn't kill Rachel Blum, so I *must* be all right!'

Alex was smiling. The smile was infectious. Jacobs began to smile again. He was a pleasant-looking man in his early thirties. Alex felt that at last he had found a friend. Jacobs pointed at the other chair. Alex sat. Jacobs gave a slight nod and leaned forward in his chair. 'Let's begin at the beginning, shall we? The very beginning. Tell me everything, in your own words.'

Careful not to mention Major Stevens, Captain Best or the envelopes, Alex told his story. When he had finished, Jacobs asked the question Alex had most feared. How had he first met Rachel?

'Through a mutual friend.'

The lawyer waited for more. At last Alex said, 'I don't want him dragged in. I'd rather not mention his name.'

Jacobs frowned. 'The Court is certainly going to wonder about the relationship between a seventeen-year-old student and a woman in the Red Light district.'

'Do I have to go to Court?'

The lawyer didn't answer the question directly. 'If I am going to help you, you must be honest with me,' he said impatiently. 'You must tell me everything that relates to the

71

case. And remember, anything you tell me is confidential and will go no further.'

Alex thought for a long time. At last he said, 'It's not that I don't trust you. It's that I gave my word to someone, someone important, not to talk about certain matters.'

'You don't seem to understand your position,' said Jacobs, with growing exasperation. 'You're facing a *murder* charge! Your whole future is at stake.'

In his naïvety, in the knowledge of his innocence, the words still meant little to Alex. He was concerned but not deeply worried. The lawyer waited for the reaction upon Alex's face, saw none and was surprised.

'Don't you realize you could spend the next twenty years in prison? Twenty years!'

'*I'm innocent!*'

'We have to prove it.'

For the first time Alex felt the jaws of the trap. He found it hard to believe, or even understand, but his worry mounted. He bit his lip and thought for a long time. At last he said, 'I can't do anything on my own. I can't say any more, I can't even decide what ought to be said.' He lowered his voice. 'You must go to the British Legation at The Hague and ask to see Major Stevens. Tell him about me. He will decide what to do, what I am to tell you.'

Jacobs looked up from the notes he was taking and stared at Alex. 'Did you say Major Stevens?'

Alex nodded.

'Haven't you heard? Don't you know what happened?'

Alex shook his head.

'I suppose there was only one Major Stevens working at the British Legation . . .'

'I'm sure there was only one,' said Alex impatiently, 'so for heaven's sake tell me! What did happen to him? Has he gone back to England?'

'He was kidnapped by the Germans along with another British officer, Captain Best.'

Alex felt his chest tighten as if a steel band had been clamped around his ribs. For an instant he couldn't believe the lawyer, then he saw his face. Jacobs was showing great surprise at the effect of his words. Alex's world was shattered, falling into fragments. First Rachel murdered, then his own arrest and now the two people he had thought indestructible, Major Stevens and Captain Best, kidnapped. He was alone, chillingly, miserably alone.

'When?' he muttered. 'When did it happen?'

'Last Thursday, the ninth. In the afternoon at Venlo.'

Alex drew in his breath. The day, the date struck him like a thunderbolt. The lawyer leaned forward again, his face full of concern. 'Are you ill? Shall I call a warder?'

Alex shook his head.

'Whatever is it?'

'Rachel was murdered that evening . . .'

The lawyer was surprised that he hadn't noticed the similarity in the dates. He sat back in his chair, on his face a quizzical look. 'Go on,' he said very quietly. 'Like Rachel Blum I'm Jewish. I've no love for the Germans.'

Alex told Jacobs everything. All those bits and pieces he had so carefully omitted from his first tale.

When Alex had finished, Jacobs stared through the barred window at the high wall that separated the prison from the outside world. For a long time he was silent, then at last he said, 'A most extraordinary story. A most extraordinary case. And too much of a coincidence. Far too much. A woman, apparently working for the British, killed on the same day that the two officers, her . . . er . . . er employers, are kidnapped.'

'Only you and I know that,' said Alex quickly.

Jacobs nodded. There was another pause, then in a most businesslike way he said, 'I'll have a talk with the Public Prosecutor. See exactly what is the evidence against you.'

After all his ill treatment, in his disorientated state, paranoia was close. Mention of the Public Prosecutor made Alex believe he had been tricked into talking about the British officers and the envelopes. He was a fool to have trusted the lawyer. Jacobs was one of the Public Prosecutor's minions. Jacobs saw Alex's look of doubt turning to horror. He shook his head and made a movement with his hands. 'Everything you have told me about Major Stevens and Captain Best is a secret between us. I shall say nothing to anyone.'

In a gesture of utter despair, Alex shut his eyes and shook his head. 'I don't know who to trust . . .'

Jacobs leaned forward.

Alex shook his head even more violently and gave a cry from the heart: '*I don't know who to trust!*'

'I am a lawyer. You must trust me. You have no one else.'

Alex desperately wanted to believe in someone and he stared at the lawyer hoping to be convinced. But inside he was numb. He could make no decision. There was no place of safety.

'I will do all I can for you,' said Jacobs quietly, 'everything possible. But I *have* to speak to the Public Prosecutor. I *have* to know his case.'

Alex still hesitated. The whole world seemed alien. 'How do I know I can trust you any more than anyone else?'

'I told you, I am Jewish. The same as Rachel Blum.'

It was the Jewishness that did it. The man was of the same race as the dark-eyed woman he had loved and still loved. Alex took the leap. It was an enormous step. He gulped down his disbelief, smothered it somewhere inside him and believed. The act of faith made him feel that there was life again. He put out of his mind the thought that Jacobs was another false god and told himself that one day there would be a spring.

'What will happen to me?' he whispered.

'In the next few days you will be taken in front of three judges of the District Court who will decide whether you should remain in custody. If they do, they will order you to be detained for thirty days. At the end of that time they will have the power to prolong the detention for a further thirty days.'

'How long can that go on for?'

'Until the Prosecutor is ready to present the case against you.'

The lawyer promised to return as soon as he had spoken to the Public Prosecutor. Alex put on his cap and mask and was taken back to his cell.

It was as the lawyer had said. The day after his visit, Alex was called to appear in front of the judges of the District Court. The panel held its sessions in a room in the House of Custody.

Outside the room a line of masked prisoners stood facing the wall with their hands behind them. When a prisoner's number was called, he took off his clogs, entered the room and stood in front of the table at which the judges were seated. He then took off his cap and mask.

'You are Alexander Richards and you are accused of having murdered one Rachel Blum. It is the Court's decision that you will be kept in custody for a period of thirty days. You may go.' That was all. He was given no chance to speak. It was a rubber stamp operation that had taken just three minutes.

Back in his cell Alex sat and brooded. He found it impossible to understand how the Dutch could be so primitive in their administration of justice. He had been born in a Dutch colony, lived all his life amongst Dutch people, but he still failed to comprehend how they tolerated this oppressive, inhuman system, this medieval way of treating people. He wondered which sadistic legal mind had invented the dreadful mask. So obsessed had been that mind with the idea of solitary confinement it had even had to obliterate human features. He thought too of the people who administered this hell. The ones he had met so far fitted remarkably well into the repressive environment. For the most part the warders were dull-witted morons recruited from the northern agricultural parts of Holland. There the people worked mostly on potato farms and lived a life of abject poverty. Anything was better than working on a potato farm. There were plenty of volunteers for the prison service. A warder was a civil servant, although the lowest paid. They didn't even need an elementary school education and there was a pension to look forward to. The only training a warder received was how to subdue a recalcitrant prisoner with the aid of a rubber truncheon.

'Some justice,' muttered Alex bitterly to himself, and then remembered that all this was happening to him before his trial. That he was innocent made it an even greater mockery.

Leon Jacobs stared across the table. 'I'm not going to beat about the bush. The evidence the Public Prosecutor has against you is enough to convict you ten times over.'

75

Alex stared at the lawyer in disbelief. 'Are you telling me that you believe me guilty?'

Jacobs shook his head. 'I'm simply saying that on the evidence you will be convicted.'

Again Alex felt that terrible, trapped feeling. He would be condemned to wear the dreadful mask for evermore. *'I didn't do it! You know I didn't do it!'*

'The Prosecutor went through his whole case,' said Jacobs sombrely. 'From our point of view it certainly looks extremely black. The police officers saw you run out of the house. They say you appeared agitated and were so keen to get away, you left the front door open. They also maintain that less than three minutes elapsed between your leaving the flat and their entrance. The medical evidence too is grim. You admitted to being with Rachel Blum from six o'clock. The doctor says that when he examined the body she had been dead for no more than an hour.' Sadly the lawyer shook his head. 'There aren't many loose ends.'

Alex was shocked at the lawyer's complacency, his apparent acceptance of the Public Prosecutor's idea of events. 'There are hundreds of loose ends. Thousands! What were the police doing there in the first place? Wasn't it a bit lucky they just happened to be standing in the Achterburgwal, watching?'

'They were on the look-out for Chinese opium pedlars.' Jacobs saw the look of disbelief on Alex's face. 'It *is* the Red Light district.'

'What about motive?' asked Alex. 'Why should I murder my best friend? The woman I loved!'

'The Prosecutor believes he has several possible motives. One is that you had an illicit relationship with Miss Blum. She wanted to end it, you didn't. When she insisted, you became angry. There was a quarrel. You killed her.'

'Do you believe that?' asked Alex contemptuously.

'It's not important what I believe. It's what the Court believes. And the quarrel story is perfectly plausible. It's happened before.'

The lawyer fell silent.

'Go on,' said Alex grimly.

'If you confess to killing Rachel Blum in an outburst of rage, the Public Prosecutor is prepared to reduce the charge to one of manslaughter.'

Alex's mouth fell open. Jacobs held up his hands. 'Listen, Alex. You still don't seem to understand how serious the evidence against you is. The Prosecutor has made a fair offer. If you are found guilty of murder, you will go to prison for at least twenty years. If you admit to manslaughter you will spend three years in a reform school. If you consider this place bad, wait until you are in a real prison.'

Alex was deeply shaken and in great despair. He had no idea what to do. It seemed that with each meeting, each event, his situation got worse.

'It would help if my own lawyer would believe in my innocence,' he said, almost pleadingly.

'I've told you,' said Jacobs gently, 'it doesn't matter what I believe. It's what the Prosecutor will say and what the Court believes.'

Alex came to a sudden decision. 'I tell you what I'm going to do, Mr Jacobs,' he said defiantly. 'I am going to go on denying that I killed Rachel Blum until the truth comes out and proves me right.'

His first meeting with his mother was even more painful than he had expected. The lawyer had been to see her. She echoed the lawyer's request that Alex should plead guilty to man-slaughter. In an emotional fifteen minutes, with a warder sitting between them, he refused. Afterwards, alone in his cell, he prayed that she had understood.

When the thirty days of his custody were nearly over, he appeared again in front of the panel of judges. With no question asked, no opportunity given to speak, the period was extended. At Christmas, Alex went to the prison chapel. Along with all the other inmates, each wearing his mask, he heard the Word of God. In the New Year, his mother came a second time, this time with a close friend of Alex's, Paul Wilking.

Wilking's visit greatly cheered Alex. Wilking was a warm-hearted extrovert who could never have believed Alex guilty

77

and considered the charge of murder quite ludicrous. As only close relatives were allowed to make visits to prisoners, Wilking was brought in as Alex's cousin. That this ruse succeeded, and the House of Custody authorities were deceived, added considerable piquancy to the meeting.

In February, Alex's thirty days of custody were again extended. In March he received a summons from the Public Prosecutor to appear before the District Court of Amsterdam on the twentieth to answer the charge of wilful murder. Alex was glad. The waiting would soon be over. In Court his innocence would be evident to all.

9

MI6 could claim to be founded at the time of the Spanish Armada by Sir Francis Walsingham. Its charter said it was to 'gather all the secrets at the girdles of the Princes of Europe and make mischief amongst the King's enemies'. The fiasco of Stevens and Best hardly lived up to the noble, or ignoble, intentions of the charter. However, there was nothing the least bit amateurish about the officer sent to Holland to pick up the pieces after Venlo.

Montague Reany Chidson was one of the ablest officers of the Secret Intelligence Service. He was cool, efficient and, if necessary, ruthless. He was no stranger to Holland, having served there previously as 'Passport Control Officer'. He was married to a Dutch woman and spoke Dutch fluently. Chidson's first job on reaching The Hague was to try and repair some of the damage inflicted by Schellenberg upon the espionage rings. There was a further complication in that no one knew what either Stevens or Best might be forced to say under Gestapo interrogation. On the latter point Chidson decided that neither man would crack. Bunglers though they had been, they were not cowards. Reassured, Chidson started at the beginning with Stevens' files.

Chidson found the notes on Alex Richards' recruitment as

a courier. He read the details of the death of Rachel Blum, the Amsterdam letter-box, and noted with a certain grim inevitability that it had happened on the same day as the abduction of Stevens and Best. At once he smelt the hands of the Gestapo. He next discovered that Alex Richards had been arrested and charged with the murder of Rachel Blum. For a while, on first examining the matter, he had wondered whether Richards was a Gestapo agent who had infiltrated the chain. He had considered the possibility carefully. It made good sense and yet Chidson was uneasy at accepting it. The age and inexperience of Richards pointed against his being a double agent. The more he thought about the matter, the more he went into it, the more convinced Chidson became that Richards was a bona fide British agent, in which case it seemed most unlikely that he had murdered a fellow member of the chain.

Chidson made it his business to find out all he could about the details of Richards' arrest and the case against him. In that he was helped by one of the remaining links with his immediate predecessor. Miss Pluck had been Stevens' secretary. It was with Miss Pluck that he discussed one of the odder aspects of the case.

'Tell me, Miss Pluck, why should two police officers happen to be so conveniently placed right by the Achterburgwal at *exactly* the right time on *exactly* the right day? Do you think that in many murder cases the police are ready and waiting at the scene of the crime *before* it actually happens? Don't you find the coincidence too much? Worse than a Thomas Hardy novel?'

Over the top of her glasses, like a slightly distraught schoolmistress, Miss Pluck looked down at Chidson. 'From the information we have been able to glean, the police officers were in that particular area watching for Chinese opium smugglers.'

'Do you believe that, Miss Pluck?'

'It may be true, Colonel, on the other hand it may not.' Miss Pluck wrinkled her nose so that her glasses rose and fell. 'It is, of course, a most unsavoury area.'

Chidson nodded. He had often seen the women in the windows. Indeed, that was why Rachel Blum had been put there.

'I always thought that Mr Richards was far too young to be sent there,' said Miss Pluck, disapprovingly.

Chidson looked up. 'Too young to murder?'

'Far too young. He is a well brought up young man, Colonel. Very well brought up.'

'And you consider well brought up young men incapable of murder?'

'I first met Mr Richards when he came to the reception. He behaved quite impeccably. That was when Major Stevens introduced him to Captain Best. When he was recruited.'

'If you are right, Miss Pluck, about good blood remaining good,' said Chidson teasingly, 'then someone else did the murder.'

'Of course they did, Colonel.'

For a while Chidson was silent. With the fingers of his right hand he drummed upon the blotter on his desk. Miss Pluck's feet were just beginning to hurt her when Chidson said, 'You do know, don't you, that it is not uncommon for a Dutch policeman to also be a Nazi? In which case it is not uncommon for certain of the Dutch police to be in contact with the Germans. It follows from that', he spoke slowly, choosing his words carefully, 'that our young man may have been set up. What I believe is called "framed".'

There was a trace of a smile on Miss Pluck's lips as she asked if the Colonel wished to go further into the background of the two policemen in question.

'Very much further, Miss Pluck. I want to know everything about them. More than their mothers know. Much more. I should also like to visit the young man, Alex Richards. So far as I remember, it is normal practice for Legation and Consular officials to visit their nationals in custody.'

Miss Pluck was pleased. She would have liked the visit to have happened long ago but, in the hiatus after the Venlo incident, the matter had been overlooked.

10

'All rise in Court!'

The Clerk's voice rang through the room. Alex had looked forward to his trial; he would be able to prove his innocence. Now, in the courtroom with the judges filing in through the large doors behind the dais, he wasn't so sure. There was nothing about the décor, the furnishings, the atmosphere or the people present to inspire confidence in any accused, let along a young man not yet eighteen. There was no jury, for the Dutch did not believe in involving laymen in the processes of the law. He was to be tried and judged by three black-gowned men with faces as dour as the room. To make matters worse, while Alex's lawyer sat at a small table in the well of the room, his adversary, the Public Prosecutor, not only entered with the judges but shared their table upon the dais. True he didn't actually sit next to them, but at the end of the long, narrow table; nevertheless he was on their level and, unlike everyone else, had no need to look up at them. On the wall behind the table, centred over the middle of the three judges, the President of the Court, was a large framed photograph of Queen Wilhelmina. Her Majesty's expression fitted the grimness of the scene.

The charge was formally read and Alex acknowledged that he understood it. He agreed that although a foreigner, a British subject, he was fully familiar with the Dutch language and needed no interpreter. His fears that the Public Prosecutor was in cahoots with the judges were increased when the President of the Court deferred instantly to Fatesma. Fatesma asked that the trial be heard in camera as the accused was a minor in a case with strong sexual overtones. After a brief discussion the court was cleared of Press and public. Left alone with nothing but the Law, Alex felt more isolated than ever.

The first two witnesses were the detectives who had made the arrest: Bearends and Deepground. Their stories corresponded in every detail. They had seen Alex run out of the house in a very agitated state. They had noted the direction in which he had gone. They had entered the house and found the woman dead. No other person had come into the house or left it during the period between Alex's departure and their own entrance. The Public Prosecutor was evidently well pleased with the police evidence for he questioned neither witness. It was left to Alex's lawyer to try and show that the case was nothing like as clear-cut. He rose to his feet and addressed Bearends.

'The staircase that leads from the street to the flat of the deceased also gives access to the first and second floor flats, does it not?'

'Yes, it does,' said Bearends in a far less respectful tone than he had used to the President of the Court.

'If that is so, would it not be possible for someone in the deceased's flat to have come down, say one flight of stairs, and entered the second floor flat without you seeing them?'

'I don't think so. I'd have heard the footsteps.'

'How could you possibly have heard the footsteps or the closing of a door if you were standing in the street outside?'

'I wasn't standing in the street for long. I entered the house immediately the accused ran out.'

'Did you look at your watch to time your entry into the house?'

Bearends gave Jacobs a sour, contemptuous look. 'Of course not.'

'You were the one who ran after the accused to arrest him, were you not?'

'Yes.'

'How did you know in which direction to pursue him?'

'I noticed in which direction he was running when he came out of the house.'

'Before the accused emerged from the house, had you expected someone to come running out?'

'No.'

'So you were surprised?'

Bearends, suspecting a trap, took a long time to answer. At last he said: 'Yes. Very surprised.'

'Now I put it to you, witness. You are walking in the street, suddenly you see a man come running out of a house. You are startled. You stop and look in the direction in which the man is running. You consider his behaviour suspicious. You decide to go and investigate why the man ran out of the house. Only then do you enter the house. Is that not the sequence of events and does not such a sequence take at least three or more likely five minutes?'

Bearends looked at the Public Prosecutor but saw no help.

'Answer the question, witness,' said the President of the Court.

'I couldn't say,' said Bearends lamely. 'I didn't time any of the events.'

It was a try. Jacobs hoped that he had sowed some seeds of doubt.

When Deepground was the witness, it was the President of the Court who asked about the possibility of someone coming down from the deceased's flat and hiding in the second floor flat. Reluctantly Deepground said he supposed it was possible. When his turn came, Jacobs put just one question.

'Did you or Sergeant Bearends ever question the residents of the first or second floor flats to find out if anyone could have entered those dwellings on the night of the murder?'

'No,' said Deepground, with considerable arrogance, and stared straight at Alex. 'We knew the accused was the murderer so we didn't think it necessary to bother the people living in the other flats.'

There was a long silence. One of the judges coughed. Fatesma closed his eyes as if saying a silent prayer. Deepground was apparently unaffected. He left the witness stand as satisfied as he had entered it.

The third witness was Dr Fischer, the pathologist attached to the police forensic laboratory. He gave the time of death as between 10 and 11 p.m. and the cause of death as manual strangulation. The Public Prosecutor rose to his feet. He looked a formidable figure staring down at the cadaverous-faced doctor. 'Did you carry out a post-mortem on the body of the deceased?'

'I did.'

83

'Did you find any evidence of sexual intercourse shortly before her death?'

'Yes. The deceased had had sexual intercourse approximately one hour before her death.'

The Public Prosecutor sat down well contented. Jacobs took over the questioning. 'Did you examine the scene of the crime?'

'I did.'

'Did you find any signs of a struggle?'

'No. The room and the body, but for the strangulation, were in good order.'

'Can I take it then, doctor, that the murderer did not first knock his victim out and then strangle her?'

'Yes, sir, you can.'

'Would you not therefore agree that the murderer must have been someone of considerable strength to be able to prevent the deceased from struggling whilst he was strangling her?'

'Yes,' said the doctor thoughtfully, 'the murderer must have been someone of considerable strength.'

'Please look at the accused and tell me if you consider him a person of such considerable strength?'

Dr Fischer took a long, hard look at Alex. At last he said, 'No, I do not think so.'

Jacobs then tried to throw doubt not only upon the exact time of death, but also of sexual intercourse. Dr Fischer agreed that such times were never scientifically exact and were therefore subject to error. Jacobs sat down well satisfied.

Fatesma at once re-examined the doctor. Slightly built though the accused was, would he not, in a wild rage, be strong enough to hold a woman in such a way that she would be unable to struggle while he strangled her? Dr Fischer thought for a long time and only momentarily glanced at Alex. He had no wish to lose his job. At last he said, 'Yes, sir. If the accused was in a blind rage he might have the strength to do as you say.' The Public Prosecutor smiled with satisfaction.

After the blowzy woman in the ground floor flat had given evidence that Alex was a frequent visitor to the house and always stayed with the deceased far longer than any of the other visitors, Alex was told to stand and was questioned directly by the President.

'Accused, you have heard the witnesses, have you any comments upon the evidence?'

'Yes, your honour, the policemen were lying when they said I ran from the house . . .'

The President knocked upon the table with a gavel. 'Accused, please watch your language. You are not allowed to call the police witnesses liars. You are, however, allowed to state that what they said was not true.'

Alex frowned with disgust at what he took to be a completely hypocritical statement. Then he noticed Jacobs shaking his head. Alex swallowed his angry words. 'Very well, your honour,' he said quietly, 'I did *not* run from the house as the policemen stated.'

'Do you admit to going to the flat of the deceased on the evening of the ninth of November 1939?'

'Yes, your honour.'

'What was the purpose of your visit?'

Alex couldn't bring himself to call Rachel 'the deceased'. 'Miss Blum had invited me for dinner.'

The judge studied Alex for a whole minute then said: 'One witness has stated that you were a regular visitor of the deceased. Now the Court is at a loss to understand how someone of your social background and young years can associate with a woman of doubtful morals. Will you therefore please tell the Court what exactly your relationship was with the deceased?'

There was a long silence while Alex bit his lip and thought what to say. He was appreciative that the President must have understood his feelings and did not try to hurry him.

'We were very good friends. I loved her.'

'Did you kill Rachel Blum?'

'No, your honour. When I left her that evening she was alive and well.'

Neither of the other two judges had any questions. The President nodded at the Public Prosecutor. Fatesma was quickly upon his feet.

'Accused, did you have sexual relations with the deceased?'

Alex had grown to hate the Public Prosecutor at that very first meeting in Fatesma's office. Now, after the personal

85

question about himself and Rachel, he hated the man even more – more than he thought it possible to hate a fellow being. There was not just something evil about Fatesma, there was something dirty.

Fatesma had pulled himself to his full height. He used every inch of his six feet as he stared down from the dais, curling his upper lip upwards. Alex could think only of an old, snarling wolf. He wanted to shriek out that his relationship with Rachel was none of the Prosecutor's business, but that would bring the wrath of the Court upon him.

'Come, come, you need not be bashful. After all, if you associate with known prostitutes, you must expect to be asked such questions. Did you or did you not have sexual relations with the deceased?'

For Alex this was a far worse, more sickening moment than any he could remember with Bearends or Deepground, even when they had beaten him and kept him standing for hours. His urge to release the fury within him was overwhelming. Then he saw Jacobs nodding at him.

'Yes,' said Alex defiantly, 'I did have sexual relations with Miss Blum.'

'When questioned by the police you denied it. Why did you lie to them?'

'I did not consider it any of their business.'

Fatesma's normally level voice was shrill. 'Neither did you think it any of their business that you had murdered the deceased. Your whole attitude in this case has been one of defiance and disrespect for authority. I put it to you, accused, that you lied to the police about having sexual relations with the deceased because *it would implicate you in the murder.*'

'That is a lie!' Alex saw the President of the Court staring at him. 'I am sorry. I mean it is not true.'

As he addressed the judges, the Public Prosecutor was triumphant. 'There once again is proof of the accused's total disrespect for authority. I have no more questions.'

Jacobs rose and tried to repair the damage. 'Was Rachel Blum a prostitute?'

'No, sir, she was not.'

86

'Was she in fact a cultured, well-educated young woman and a graduate of Berlin University?'

'Yes, sir. That is correct.'

'Did you quarrel with the deceased on the night of her death?'

'No, sir, I did not.'

'So there can be no question of your having been in a wild rage that night?'

'No, sir, absolutely not.'

Jacobs sat down, relieved at having retrieved something. The Court adjourned until the afternoon.

They were eating *Uitsmijters* – open sandwiches – and drinking beer. Bearends was staring at Deepground's hands on the beer glass. He watched them each time the Detective Constable raised the glass to his lips. Bearends found the hands fascinating, compulsive. He admired, even envied Deepground's hands, but his admiration didn't stretch to the owner. Deepground was his colleague, but Bearends despised him and always had. Deepground had joined the Party without a second thought. It had been easy for him. He had seen no problems, no contradictions, nor felt any pang of conscience. Now he enjoyed the thuggery of it all.

'Bastard Jewish lawyer!' muttered Deepground. 'His day'll come, you see.'

'We should have checked the occupants of the other flats. We should have questioned them.'

'You weren't to know . . .'

'It was a mistake. A foolish mistake.'

'If it was a mistake,' said Deepground slowly, 'and the way I see it, it wasn't necessarily a mistake, then the mistake was Fatesma's. He's the one who planned it all. He's the brains behind it.'

Bearends stared into Deepground's face. Even knowing Deepground as well as he did, the way the man had just spoken astonished him. It was as if Deepground had had nothing to do with the events in the Achterburgwal – as if he hadn't even been there.

87

'Fatesma had to do with the overall strategy,' conceded Bearends, 'but he left the details to me.' The way Bearends spoke, the words were supposed to leave his junior in absolutely no doubt that while Fatesma may well have been the prime mover, Bearends was the tactician, the man in charge of the fine tuning. He was certainly no roughneck like Deepground.

'I still don't see that it matters,' said Deepground, taking another mouthful from the glass. 'The buggers won't get away with it, either of them. Fatesma will see to that.'

'It was still a slip-up. We can't afford slip-ups.'

Bearends prided himself upon always doing a thorough job. Jacobs' questions about the occupants of the flats and the possibility of someone taking refuge in the second floor flat had not just angered him, they had deeply hurt that pride. If Bearends hadn't been in the police force he would have made an ideal corner shopkeeper or the clerk of a small stores. Although he treasured his mind – and after all, it did differentiate him from Deepground – it was a very limited mind. His horizons were close. The rank of Detective Sergeant eminently suited him. He had none of the outlook of Fatesma. He had no real desire to change Holland or society. He had never visualized the New Order goose stepping down the Leidsestraat or the black and scarlet banners paraded outside the Royal Palace. The secrecy of the Party was a considerable attraction. He preferred to burrow away within its clandestine organization. There was something schoolboyish about it that appealed to Bearends. Yet he had greatly enjoyed the camps in Germany. Indeed, he had surprised himself how much he had enjoyed them.

'There could be more behind this than we know,' said Bearends darkly. 'Our friends could be involved.'

Deepground grinned. 'If they are behind it, they've got nothing to cry about. We got the Jewish girl nicely, so they can't grumble at that. And we haven't done badly with the lad. He certainly got thoroughly confused when we picked him up. That worked well enough. At least our friends'll know that all that training we had didn't go amiss.'

For a while they ate and drank in silence, then Bearends

said: 'Don't you ever have doubts? I mean, don't you ever wonder . . .?'

'Wonder?'

Bearends shrugged. It was like talking to an ox. 'Ask yourself questions?'

'I could do with a bit more money. A rise.'

'I'm not talking about money!' said Bearends angrily. 'The trouble with you is that everything is so bloody straightforward.'

Deepground shook his head. 'If you ask me you're making a mountain out of a molehill. It's all quite clear. Plain sailing. If there weren't any Jews or Communists, then there wouldn't be any trouble.'

'You really believe that?' asked Bearends in astonishment.

'Of course I believe it. It's true, isn't it?' Deepground emptied his glass. 'You stop worrying. It won't do you any good. That lawyer'll get his comeuppance. The lad too.'

'They could find him innocent,' said Bearends quietly. 'They could believe the Jewish lawyer, that the murderer went into the second floor flat. It will be our fault if they do. If we'd checked, taken the trouble to ask a few questions . . .'

Deepground picked up Bearends' empty glass. 'I said, stop worrying! It's not the end of the world. Even if they do find him innocent, Fatesma'll fix it for next time.'

Bearends nodded. Fatesma would appeal to the Amsterdam High Court. There he would call the residents of the lower flats to state under oath that no one had entered their premises on the night of the murder.

'You're right, Deepground,' said Bearends slowly, 'I do worry too much. I've always worried. It's been a failing of mine. I take after my mother. She never stopped worrying.'

Deepground grinned and went to the bar with the empty glasses. Bearends watched him. He would never understand Deepground's simplistic attitude, but there was no doubt that the Movement needed hands like that. They could be very useful.

*   *   *

Colonel Chidson was far from happy. Indeed, he was exceedingly angry. He had passed his request to see Alex Richards through the normal channels and had now learned that the request had been refused. He had made instant enquiries as to why such a perfectly normal request should be turned down and discovered that it was the Public Prosecutor handling the case who had issued the orders that no one other than his lawyer and very close relatives was to see the prisoner.

'What do you make of it, Miss Pluck? To me, the whole thing gets more and more fishy with each day. Why should a Public Prosecutor make such an extraordinary order about a British national? Especially when that national is a minor?' Chidson looked up at the plain, spindly woman with the grey hair and lined, hawkish features. 'We shall have to go higher, Miss Pluck. To the very top.'

'You wish me to get the Envoy on the phone, Colonel?'

'Please. If J. Fatesma, Master at Law, Public Prosecutor of the District Court of Amsterdam, wishes to be difficult, then we must go to someone who will teach him not only manners but his job as well. We must ask the Envoy to speak with the Dutch Foreign Minister.'

Miss Pluck was pleased. She was already deeply upset at the prospect of the young British boy enduring the rigours of a murder trial without help from his own Legation.

'And after that, Miss Pluck, I intend to call upon my old friend, Colonel van der Plassche. It may well be that not only are our two policemen members of the Nazi Party, but Mr J. Fatesma as well. If anyone knows, it will be the head of Dutch Security.' Chidson paused, then said, 'What do you think to that?'

'They would hardly be current members, Colonel,' said Miss Pluck, remembering that Dutch law forbade civil servants from being members of the Nazi Party.

'Then perhaps they have resigned their membership and not their convictions?'

Miss Pluck nodded. It was a perfect possibility and one that suited her tidy mind.

★   ★   ★

Fatesma's address to the judges was devastatingly simple. On the accused's own admission he had formed an illicit association with the deceased, visited her regularly, and was with her on the night of the murder. The medical evidence suggested that death occurred between 10 and 11 p.m. Two police officers saw the accused run from the deceased's flat at ten minutes to eleven in such an agitated state he left the front door open behind him. The accused was pursued, apprehended and himself identified the body as Rachel Blum. The motive was clear. The woman wished to end the affair, there was a quarrel and in a fit of rage the accused strangled her. As to character, the Public Prosecutor had never met so young a person already so depraved. Even at his early age he had no respect for authority and had all the makings of a hardened criminal.

Alex no longer heard the words. He was studying Fatesma as the Public Prosecutor addressed the court. In Fatesma's office the time had been short, the personal rancour violent. He had left with a fleeting glimpse of the he-devil that tormented him. Now it seemed, with Fatesma droning away, he had all the time in the world to complete the study.

Fatesma had changed. He was now a great black beetle with a large, heavy head. Not that all of him was black. In the courtroom lights his face seemed almost yellow. After a while Alex had to concede that what he considered so ugly and evil, others might see differently. There was a certain sinister, arrogant handsomeness in the rugged, lined face. If Fatesma had had a good shock of hair instead of the few thinning strands, he might have been considered quite good-looking. Vaguely Alex wondered what Fatesma's wife and the rest of his family made of this strange, black beetle with the sallow face that had taken such delight in hating the man he was prosecuting. Then he decided that such a person as Fatesma couldn't have either a wife or a family. There was no blood in his veins, only ice. For a second time, and upon this occasion with far more deliberation, Alex committed every detail of that face to memory. From the upward curled lip to the lugubrious jaws, Alex made a mental dossier of every feature.

Bearends and Deepground, although discharged as witnesses, had remained in Court. Alex studied them too. When he stared at Bearends, and Bearends spotted him doing so, it seemed to Alex that the Detective Sergeant, quite unlike Fatesma who seemed to glory in staring at Alex and hurling his wrath and sarcasm upon him, turned his head away in some confusion. Indeed, when Bearends began to pick his nose, Alex knew that the man was not at ease. Bearends' companion Deepground, on the other hand, showed no such concern. He appeared as untouched by the proceedings as if he had been having supper at home or resting in the garden. Only when the Public Prosecutor said something particularly virulent did Deepground's face light up. Alex took in every detail of the two detectives as he had taken in every detail of Fatesma. Bearends' neat, well-proportioned face, his almost delicate features, blue eyes and small mouth with its slight grimace as if he had just tasted something sour; Deepground's much larger head, big mouth and cold, grey eyes, his shoulders, broad and slightly hunched, were all scored into Alex's memory. He would never forget them. They would remain for ever with him alongside the sight of Rachel lying dead upon the bed.

Alex had no idea why the two detectives should have perjured themselves as witnesses and saw all three men merely as his enemies and tormentors. He had no conception of them as murderers. In spite of his treatment, his youthfulness saved him from reality. Much of his innocence was still intact.

He was back concentrating upon Fatesma when the Public Prosecutor asked for the maximum sentence. Imprisonment for life.

It was the turn of the Defence. Jacobs asked to be allowed to indulge in conjecture just as the Public Prosecutor had. The accused had certainly been with the deceased that night – who, far from being a woman of ill repute, was a woman of excellent character – but he had left her alive and well. Being young and happy, he had bounded down the stairs three at a time. The watching police had mistaken this for an agitated escape. While the police were watching the accused, the real murderer had stolen out of the flat on the second floor, gone to the third floor and there murdered the deceased. With the narrow, winding staircase that the house possessed it was impossible to stand at the entrance to one flat and see the door of another on a different level. For motive, Jacobs reminded the Court that Rachel Blum was a refugee from Nazi Germany. The Nazis, unhappy that she had escaped them once, had sent an assassin to Amsterdam to kill her. Jacobs asked that the accused be found not guilty of murder and released from custody. He sat down, wiped his forehead and hoped he had made the best of an exceedingly difficult case.

The President asked Fatesma if he wished to reply. Fatesma scrambled to his feet. He was at his most theatrical, his tone suddenly changing from one of deeply felt offence to sharp ridicule. As his voice and manner changed so did his face and eyes. He used every nuance in the lawyer's arsenal of acting. He professed to be outraged by the Defence Counsel's plea: 'First and foremost I must protest at Counsel using this Court to level completely unfounded accusations against the friendly government of a neighbouring state. The very idea that the German government would send an assassin to murder someone living in our country is preposterous!' Fatesma reminded the Court that in his plea only the cause of the quarrel was conjecture. His evidence might be circumstantial but murders were seldom committed in front of witnesses. With one final, stabbing glance at Alex, he reaffirmed his demand for life imprisonment, bowed to the judges and sat down.

The President announced that judgement would be given in two weeks' time, at ten o'clock on 3 April. Alex went back to the House of Custody.

'You mustn't raise your hopes too high, Alex, but there may just be a chance that the Court finds you not guilty.'

'They *must*!' shouted Alex. 'Especially after your story of the murderer slipping in and out of the first floor flat. I was watching that horror Fatesma, he certainly looked sick.'

Jacobs shook his head. 'The trouble is he can have a second go at you.'

'A second go!' cried Alex in disbelief.

'If you are found not guilty he will appeal to the Amsterdam High Court. They will try the case all over again. This time Fatesma won't be caught out. He'll call the people in the flat below to prove that no one entered there on the night of the murder.'

'That's monstrous! I can't be tried *twice* on the same charge!'

'In Holland you can.'

Alex held his head in his hands. They were changing the rules as they went along. The scent of victory, that a moment ago had seemed so sweet, had turned bitter. Liberty was slipping inexorably away and there seemed nothing he could do about it. Despair welled up and choked him.

'They can really try me again?'

'I'm afraid so, that's the law.'

Back in his cell, Alex lay on his cot and cried. He needed sleep, oblivion.

Later that same afternoon, Alex was taken to the visitors' room a second time. There a distinguished-looking man, with a small moustache and a very upright bearing, was waiting. Chidson looked at Alex's bizarre headgear in astonishment. 'Do they make you wear that damned awful thing all the time?'

'Only when I'm out of the cell.'

Chidson shook his head, muttered, 'Sadistic sods!' then stuck out his hand. 'I'm Chidson, Colonel Chidson from the British Legation in The Hague. I'm the new Passport Control Officer. I've come to have a chat with you. It's high time we got together.' He waved Alex towards the other chair. Alex sat; his mood had changed. He was suddenly filled with suppressed excitement but he dared not let hope take over completely for he had had too many disappointments recently.

Chidson stared at the warder. The warder left the room. Chidson leaned forward and said, 'I've been sorting out the pieces to get a complete picture of exactly what happened. I tried to attend your trial yesterday but, as you know, the wretched affair was held in camera. So please tell me, in your own words, exactly what happened that night Rachel Blum was murdered.'

Alex told Chidson everything.

'Are you sure you didn't run out of the flat as the police claim?'

'Certain.'

94

'Did you or did you not leave the front door open as you left?'

'I am sure I closed it, sir.'

'Good,' said Chidson in a crisp, matter-of-fact way. 'Everything makes sense. It's exactly as one would expect it. Now don't worry too much about what is going to happen to you. If you are found guilty you must appeal. When the appeal is heard I promise you'll go free.'

'*Promise?*'

Chidson nodded.

Alex's face lit up. 'You don't believe I killed Rachel, do you?'

'Of course not. Never did. It's a damned stupid idea!'

There was a long silence, then Alex said: 'Do you know who did kill her?'

'I've a good idea . . .'

Alex felt his own heart beating. 'Please tell me . . .'

'I will tell you when you are free again. At the moment you couldn't handle it.' Chidson got up. 'If the verdict goes against you I'll get in touch with your lawyer and give him the evidence he needs to get you acquitted on appeal.'

Alex was taken back to his cell. If he was dismayed at the way the trial had gone and his lawyer's words about a second trial should he be acquitted, he was considerably cheered by the precise-speaking Colonel Chidson. He had no idea that the confidence Chidson had exuded was in some contradiction to his words when talking to his secretary. Nor did he know that Chidson had yet to clear with London the question of any British representation at a future trial. That Rachel Blum and Alex Richards were part of a British espionage network operating in neutral Holland was still something the British government might not wish to broadcast too loudly.

On 3 April 1940, Alex was found guilty of murder and sentenced to imprisonment for life. It was his eighteenth birthday. The sentence and the words of the sentence, 'solitary confinement for the rest of his natural life', cut deep into his soul. He saw no hope, no future and his world was filled with hatred and bitterness. Then he remembered the British Colonel with the upright stance and military bearing. He hoped that the word 'promise' was still relevant and meant exactly what it said. After all the treatment he had had, the lies he had listened to, the 'justice' he had seen done, he had doubts.

Chidson had worked it all out. He had even obtained permission from London for a member of the Legation to testify that both Rachel Blum and Alex Richards had been working for Major Stevens. The defence lawyer would question the two police witnesses about their past membership of the Nazi Party. The Court would realize that only Bearends and Deepground had the time and motive for the murder. Alex would be freed. All these were mere plans when events swept them away. On 9 May, three weeks before the date for Alex's appeal to be heard, Chidson learned from a contact in the Abwehr of the imminence of the invasion of Holland. That same day, Hitler confirmed 'Operation Case Yellow', the attack in the west. Just after dawn on the tenth, along a front of a hundred and seventy-five miles from the North Sea to the Maginot Line, German troops crossed the borders of Belgium, Holland and Luxembourg. For the Dutch, the fighting war lasted five days. For Chidson it was the busiest five days of his life.

11

They raced through the deserted streets of Amsterdam as if on the Donnington Circuit. The van was from the Legation, the men from the destroyer. Chidson had his orders, half of which he had already carried out. The Dutch royal family and government were now in England, the diamonds were not. Chidson had returned to Holland for the second part of his task. For this he needed a small private army. From HMS *Hereward* waiting at Ijmuiden he had acquired a sergeant and nine marines, all draped with weapons ranging from hand grenades to Stens.

'Right! Hard left!' Chidson pointed, the driver swung the wheel, the van careered around the corners. They were making for the Jewish Quarter in the centre of the city. In the Nieuw Market was the Diamond Exchange. The large stocks of industrial diamonds held there must not fall into German hands.

Chidson glanced up at the sky. He believed that the parachutists had been confined to the bridges and airfields around The Hague. He had already circumnavigated them safely on his earlier mission. But the Fallschirmjägers' fame and notoriety had spread far. Rumours were rife. They were to be found behind every tree, upon every bicycle. To the people of Amsterdam the war was one of terror from the skies. But Chidson knew more.

After meeting stiff resistance from the Dutch, the ground forces of the Wehrmacht's Eighteenth Army had now overrun eighty per cent of the country and were at the doors of 'Fortress Holland', the small rectangle of land on the west encompassing Rotterdam, The Hague and Amsterdam. Whilst the advance had actually been halted on the bridges to Rotterdam and many of the parachutists had been driven from their objectives, Rotterdam had been bombed. The heart of the city had been destroyed. Dutch capitulation was imminent. Time had never been more precious.

Chidson pointed towards a large three-storey building. The driver braked. Chidson jumped from the van, the marines clattered out behind him. While the marines deployed along the front of the building, Chidson and the Sergeant hurried inside.

The Amsterdam Diamond Exchange operated like a nineteenth-century English corn exchange. Individual diamond merchants met and did their business under one roof. All the members were Jewish, many wore their traditional skull caps. When Chidson, in uniform, tin hat and revolver, burst in followed by the Sergeant with a Sten, the chatter stopped. The merchants watched in sulky silence as the Englishman explained, as calmly and rationally as he could in the circumstances, the purpose of his precipitous visit. Within twenty-four hours the Germans would be in Amsterdam. They would most certainly seize everything they wanted to help in their war effort. The industrial diamonds within the Exchange would not be spared. Britain needed those diamonds for her own war effort, and could never allow them to fall into the enemy's hands.

Chidson saw the stony faces around him. 'You have my promise', he cried in a loud voice, 'that after the war my government will pay for every single diamond!'

Chidson's promise had no effect. Nor apparently did the threat of approaching Germans. If the diamonds were to go, the merchants wanted their money now. And they wanted it in cash. 'You might not win the war,' said one old man shaking his head.

If the moment hadn't been so serious, the ludicrousness of the situation would have made Chidson laugh. He was one of the few Englishmen fully aware of how the Nazis had treated the Jews in their own country and of their terrible fate in newly conquered Poland. The death of Rachel Blum in a neutral land was fresh in his mind. There were German paratroopers thirty miles away at The Hague, a Panzer division forty miles away at Moerdijk. The Jews he was talking to, so desperate to keep their small glinting stones, would most probably lose everything including their lives. Yet he could not bring himself to tell them. Illogically, he understood exactly how they felt. He might even feel the same himself were he in their position. He remembered stories of passengers running back into their staterooms in the sinking *Titanic* just to rescue their belongings and never being seen again. In their insular way, the merchants had every right to be horrified at being told to hand over their treasure in the hope of some future payment when the world once again returned to sanity. But this was war. Time was exceedingly short and when the Germans did arrive there would be no niceties.

The diamonds were in a massive safe in the vault. Chidson demanded the keys to the safe. When he was refused he called in the marines. Quickly and deftly they laid their charges, primed them and blew the safe open. The diamonds were hurriedly loaded into sacks and the sacks put in the van. As

Chidson and the marines withdrew, the merchants sprang into life. They produced receipts and demanded Chidson's signature. Chidson quickly obliged. A sort of honour had been saved.

'Home, sir?' asked the driver. 'Back to the docks?'

Chidson shook his head. 'Leidseplein. We've got one more job.'

The driver was puzzled. He thought the mission had been accomplished. 'Where, sir?'

Chidson pointed. 'I'll show you the way.' He glanced up at the sky. 'And step on it. As fast as you can.'

They raced south to the flower market. There they turned right then left into the Leidsestraat. At the bottom of the street, in the square, Chidson pointed again. They screeched to a halt fifty yards from the grim façade of the House of Custody.

Chidson left a corporal and five marines to guard the van with the diamonds and took the Sergeant and the remaining three marines with him to the prison. He showed his permit for visiting Alex at the lodge window and when the door was opened, shoved it wide with his foot. Chidson, the Sergeant and three marines raced inside. Leaving one of the marines to guard the lodge, Chidson took the porter's keys and with the rest of his rescue party hurried to the Governor's office.

The Governor was talking with the Chief Warder when Chidson burst in. The Governor saw the Colonel and the marines and at first thought they were Germans. Then he noticed the helmets.

'Who the devil are you, coming in here like this?'

'My name is Chidson. I'm from the British Legation. The Germans are about to occupy this city. You have a British prisoner here who must not fall into enemy hands. His name is Alexander Richards. I want him released now!'

The Governor got up from his desk. 'Have you got an order from the Court authorizing me to hand this prisoner to you?'

'There is a war on,' said Chidson, coolly. 'The Germans are at the gates of Amsterdam. There isn't time for a Court order.'

'Too bad,' said the Governor, surlily. 'Without that Court order I'm not handing over any prisoner to you or anyone else.'

99

Chidson's face changed. All his attempts at civility vanished. He indicated the marines. 'These are my authorization. Armed marines. And there are more outside.' He took a Sten and cocked it. 'I want Alex Richards and I want him quick.' He fired the Sten into the wall above the Governor's head. The Governor fell flat across his desk. 'Quick!' shouted Chidson. 'Alex Richards or next time I won't aim so high.'

The Governor grabbed a ledger and opened it. 'A3-10, Chief, go and get him!'

As the Chief Warder made for the door, Chidson ordered the Sergeant to go with him. 'If he gives you any trouble, shoot him,' said the Colonel in Dutch.

Alex was folding envelopes in his cell. When the door was flung open he was about to retreat to the end wall, as required by the regulations. Then he saw the Sergeant and the English uniform.

'Are you Richards? Alex Richards?'

Alex nodded. He was too surprised to speak.

The Sergeant beckoned. 'Come on, lad, you're going home.'

Out of habit, Alex picked up his cap and mask. The Chief Warder told him to put it on. 'Get stuffed!' cried Alex, and ran after the Sergeant.

They hurried back to the Governor's office. Chidson clasped Alex's hand. 'I'll explain later,' he said. Alex was still looking at the Governor, the bullet holes in the wall and the Sten guns when Chidson waved towards the door. With the British party leaving, the Governor recovered some of his composure. 'You won't get away with this!' he shouted. 'I'll have the police after you!' Alex remembered that he was still holding the cap and mask. He turned and flung it at the Governor. 'Here, you bloody sadist! You wear this! It suits you better than me!' To Alex's joy the hated headwear struck the Governor full in the face.

Back in the van they drove at breakneck speed for Ijmuiden. On the way, Chidson had to explain to Alex that the Germans had invaded Holland. In the House of Custody, no one had thought fit to tell the prisoners.

★ ★ ★

They stood at the stern, the White Ensign above them snapping in the wind, the smoke from the destroyer's funnels drifting low across the sea, the white wake zigzagging back towards the horizon until, two cable lengths away, it was almost imperceptible. They were at full speed, at action stations, and the coast of Holland was now no more than a thin line.

'Who killed Rachel, Colonel?'

Chidson stared towards the horizon. He answered in his usual clipped, matter-of-fact sentences: 'One or other of the two detectives. Bearends or Deepground. I don't know which. The planning, however, was done by Fatesma, the Public Prosecutor.'

Chidson allowed himself a glance at Alex. The young man was staring at Chidson with a puzzled, disbelieving frown. His mouth was open. He began to shake his head. 'It doesn't make sense. I can't believe it . . .'

'It makes perfect sense.'

'Why kill Rachel and blame me?'

'It was the long arm of the Gestapo. The detectives and the Public Prosecutor were Dutch Nazis. They did as they were told. It was all quite neat and well-timed. Major Stevens, Captain Best, Rachel Blum the letter-box, you the courier, all got rid of at one stroke. To that we must add the people in Germany.' Chidson shook his head. 'They did a lot of damage. Too much.'

Alex wasn't thinking of the espionage chain. He still had no idea what was in the envelopes. Indeed, he had almost forgotten about the envelopes, he had made so many more thousands in prison. He was thinking of Rachel and the murder.

'You mean they were waiting for me to come out of the house . . .?'

'They had already checked up on your movements. Your routine. They knew you went to Rachel Blum's every Thursday. When you came out of that door, one followed you to the station to arrest you. This gave the other time to ring the bell and go upstairs when Rachel opened the door. You can imagine the rest.'

'Deepground . . . the gorilla,' muttered Alex, 'he was the

one who went upstairs.' Alex shut his eyes. 'The bastard would have enjoyed it, too.'

Chidson's words had opened a Pandora's box. Alex had a surrealistic vision, a nightmarish medley of sights and sounds. The menace of Deepground behind him as he stood swaying in front of the desk, the thud of the detective's fists and boots, Deepground bearing Rachel back towards that bed, even his great hands unable to throttle the scream; Bearends, who knew the truth, tormenting him with questions; the large, ugly face of Fatesma, the hideous spider in the middle of the web, the man with puppets at his fingertips, the inquisitor-in-chief and chief torturer, obliterating everything. The three men he hated, with a hatred so blind that, had he been able, he would have returned to Holland with no other thought than revenge.

Tears were running down his cheeks. He was just eighteen. Many boys of his age had experienced no more than school. In seven months he had gone from the youth with the idyllic love affair to the man who had seen that love murdered and had himself suffered treachery, despair and fearful privations.

Chidson pointed towards the fading coastline. 'I wonder when we shall all be back?' he said, quietly.

Alex looked in the direction of Chidson's arm but he didn't see Holland nor even the drift of dark haze that marked burning Rotterdam. He saw Rachel in her black dress, lying on her bed, frail and motionless. He continued to see her when, six hours later, he landed at Chatham, still dressed in his coarse prison clothes, but minus the cap and mask.

12

'Can you come up and see me for a minute, Monty?'

'Now, sir?'

'We'd best get on with it.'

Chidson put the phone down, glanced at his watch and got up from his desk. Much of SIS, the Secret Intelligence Service, had moved out of London to the large, gloomy, Victorian mansion at Bletchley Park, but the headquarters still operated in Broadway and Queen Anne's Gate. Chidson went up the single flight of stairs. He was in his fifty-second year. He was just as upright and walked in the same military way, but his hair was a shade greyer. Since coming back from Holland in the *Hereward* just over a year ago, he had collected a DSO – for saving the industrial diamonds – but he had been desk-bound. Now he could do with a spot of action. He hoped Menzies was going to provide it.

Brigadier Stewart Menzies looked up from the file on his desk and waved Chidson towards a chair. 'How are you, Monty?'

'Well, sir, very well, but I could do with a bit of exercise.' Chidson patted his Sam Browne belt where it bisected his stomach. 'I never thought I'd be a subject for middle-aged spread.'

Menzies seemed not to see the humour in the remark. He peered at Chidson then down at the file. Chidson had to wait. He knew when he came in that, however urgent the matter, he would still have to wait. It always took a minute or two for Menzies to broach a subject. Menzies, the ex-Etonian old Guardsman, always did things carefully, adroitly. He never rushed matters. He was the epitome of the unhurried, unruffled English Establishment.

Menzies indicated the file and spoke very slowly, emphasizing each syllable. 'An extraordinary bit of luck, Monty, a most interesting report, most interesting. It's from our Abwehr man in Berlin. He says that there exists a plan, a sort of master map of the whole of the planned defences of Hitler's so-called "Atlantic Wall", right the way from the north of Holland to the French border with Spain.'

Menzies looked up from the file and stared at Chidson.

'Quite a gem . . .' said Chidson laconically.

'Exactly. And there apparently exist several copies of that map. One is of particular interest to us for it is in the possession of the German Admiral in charge of naval defence!'

Menzies stopped as if he had just produced a rabbit out of a hat.

Chidson grunted. He knew exactly what was coming. He

also saw the possibility of his spot of action. 'Den Helder . . .' he muttered, suppressing his excitement, 'the Kriegsmarine . . . their naval defence headquarters are at Den Helder.'

'Correct, Monty, *Holland*. We're talking about Holland, your second home.'

Menzies was looking straight at Chidson. They were men of similar age, but two ranks now separated them. Menzies in his day had been a considerable athlete, now he left physical activity to others. Chidson, on the other hand, considered himself still active. In spite of what had been happening to the country, he had enjoyed those five days in Holland. It had been exhilarating racing about with armed marines. The memories were vivid and helped to keep him young.

'The map is kept in a safe in the Admiral's office . . .'

It wouldn't be like riding in the van this time. Holland was swarming with Germans. It would be a clandestine, stealthy operation and damned difficult.

'The Chiefs of Staff want a copy. I don't need to tell you, Monty, how vital it would be in planning the invasion.'

'A very tall order, sir.'

'You haven't heard all. When we do get a copy of the map, the Germans must not be aware of it. Otherwise, of course, they'll only change the wretched plans.'

Menzies had a handsome office and a strange one. There was a door and a staircase that only Menzies used. It was part of the 'image' of being head of MI6. Chidson looked from the private door to the view of Whitehall and St James's Park that filled the window behind Menzies' head.

'Do the Chiefs of Staff have any suggestions as to how we go about getting a copy of this map without the Huns knowing?'

Menzies smiled. 'You know damned well, the details are always left to us.'

Chidson said nothing.

'You're the Dutch expert, Monty,' said Menzies. 'I'm hoping you can come up with something.'

'What about time-scale? How long have we got?'

'With the Chiefs of Staff, everything is urgent. In fact we've got time. We're in no position to mount an invasion for another couple of years at the earliest.'

To many even such a cautiously expressed opinion might have sounded optimistic, but there was an embryonic Combined Operations, Britain did have a few landing craft and had mounted a small, successful raid upon the Lofoten Islands. It helped now that Germany had turned the bulk of its forces upon Russia. But to launch a full-scale invasion upon the Continent . . . Chidson shook his head. We needed America.

'I've had the air photos checked,' said Menzies. 'Also reports from agents. Most of the fortifications shown on the map are in the preliminary stages of construction.'

'How old is the information?' asked Chidson. 'Are we certain the map is still at Den Helder? It hasn't been moved?'

Menzies shook his head. 'It's still there.'

'A map that has to be photographed . . .' mused Chidson. 'How big is it?'

Menzies scanned the report. 'It doesn't say . . .' He looked up. 'We'll find out.'

Menzies gave Chidson the report to read. Chidson read it, asked a few more questions then went back to his office. At lunchtime he went for a walk; it took him away from his desk and the telephone and helped him to think. The July day was warm but with thin, high cloud, the shadows were merely faint and promising. The park looked resplendent. So did the London buildings, in spite of their grime and the sandbags around the offices in the Horse Guards Parade. Chidson imagined that Holland was enjoying much the same sort of weather. The Hague, once known as 'The Spy Capital of the World', with its suggestion of eighteenth-century France, its parks and gardens, would be particularly beautiful. Den Helder was a different matter. He'd only been there once and he hadn't been impressed. But then flat habitations by the sea had never impressed him. The job would be difficult and nasty, but it would be exciting. He spoke fluent Dutch and German. He would like to go.

For the next forty-eight hours Chidson was busy contacting his Dutch friends, many of whom now lived in England. By the evening of the second day one matter haunted him. He had been working on the assumption that he would go himself. If Menzies thought otherwise, and Chidson had to consider the probability, he would have to find an alternative. He had racked his brains but after the ravages that followed Venlo and Dunkirk, agents with the necessary qualifications, perfect Dutch and German and the athletic build and guts to do the job, were rare. In the end he could think of only one person and he thought of that person with some reluctance.

On the third day after his briefing by Menzies, Chidson was back in his chief's office. Before sitting down he placed a large key upon the desk. Menzies stared at the key, then gingerly picked it up and examined it. Finally he looked up questioningly.

'The key,' said Chidson.

Menzies wrinkled his forehead. His close-cropped silver-grey hair moved on his scalp. 'So I see,' he said with the trace of a well-bred Scottish accent. 'Key to what?'

'The safe.'

'The safe . . .?'

'The key to the safe of the Admiral's office at Den Helder. The safe in which the map is kept.'

Menzies stared at the key with amazement. 'My God, Monty, where on earth did you find it?' He looked up at Chidson. 'You haven't been over there, have you?'

Chidson laughed. 'I've had a chat with Furstner.'

Menzies nodded. Admiral Furstner, Commander in Chief of the Royal Netherlands Navy, had escaped to England and now had his headquarters in London.

'In the good old days, Furstner's HQ was Den Helder.' Chidson indicated the key. 'Being a well-trained, thorough naval officer, before he left for good he emptied the safe, locked it and put the key in his briefcase.'

'And you think it's the same safe there now?'

'Why alter it? I'm assured it's a perfectly good safe. The Hun might seem super-efficient, but he won't be above using a good Dutch safe.'

'Go on . . .'

Chidson opened his briefcase and took out a folded sheet of paper which he laid on Menzies' desk and proceeded to unfold. Menzies let out a low whistle.

'The barracks . . .'

'Den Helder naval barracks. Up-to-date when Furstner left

fifteen months ago. I've asked the RAF for new photos. When we get them we can see if the Hun have made any changes.'

Menzies examined the drawing of the barracks, then again picked up the key. 'Does Furstner know what this is all about?'

Chidson shook his head. 'He hasn't the faintest idea. He just lent me the key.'

For a moment they were silent then Menzies said, 'We have the layout of the site, the key to the safe. All we want now is the burglar.' He looked at Chidson. 'Any ideas?'

Chidson hesitated then blurted out: 'Why not let me go, sir?'

A thin smile spread across Menzies' face. 'I expected you to say that. I knew you'd say it. But you know as well as I do it's just not on.'

'Why not? I speak Dutch and German fluently, I know Holland well. I'm certain I could do the job.'

'You probably could, Monty, but you're a backroom boy now. I can't afford to lose you, not after Stevens and Best. I need you here.'

Chidson had tried, it was his nature to try. He knew Menzies would refuse him and he knew that Menzies was right. Even if they were in the middle of a war, he supposed, with reluctance, that when he really considered the matter rationally, his daredevil days were over.

'So who is there?' asked Menzies.

Chidson had the answer although it worried him to give it. 'If you don't want me to go, then there is one other person.' He hesitated, then very quietly said, 'The only one I can think of, the only one capable of doing the job . . .' He stopped.

'Go on.'

For a long time Chidson said nothing. At last he said, 'Young Alex Richards, the chap who worked for Stevens as courier. His mother is Dutch, he speaks Dutch and German fluently and he knows his way about Holland. He's got all the qualifications.'

Menzies remembered Richards, the lad who stood trial, the lad Chidson had got out of prison.

'When he came back,' said Chidson, 'he joined the RAF as aircrew. It's what he wanted to do. He sailed through elementary flying training school and got himself into Fighter Command. I've checked, he's still alive and flying, or he was yesterday.'

'Have you spoken to him?'

'Not yet.'

Menzies looked thoughtful. 'If I remember rightly, he had a bad time in Holland.' He looked into Chidson's face. 'Do you think he'll want to go back?'

'He's at Manston. With your permission I'll go down tomorrow and ask.'

Menzies stared up at the ceiling. 'In view of the uncertainties of war and the short life expectancy of a fighter pilot these days, have a word in the right quarter and see that our young man doesn't do any more flying until you've seen him.'

Chidson nodded. He would have done that anyway.

Chidson was at the door when Menzies said: 'You wanted to know the size of the map. It's enormous, bloody enormous. Ten feet long, two feet wide.'

Chidson shut his eyes. Even if they could get hold of it, it would be a devil to photograph.

13

They met in the officers' mess. It was six months since Chidson had seen Alex. In February, at their last meeting, although a pilot officer with his wings, Alex had still been the thin, somewhat angular youth that Chidson had plucked so dramatically from the House of Custody. Now, as a flying officer with a newly acquired DFC, he was still lean but his shoulders had broadened, his cheeks were full and gone from his eyes was the tired, haunted look he had brought back from Holland. He now had the face of a man used to making decisions and, when he spoke, his voice was brisk and controlled.

Alex grinned. 'I knew you must be behind it, sir. That grounding.'

Chidson indicated the thin mist that covered the airfield and cupped his hand behind his ear to indicate the silence. Alex laughed. Since it was his mess, Alex bought the drinks. When Chidson led the way to a table in the farthest corner of the large room, Alex knew that the meeting was not to be purely social.

Chidson started by asking about current operations. Alex's eyes lit up. He was now upon his favourite subject, flying.

'We get one or two sneak raiders, otherwise it's mostly sweeps over northern France.'

'Have you seen Holland again?' asked Chidson almost casually.

Alex smiled. 'We were over Ijmuiden the other day escorting Blenheims.' He waited, and at last said: 'Why the grounding, sir? It was almost as if you were frightened of losing me.'

'Still enjoy flying?'

'Very much, sir. Very much indeed.'

'Would you like a break from it for a while?'

Alex hesitated, then said, 'That depends . . .'

Chidson remained silent, not quite sure how to continue. What had seemed a reasonable task in Menzies' office now had its problems.

Alex looked at the Colonel with increasing suspicion. His eyes narrowed. 'You asked if I'd like a break from flying. You also mentioned Holland . . .?'

'Ever thought of going back there?'

Alex's eyes clouded. 'One day perhaps . . .'

'How do you feel when you cross the coast and fly over the place?'

'Strange. Most of the time I try and put it out of my mind.'

'I'll come to the point.'

Alex smiled. 'Good. I'm sure you haven't come down here, Colonel, to ask me what it's like to fly *over* Holland?'

Speaking quietly, unemotionally, Chidson gave a detailed account of the map showing German coastal defences, where it was kept and the Chiefs of Staff's request for a copy. Although he was leaning back in the old, cane chair with all the studied nonchalance of the fighter pilot, Alex listened intently. When Chidson finished there was a long silence. Chidson knew better than break it. He could imagine the younger man's thoughts. He hadn't actually asked Alex if he would undertake the job. There had been no need. The recital of the details had been enough. Chidson would never have come to Manston merely to relate a story. Alex knew what was wanted of him.

Chidson's appearance in the mess had triggered off a whole cavalcade of memories most of which Alex had been struggling to forget. The thought of going back to Holland, to the land of those memories, was disturbing if not horrific.

'The last time I got involved with the Secret Service, I ended up in a hell of a mess.'

Chidson caught the bitterness in the voice. 'I know. I'm only too aware of it. That's why I wanted to go myself.'

Alex looked straight into Chidson's face. Chidson was old enough to be his father. 'You wanted to go yourself?'

'Why not? I know Holland well, it's my old stamping ground. Anyway, it's really my job.'

Alex laid his head back and half closed his eyes. He was looking at the rafters of the mess ceiling, but he saw many other things. 'It's not going to be a particularly easy thing to do, is it, sir? I mean, getting a map out of a safe in a German admiral's office?'

'Damned difficult. The only things to help you, give you a fifty-fifty chance, are training, very thorough training, good briefing, surprise and your own guts. You'll have one advantage over the Hun, you'll be operating in Holland, not Germany. The locals will be on your side.'

Alex smiled grimly. 'Not all of them.'

Again they fell silent. At last Chidson said, 'I'll come clean with you. I've no right to ask you to undertake this, none whatsoever. The trouble is, and you'll discover this for yourself as you get older, only a very few people are capable of doing extraordinary things. The average man may be a damned fine chap, the salt of the earth and all that, but he is only average. This means that the above-average fellow, the one who can do the extraordinary things, gets called upon over and over again. I've seen it with battalions in the last war and with men. A good battalion spends too long in the line. A good NCO goes on throwing bombs into an enemy sap time and time again.

And the awful thing is that you go on expecting him to do it.'

'Who else have you got?'

Chidson shrugged. 'No one at the moment.'

'I thought you had plenty of agents in Holland. I thought it was the one country where Britain had a good network?'

Chidson shook his head. 'You forget poor old Stevens and Best. The Huns have played havoc with our networks ever since that damned Venlo affair. We're only beginning to see the full extent of the damage now.' Chidson glanced at Alex. 'I can see this is no way to get you all enthusiastic about going back there, but it's only fair that you should know the realities.'

Chidson stopped. He was talking in a matter-of-fact way about one of the cruellest, most pitiless and deadly of all war games. It now seemed apparent that Stevens and Best, presumably under duress, had told the Gestapo much that the SIS would have wished to have kept secret. Here he was persuading a young man who had already suffered enough to go back into that fearful climate. He had already applied moral blackmail when he had said that SIS had no one else. Chidson hated what he was doing and wished Menzies had let him go. The terrible thing was that he must keep on until he had, or was fairly sure of having, Alex's agreement. He must keep his own feelings out of it. What he was doing he was doing for the war effort, for the country, for freedom, for all the hundreds of other reasons pronounced daily, no doubt on both sides, to persuade men to give their lives.

'All our lines of communication have been cut since Dunkirk. We've got to build everything up again . . .'

'This map of coastal defences . . .' began Alex, and stopped.

Chidson dropped his voice. 'The point is, we're already planning the return to the Continent.'

Alex nodded. It was logical and he had assumed it was happening – after all, the war had to be won – but to be actually told that plans were already afoot for a landing somewhere along the Occupied coast was quite different. It made the whole affair infinitely more real, not just some sort of hazy dream.

'You can see now why the possession of that plan is so important.'

All this was top secret. Chidson could say no more. Indeed, the less Alex knew the better. All he needed to know were the details of the map. But Chidson had one more element of moral blackmail. 'When the day does come, data on their coastal defences, calibre of guns, arcs of fire, thickness of concrete, all the technical details, will save thousands of lives.'

Alex understood perfectly. It was his life for the infantry and tanks plodding off the beaches. For a moment it seemed awful, then he realized that in a way it was what he was already doing. No one in 1941 would want to insure the life of a fighter pilot operating over northern France.

'I need time to think, Colonel. There is so much involved.'

Chidson understood. 'You have my number in London.'

Alex nodded. He walked with Chidson to his car. As he was about to leave, Chidson said, 'If you decide to turn down this job, there will be no hard feelings on my part. None whatsoever. Most people would think you'd done more than enough already.'

Alex saluted and watched the car drive away. He was suddenly alone with his memories: memories none of his other colleagues at Manston, for all their camaraderie, could share.

Alex lay awake late into the night. The turmoil in his mind after Chidson's visit surprised even himself. There was a period in his life that he had consciously tried to forget, memories he had deliberately suppressed. On the ground, there was other human company. Men who lived for the moment, and Alex lived with them. In the air, such memories were too dangerous. Flying, he had to concentrate every second. He had to watch the alien sky. His mind had to be clear, his body alert. Now in bed it all came back. His memories, bitter and fresh; what he saw as his duty, muddled and indistinct.

He loved the job he was doing. To be a fighter pilot had always been his dream; he hated the thought of giving it up. He was lucky to be a fighter pilot. Now, when people got their wings, they were being posted to bombers. He wouldn't have wanted to be in bombers. To leave his squadron, the people he flew with, in whom he had confidence, would be like leaving home again. In the darkness of the night, it seemed to him that even if he returned from Holland, he might never come back to the squadron. He might find himself posted anywhere. Yet he hated the thought of letting Chidson down. If anyone else had asked him to take on this mission he would have refused outright. But there were few things he could not do for the man who had rescued him from that Dutch prison and thereby almost certainly saved his life. Alex had few illusions about what would have happened to him had he still been there when the Germans occupied Amsterdam. And that brought up the Germans and above all the Gestapo.

Thoughts of the Gestapo added yet another world to his night. Holland would be full of them. They must have details of him or they wouldn't have been able to set the trap for him. They were the unknown enemy. So far as he knew he had never met a Gestapo man. But he had met their Dutch counterparts. If he took on this job he would run the risk of again falling into their hands. What would happen if he ran into Bearends or Deepground? They might well recognize him. What if he was arrested on some minor charge and brought before Fatesma? Fatesma would certainly remember him. In the darkness of his room he saw Bearends, Deepground and Fatesma. He saw the Governor of the House of Custody and frightened eyes peering through the slits in the masks they had had to wear, but above all he saw the three Dutch Nazis. For fifteen months he had struggled to bury their faces. Now they were back. Every feature he had so carefully etched into his memory had returned.

In Alex's mind, just before dawn, Fatesma, Bearends and Deepground turned into the crew of a Heinkel. He no longer feared them. He came up beneath them and emptied all his ammunition into the plane's belly. He watched the plane spiralling down, burning, and his joy was unbounded that no parachute blossomed. He flew over their funeral pyre and did a victory roll. Then he fell asleep.

He woke up late and ate an enormous breakfast. He was still grounded but in any case the mist still hung and there was no flying. He took his cup of coffee with him to the telephone.

'I'll go, sir.'

113

At the other end of the phone there was a pause, then Chidson said: 'Are you quite sure, Alex? Absolutely sure?'

'Yes, sir. If you think I can do it, then I am prepared to go.'

Chidson drew in his breath. 'Good man, Alex, good man. I'll arrange with your CO for you to have leave of absence. I'll do that at once. How soon can you come up to London?'

'This afternoon.'

Chidson still had a lot to do, a lot to settle. He was delighted with the young man's keenness but he wanted more time himself. 'Make it the day after tomorrow.'

Alex was disappointed. Now he had made up his mind he wanted everything to happen quickly.

'The day after tomorrow?'

'I can't manage anything earlier and the person I want you to see is away. Give me a buzz about the time of your train and I'll get my driver to meet you at Victoria.'

14

'We're going to see Brigadier Menzies. My chief and now your chief.'

Alex nodded.

They went up the flight of stairs in Broadway. Chidson introduced Alex. Menzies waved them towards two chairs then looked intently at the young man and for a long time said nothing. His sharp eyes focused first on Alex's face, then on the blue and white striped ribbon of the DFC above the breast pocket of the tunic. At last he seemed satisfied.

'I understand Colonel Chidson has briefed you?'

'Yes, sir.'

'The job we want you to do is going to take guts and a whole lot of other things including a good slice of luck. I know you have the guts, I hope we can teach you the other things. As for luck, Monty and I will be praying for you and let's hope that fortune favours the brave.'

Alex allowed himself a grim smile. He glanced at Chidson but Chidson was watching Menzies.

'To put the matter quite bluntly, so you have no doubt whatsoever of what you are taking on, this is an espionage mission behind enemy lines. Before you go you will have to train in the dirty business of behind the lines operations. You will have to learn to shoot, knife and strangle a man with your bare hands. You will have to learn to act. To appear drunk but remain absolutely sober. It's like being on patrol all the time, watching for the Hun in the sun all day and all night for days on end.'

Alex suddenly realized that he was sitting forward in his chair. The palms of his hands were wet. He felt a shiver of excitement down his spine.

'Secrecy is of the utmost importance. You must not discuss this matter with anyone, except of course Colonel Chidson and myself. It that quite clear?'

'Yes, sir.'

'We know what our objective is, what we want to achieve. Colonel Chidson will help you get to know the layout of those barracks until you know them as well as your own mess at Manston. You must be able to find a drainpipe blindfold. Come back to me when you've worked out just what you're going to do. I want to hear every detail.'

Menzies got up. Chidson and Alex got up. Menzies looked straight into Alex's face.

'Are you quite sure you want to undertake this job?'

'Quite sure, sir.'

Menzies put out his hand. 'Welcome to the Secret Intelligence Service. I trust you will be as successful in this as you have been in the RAF.'

From Menzies' office they went into the projection room. Chidson switched on the epidiascope. 'Ever been to Den Helder?'

'Never.'

'Not the most prepossessing place, especially in mid-winter when you'll get there.'

'Mid-winter?' asked Alex in astonishment.

'I'm not letting you go half-prepared. Before you leave these shores you'll really believe you're your new persona. For that you'll need five months' training.'

The first aerial photo came up on the large screen.

'Ever flown over Den Helder?'

'Not consciously.'

Chidson used his pointer. 'That's the naval barracks. And there's the pearl in the oyster, Admiral Furstner's old office.'

Chidson moved the pointer to a large, dark Mercedes parked outside the building. 'You can just see the metal pennant on the car's front bumper. That's an admiral's pennant. Since the car is parked outside Furstner's old HQ, we may consider that we've had our first bit of luck. We can take it that the German Admiral is using the same building.'

'Do we know the name of this admiral?'

Chidson smiled. 'I do, but there's no reason why you should. Indeed, there's every reason why you shouldn't.'

Alex had his first glimpse of how SIS thought.

'The Germans', said Chidson, 'have their faults, but one thing can be said in their favour. They are a hospitable, garrulous lot. Quite unlike us stiff, stuffy, formal British.'

Alex was wondering just where this eulogy of the Germans was leading when Chidson began to explain.

'You're a fighter pilot. Flying, air fighting, aeroplanes are all second nature to you. We've got to get you into a German naval barracks. When you are in there you must have the run of the place. That means you've got to be in the German armed forces. Now, in view of your experience, your most natural role would be as a Luftwaffe pilot. It's no good a plumber pretending to be an accountant. He'll give himself away sooner or later. Supposing for one reason or other, a Luftwaffe pilot, an officer, were to visit the naval barracks at Den Helder, Hun hospitality would ensure that he was well received. He would be able to move around freely without raising suspicion.' Chidson looked into Alex's face, and spoke very slowly, carefully pronouncing each word. 'In the night, perhaps after a party, he should be able to get into the Admiral's office . . .'

'It's possible . . .' said Alex quietly, thinking how simple Chidson was making it all sound. 'But what is a Luftwaffe officer doing in a naval barracks?'

'Ever flown a Messerschmitt?'

Alex was surprised by the apparent sudden switch in the subject. 'I've seen plenty . . .'

'You ought to at least sit in one. Handle the control, familiarize yourself with the cockpit layout. There's one at Farnborough. They're a bit proprietorial about their Enemy Flight, but I'll see what I can arrange.'

Alex's appreciation of the thoroughness of SIS increased with every minute.

'You asked why a Luftwaffe officer should be visiting a naval headquarters.'

Alex nodded. 'It seems a bit incongruous.'

Chidson bit his lower lip. 'I can think of half a dozen reasonable reasons, reasons that would satisfy a detective story, but I can't think of an *absolutely foolproof one*. I want *you* to think about it. After all, it's you who is going to be doing it. Sleep on it. Something will come by the morning.' His voice changed from the conversational to the crisply efficient. 'But remember, it must be foolproof. You must be in those barracks naturally. Those Hun matelots have got to *want you in there*.'

For the rest of that day, Alex considered the problem. A Luftwaffe officer, wherever he was wandering, must come from some base. At some point during a conversation he was almost certain to be asked where he was stationed. It would be all too easy for a suspicious German navy man to phone and check. So he must not be stationed in Holland. In which case what was he doing there? On a course? Passing through? By ten in the evening, without a foolproof solution, he was mentally exhausted and fell into a deep sleep.

It came to him while shaving. All his best ideas came to him while shaving. He got to Chidson's office early and waited impatiently for the Colonel.

'I'm on leave looking for a girlfriend. A Dutch girlfriend.'

'Go on . . .' said Chidson.

'I'm not stationed in Holland at all. I'm a Luftwaffe officer on leave from the Russian Front. That's a long way away. Difficult to check up on.'

Slowly Chidson nodded. 'We want a fighter squadron stationed in Holland in 1940 and transferred to the Russian Front in the spring of this year. And while you were in Holland, you fell in love with a girl there. Now, with a bit of leave, you've come back to see her.' He considered the words as one might consider the first sip of a fine wine.

Alex looked anxiously at Chidson. 'Does it sound all right? Will it do?'

Chidson got up and started pacing the room. After a while he said, 'Of course, we'll have to work on the girl. If you start telling the hearty, lecherous Huns over a glass of schnapps that you've come half across the world looking for a Dutch girl, they'll want to know all about her.' He stopped and shook his head. 'However, that's not difficult. We can think up something. Of course, you won't be able to find the girl. She'll have moved. Perhaps even been taken away.'

Chidson sat, his thumb and forefinger stroking his chin. 'You know, Alex,' he said after a while, 'there's still something missing. I like the idea of you being on leave from the Russian Front, that's good. Excellent. But there's still something odd. You're walking about Den Helder, a small port, mostly naval, all on your own looking for a girl. You go into the bars. Most are filled with ordinary ratings. You find the one the officers use. You go in again on your own. You get to know people . . .' Chidson stopped and shook his head. 'It won't do. *You're always on your own!*'

Alex wanted to be on his own. He felt his stomach sink. 'You mean I've got to have someone with me?' he asked, hoping his voice didn't betray his anxiety.

'In one way it doubles the risk, in another way it halves it.' Chidson was silent for a long time. At last he said, '*Two* officers walk into that bar, not one. *Two* Luftwaffe officers would look much better. Two chums spending their leave together in Holland would raise far less suspicion than one on his own. Single people, single strangers, are always suspect.'

From the first mention of the plans in the safe to the acceptance of the job, Alex had visualized himself being on his own. At no point had he visualized a companion. When he had been considering the matter, before making up his mind, he had thought of himself operating alone. Indeed, he now realized that had he been told there would be another person with him, in all probability he would have refused to go. He had more to do than Chidson knew or could ever guess. The idea of a number two did not appeal to him. 'I'd rather be on my own,' he said bluntly. 'I like operating on my own.'

'You don't go on patrols on your own,' said Chidson quickly. 'You're normally part of a flight or squadron.'

'This is different . . .'

Chidson shook his head. 'It won't look right. I've told you, people on their own, strangers, are always suspect.'

'He'd have to speak fluent German . . .'

'That's not too difficult.'

'He'd have to be young . . . a pilot . . .'

'You could cover for him not being a pilot.' Chidson stopped, then said, 'More important, you've got to get on with him. Trust him. Trust him with your life.'

Alex waited, wondering where such a person was to be found, hoping he didn't exist.

'We need an Austrian or German,' mused Chidson. 'Unfortunately we've deported a lot of them.'

'We've also got to make sure that anyone who comes out of Europe is clean,' said Alex doubtfully. 'If I really do have to be with them, then I hope to God MI5 has given them the complete going over. I wouldn't want to get out there and find that the chap's got a chum in the Gestapo.'

Chidson wasn't listening; he had his own thoughts. 'There's a Pioneer Corps unit in Wales at some godforsaken camp near Cardiff. They were formed from German and Austrian refugees. They've had clearance, all of them. There must be some young ones amongst them, someone with enough guts who's dying to hit back at Hitler.'

Alex knew that he had lost the battle. Reluctantly he accepted that Chidson was right. Philosophically he decided that what he wanted to do on his own, he could still do. His private war need not necessarily be impaired. Presumably, if there were to be two of them, he would be the senior, in which case Alex could make his own opportunities.

'You win, sir,' he said quietly. 'As long as you're sure of the man, he's all right by me.'

'He'll be as good as you, Alex, I promise,' said Chidson with a twinkle, 'and when you're out there, you'll be damned glad you've got him. It's not all action, you know. For a lot of the time you'll be holed up in a safe-house, and that's no fun on your own.'

Alex decided it would work. Suddenly he came right round to Chidson's way of thinking. 'For that matter, I don't suppose it's all that much fun walking into a café full of Germans on your own either.'

'A nanny would be comforting,' said Chidson sombrely.

Chidson put the proposition to Menzies. Menzies liked the plan so far and agreed to the doubling of the force. The following day Chidson again saw Alex. 'Next job', said Chidson, staring into the younger man's face, 'is for you to find the number two.'

'*Me*, sir?' said Alex in astonishment. 'You've got far more experience in judging men than me.'

Chidson was smiling. 'I don't dispute that, but remember, we need someone *you* can get on with so you'd better go out and select him yourself. First thing tomorrow it's down to the Welsh mountains for you. I've rung the camp, you'll get all the co-operation you need. After you've chosen him, I'll check him.'

Alex was happy. If the man was his own nominee, the trip to Holland should still be fruitful in more ways than one.

Middle-aged, grey-haired sometime professors, doctors, lawyers and accountants, draped in ill-fitting battledress, gauchely saluting a young flying officer, did not appear promising material for transformation into a daredevil Luftwaffe pilot cum agent. Certainly not promising material for a companion upon a hazardous trip behind enemy lines. Alex had accepted the need for a number two. The main mission and his private mission were going to work perfectly well as a duet. But by lunchtime Alex was depressed. As depressed as the inclement Welsh summer weather and the dreary camp environment.

There was nothing and no one in those shiny, wet Nissen huts to inspire him.

At four o'clock he was brought a cup of tea by a young lance corporal. Alex indicated where to put the cup. The Lance Corporal put the cup down then stood, hesitant.

'Can I ask you something, sir?'

Alex looked up from the files of the men he had still to see and nodded.

'There's a rumour in the camp that you're here to interview men for a special mission?'

Alex raised his eyebrows. 'Is there? Thank you for telling me. However, my advice to you is to take no notice of it.'

The Lance Corporal looked crestfallen. 'You mean it's not true, sir?'

'Exactly. It's not true. It's typical of the sort of rumour that goes around a camp in the rain. The sort of rumour not to listen to.'

To Alex's surprise the man didn't go but went on standing there. Alex looked up at him questioningly. 'Well?'

'With you being an RAF officer, sir, we thought it might have something to do with parachuting.'

Alex thought for a moment and then said, 'What's your name?'

'Grosman, sir. Abraham Grosman.'

'You are Jewish?'

'Half Jewish, on my father's side.'

'And that's why you got out of Germany?'

'Yes.'

Alex indicated the single hard wooden chair. 'Sit down and tell me about yourself.'

The Lance Corporal sat. 'There's not much to tell, sir. I was born in Berlin, brought up there and did all my schooling there. My father was a doctor and I was going to study medicine too. However, the Nazis had different ideas. Compared to a lot of others, we were pretty lucky. You see, my father was never fooled about Hitler's intentions. He knew what was going to happen and he got us out of Germany before things got too bad. Before they stopped the Jews leaving. We lived in Holland for a while then came to England in May last year. I volunteered for the RAF but finished up here.'

Alex looked closely at the Lance Corporal. They were about the same age. Grosman could not be more than twenty. He was tall, slim and, even sitting, he was erect. He had a fine face, thin like his body, and the features were clear cut, the bones apparent. About his pale blue eyes and firm mouth there was a look of character and determination. He gave the appearance of being in command of himself, able to live hard. Watching him, talking to him, Alex felt a surge of confidence. It was all so different from the interviews with the intellectuals.

'Don't you like it here?'

'It's an awful place, sir. We're just labourers. That's all they want us for.'

Alex took a long time to speak. He was beginning to understand what Chidson had gone through at Manston. Only Chidson, being older, must also have had some parental feeling. It seemed at that moment to Alex, as he considered Grosman's face, that he had in his hands the man's fate. If he liked Grosman too much, thought him uniquely suitable, he could be the cause of his death. He hated such responsibility.

'Would you ever go back to Germany . . . or, perhaps, Holland?'

'In the right circumstances, sir. I mean, if it meant having a go at the Nazis.'

'It wouldn't be like fighting as a soldier . . .'

'If I stay here I won't be fighting like anyone. I'll just be digging ditches, filling sandbags and making roads.'

Alex smothered a smile. Very quietly he said, 'The man I want may not necessarily have to parachute but he must certainly be prepared to do something dangerous. Very dangerous. He must be prepared to risk his life.'

'And he has to speak German?'

'Perfectly.'

'In which case, sir . . . German is my mother tongue.'

Alex shook his head. 'The chips will be stacked against you,' he said warningly.

Grosman said nothing.

'You know what I'm saying?'

'Of course I know what you're saying, sir.'

'It's a dirty war, the war I'm thinking about. You don't always know who are your friends, who are your enemies.'

'It's a dirty war here too, sir. Filthy.'

Alex smiled. 'You are still interested?'

'Very much, sir.'

There was no hesitation. Alex was surprised.

'The Gestapo must know about you . . .'

Grosman shrugged.

'There's nothing nice about the Gestapo, I can tell you!'

'I want to see action, sir! I don't want to rot away here until the end of the war. We'll never see action in the Pioneer Corps. Certainly not out here in Wales. They've put us as far away from the war as they can.' Grosman lowered his voice. 'You see, sir, they don't really trust us.'

It was the word 'trust' that did it. Alex looked hard into Grosman's face. At last he said, 'I'll look at your file.'

Grosman gave a great grin. 'Thank you, sir. Thank you very much.'

Alex expected the Lance Corporal to go, but to Alex's considerable surprise Grosman still stood his ground.

'Just two things, sir. Do I do whatever this is on my own?'

'No. If you do it at all, you do it with me.'

Grosman nodded.

'And the other thing?'

'The reason I asked, sir, was because I have a friend. A mate. He's here in the camp. He's dying to get out too.'

Alex looked at the Lance Corporal in astonishment. 'For God's sake, Grosman, I haven't come here to recruit a whole squadron!'

Grosman was not abashed. 'He knew I was coming to see you and I promised to put in a word for him.'

'I'm only looking for *one* man,' said Alex sharply.

'He might be better than me. More suitable.'

Alex's astonishment grew. The man's precocious naïvety reminded Alex of himself when he first met Rachel Blum. Then he had refused to accept 'no' for an answer. Now Grosman was doing much the same thing.

123

'If you saw him, sir, then after you'd seen him, you could take whichever of us you thought the better.'

'You're jumping the gun, Grosman, I might not take either of you.'

There was a long silence. Alex stared at Grosman but Grosman didn't flinch. 'What's your friend's name?'

'Meisner, sir. Hermann Meisner. He's about my age and he's also German by birth.'

Alex indicated the door. 'Go on, send him in to me.'

Unlike his friend, Hermann Meisner had not yet acquired a stripe. He was a Pioneer Corps private, just about the lowest creature in the British Army. He was slight without being actually thin. Like Grosman there was no fat on his face. His nose was long and broad at the nostrils. Alex had little doubt that he too was Jewish or partly Jewish. Above his dark brown eyes, his most striking feature was the untidy mop of thick black hair that stuck out from beneath his cap. Meisner came from Mannheim, he was twenty years old and would have been a dentist but for the anti-Semitic laws of Nazi Germany. He had completed his education in Holland and like Grosman had fled to England when Holland was invaded. Like Grosman his attempt to fight back had ended up with him in the Pioneer Corps. He too craved for action.

Alex took to Meisner as he had taken to Grosman. He found it difficult to separate one from the other. It seemed to him that together they were more than double either one of them. Eventually he put the same question to Meisner that he had put to Grosman. Would he be prepared to go back to Germany or Holland with all the dangers that entailed? Again there was no hesitation in the answer. Alex examined the files of both men and checked that they had been cleared by MI5 before being allowed to join the Pioneer Corps. He could see only one course of action. He would take both Grosman and Meisner back to London and ask Chidson to make the final choice.

Chidson interviewed both men. Indeed, he spent the best part of a day with one or other of them. Like Alex he found it difficult to choose between them. He too believed that they were better together, that they complemented one another. In the end he decided to send both. Meisner he considered a little too Jewish-looking to pass as a Luftwaffe officer but decided that he would make an excellent back-up man. Meisner would be trained as a wireless operator. In accordance with established SIS policy neither was to be given any details of the mission until shortly before they set off. However, in fairness to them, so that they could still back out if they wanted to, Chidson told them that they would be going behind enemy lines and operating in an occupied country. Both men seemed to take the news calmly and remained adamant that they wanted to go.

15

They trained throughout the autumn. The training was done by SOE, the Special Operations Executive. SOE was divided into sections, each being responsible for action in a particular country. Each country section had its own training school. Chidson did not want to send Alex, Grosman and Meisner to the Dutch section, where they would have mixed with Dutchmen being trained for action in Holland. In spite of the rivalry between SIS and SOE, for the latter, much to Menzies' chagrin, had got themselves involved in espionage, Chidson managed to have a new German section especially created. It was in this section, in a training school in Inverness-shire, that the three SIS recruits began their toughening up.

With full packs they carried out long day and night exercises. They were taught how to handle German weapons, unarmed combat, quick reaction shooting and silent killing. In September they were posted to Ringway Aerodrome, Cheshire and given a five-jump parachute course. Next they went to a training school near Beaulieu in the New Forest where they learned safe-breaking, lock-picking, secret codes, the use of infra-red inks, and infiltration into carefully guarded houses under cover of darkness. There they also studied the complete documentation used by the German forces in Holland and German uniform recognition for all three services and the SS.

The Third Reich was a country of uniforms. It seemed to be held together by them. No other warring nation had such a complexity of cuts, colours, flashes and badges. It seemed that everyone in Germany must be entitled to wear at least one uniform, often two. The subtle differentiations were astonishing. Alex, Grosman and Meisner were questioned on insignia and badges of rank until they were dreaming of them. At Beaulieu they also learned the arts of camouflage, personal disguise and forging documents. After that the trio were split up. Alex and Grosman were sent on a military intelligence course at Minley Manor near Camberley, Meisner went to train as a wireless operator with the Royal Corps of Signals. At Minley Manor, Alex and Grosman learned, amongst many other things, document photography with a sub-miniature camera. From Minley, Alex paid a visit to Farnborough where he had the odd experience of seeing a Messerschmitt 109 E in RAF roundels. He sat in the cockpit and familiarized himself with the controls. From a test pilot he learned how the plane handled.

By the middle of November they were fully fledged agents. Grosman and Meisner were given temporary commissions as second lieutenants in the Intelligence Corps. All three returned to London to be given their respective covers and for two of them to learn, for the first time, the nature of their task.

During their training, Chidson had worked out all the finer points. Alex was a Luftwaffe Hauptmann, Erich Baader, serving with Jagdgeschwader 51 now operating on the Russian Front near Smolensk but in 1940 and during the early months of 1941 stationed in Belgium and Holland. Grosman was Oberleutnant Kurt Wiegand of the same Jagdgeschwader. Meisner was an SS-Obersturmführer of the Security Forces. The Colonel had also located a safe-house in the town of Alkmaar. The house belonged to a Dutchman who had recently escaped from Holland to England. The man had no family and the house was empty. Alkmaar was only forty kilometres from Den Helder and there was a railway between the two. In spite of their parachute training they were not to be dropped into

Holland. SOE were training Dutch agents who would shortly be parachuted. Chidson did not want his men to arrive in the same way. He had therefore arranged with the Director of Naval Intelligence for them to be taken by submarine to the Dutch coast. The point he had chosen for the landing was on the relatively uninhabited shore just north-west of the small town of Bergen.

'Any of you ever been there?' asked Chidson.

All three shook their heads.

Chidson indicated on the map. 'Due west of Bergen where this road ends, there's this tiny hamlet. Half a dozen fishermen's cottages, Bergen aan Zee.' His finger moved. 'It's just north of there, three or four kilometres up the coast. That's where I want you put down. The place is as bleak as the Sahara. Nothing but sand dunes. There won't be a Hun for miles.'

They examined the map and the air photos. For all of them, the layout of the towns, roads, rail and waterways of the area in which they would operate brought the project into its first, vivid prospective.

'Now,' said Chidson looking at each man in turn, 'you know the job, where you're going to land, where the safe-house is, and your cover. That's how I see it. I want you to tell me how you see it. I want you each to be devil's advocate. If there's anything wrong, anything that stands out as odd, now is the moment to put it right.' Very quietly he added, 'We haven't got much longer.'

'I think we should all have SS uniforms, sir,' said Alex, 'not just Meisner.'

Chidson frowned. 'We've been through it all, Alex. You're a pilot, a flyer . . .'

'I don't mean that the SS should be our main identity, sir. The main cover stands . . .'

Chidson was not happy. He believed he had dotted every 'i' and crossed every 't'. He looked from Alex to Grosman and back to Alex. 'That would mean providing *two* covers. That could be messy. Damned messy.'

Alex had his reasons for wanting SS uniforms, one private, the other public. Now he put forward the latter. 'We shouldn't land in Luftwaffe uniforms, Colonel. It just won't look right.'

He indicated on the map. 'Alkmaar is eight kilometres from the sea. Assuming we are landed at the correct place on this quiet stretch just north of Bergen, we've still got to walk to the village and probably get the first bus in the morning for Alkmaar. It's winter. What are two Luftwaffe officers and an SS man doing walking along the shore? Indeed, what are they doing in a one-eyed little hole like Bergen in the first place? I'd feel much safer if we landed in SS uniforms. From what we've been told, the SS have got the run of the place. SS officers aren't likely to be stopped and questioned.'

Chidson accepted that Alex had a point. Somewhat reluctantly he agreed to provide SS uniforms and a second cover for Alex and Grosman. They went on and discussed the plan in every aspect. They could find no evident fault. All they had to do was to assimilate their respective characters. They decided that if there were questions on flying, Grosman would have to fend them off. Alex would have to answer them. Provided they stayed together, with Alex being the senior, that wouldn't be too difficult.

When they broke up for the day, Chidson announced their next move. From tomorrow they would be billeted with the Navy at Chatham.

Chidson unrolled his map. The Lieutenant Commander with the ginger beard and ginger eyebrows unrolled his charts. He knew he had to deliver three agents to the Dutch coast as soon as practicable, but that was all he did know. With that limited knowledge he had done his homework. Chidson indicated the bleak coastline just north of Bergen.

'Eight kilometres, five miles, without a decent habitation. Sand dunes and neither a Dutchman nor a German to be seen. That's where we want to end up.'

The Lieutenant Commander consulted his charts. Given the right tides and weather, they could be taken to within five hundred yards of the beach. From there on it would be a matter of rowing them ashore in the rubber dinghy.

'When will the tides be right?' asked Chidson bluntly.

'The twelfth would be best.'

Alex counted on his fingers. Today was the seventh. The twelfth was in five days' time. The three looked at one another. Suddenly they were one stage further than the map. Within a week the blue, white and yellow of cartography would be an icy sea, sand, shingle and a Dutch road.

'Sunset on the twelfth is at 15.51. If we slip out soon after that, we should be off your coast at about 03.00 hours.' The Leiutenant Commander looked at Alex. 'Sunrise won't be until about 08.00 hours. That gives you a good four hours of darkness and allows us a little time should there be some unforeseen event. Does that sound all right?'

Alex looked at the others. Grosman nodded. Meisner bit his lip, then he too gave a slight nod. 'Fine,' said Alex. 'Fine.'

'We go on the twelfth . . .' said the Lieutenant Commander.

'The twelfth . . .' said Alex softly.

'That's fine,' said Chidson cheerfully. 'We'll get it all over by Christmas, then you can relax.'

It was a difficult five days. They had their own personal war to contemplate and anticipate. In detachment, it was obsessive and frightening. But their own personal war was made even sharper by the great, external war. In the afternoon of the first day of their purdah, they heard the news of Pearl Harbor. Any elation that the United States had been drawn into the conflict was offset by the battering to the American fleet. From that point on the external war seemed to go from bad to worse. When they heard that the *Prince of Wales* and the *Repulse* had been sunk off the coast of Malaya, they forsook the outside world and went into themselves. They ceased to talk and sat in their quarters staring out of the window at the bleak December days. When they felt their hands they noticed that they were cold. When they looked at them carefully or rubbed their fingertips along their palms, they noticed that they were damp. Then Chidson returned and they had no more time on their own. Chidson filled their minds.

For hour after endless hour, from early in the morning until late in the evening, they went over their cover stories. They dived into their individual worlds of make-believe. Alex grew to know Erich Baader and Jagdgeschwader 51 better than he knew his mother and their old flat in Amsterdam. He knew the girl he had come to find. He could describe her and what she had worn when he had last seen her. He had never known where she had lived for they had always met away from her home. But he still had a tattered letter from her. He knew the name of the commanding officer of his Jagdgeschwader and he was delighted that they had just received the new Messerschmitt Bf 109G-1s. True there had been one or two hold-ups on the Eastern Front but until the onset of winter, which had closed everything down, overall progress had been spectacular.

In the afternoon of their last day, Chidson began a systematic clothing check. All three were stripped naked then handed the clothes they were to wear. Each item was meticulously examined and anything that might betray the wearer removed. The uniforms were exact copies of the German originals tailored by continental tailors working for SOE. Apart from Luftwaffe and SS uniforms, the three were also issued with a suit of civilian clothes. They dressed in the SS uniforms and packed the Luftwaffe uniforms and civilian clothes into suitcases of German manufacture. Into Meisner's suitcase went the wireless transmitter. Identity cards and ration cards were carefully checked and handed over. Besides his Luftwaffe and SS identity cards, Alex had a Dutch civilian card in the name of Cornelis Verloop. Alex was given a considerable quantity of Dutch and German money and all three were issued with loaded Luger pistols. Into Alex's suitcase went two sub-miniature cameras complete with films. Finally Chidson gave Alex two keys: one to the safe-house in Alkmaar, the other to the safe in the Admiral's office in Den Helder. As he handed over the key to the safe, Chidson smiled and said, 'Don't forget to bring it back with you. I've only borrowed it. Admiral Furstner has a long memory.'

It was a moment of levity which ceased the instant Chidson looked at his watch. 'Time to go . . .' The Colonel looked at each of them in turn. He looked them full in the face, straight in the eyes. 'It's a difficult moment,' he said in his clipped, precise way, fighting the emotion welling within him. 'There's a lot one wants to say but doesn't know how. This is the time one wishes one knew a good line from one of the poets. However, I'm sure you all know how I feel. I hate sending you out on such a dangerous job and I would give anything to be with you.' For Chidson, during a time of emotion, it was a long speech. It had considerably taxed his ability to remain undemonstrative. Somewhat gruffly he added: 'Good luck and God bless.' At this point Chidson substituted actions for words. He shook hands with each of them then brusquely indicated the door.

They went out into the cold December twilight. A faint breeze blew from the north-east but scarcely enough to ripple the surface of the water. Outside the building they felt embarrassingly conspicuous. It was bizarre to be walking through a British naval barracks in German uniforms, but in the half-light no one noticed. They even received a salute from a naval rating. They walked between the buildings, past the dark shape of a frigate to a jetty on its own. A gangway led down to the hull of a submarine. On the jetty there was a further handshake with Chidson and an individual, soft 'Goodbye'. Then they were over the tiny patch of dark water and in the care of the boat's First Lieutenant.

They gave their suitcases to two sailors and followed the First Lieutenant up on to the conning tower. Around them the blackout was complete. The only lights were the sidelights of a lorry as it moved slowly along the quayside. As his eyes grew more accustomed to the darkness, Alex began to make out the figures on the bridge. Wrapped in duffle coats were a petty officer and two ratings; one of the ratings was the signaller. The captain of the boat, the Lieutenant Commander with the ginger beard and ginger eyebrows, had the collar of his sheepskin jacket turned up against the night air and was leaning over the bridge rail. He turned his head, saw the three SIS men, glanced at their uniforms, raised his eyebrows and smiled. Alex would like to have spoken to him, said something personal, something like 'Hullo, Frank,' but he did not know the man's name. Names had not been mentioned at their previous meeting. They were just nameless men on a submarine's bridge. Four in British naval uniforms, three in German

SS uniform. It was even more bizarre than walking through the barracks.

There was radio silence. The signaller's lamp clattered out the request to 'Cast off'. A bright light from somewhere ashore answered.

'Ring down, stand by.'

The steel deck beneath their feet began to vibrate. The gentle hum of the electric motors that had been providing the boat's power and lighting was drowned by the rough beat of the diesels.

'Let go forrard, let go aft! Slow astern together!'

To the thump of nineteen hundred brake horsepower, the two hundred and twenty feet of steel that was to be their home until three o'clock the following morning and was to take them to the cold, inhospitable waters off the Dutch coast slipped slowly, stern first, out into the Medway.

'Slow ahead together! Steer zero-one-zero!'

As they increased speed, so the breeze picked up and the chill increased. Behind them and to starboard were the buildings of Chatham and Rochester, a darker backdrop against the dark sky. Alex thought he could make out the great Norman keep of the castle and he indicated it to his two companions. They peered, but no one could be sure. They passed the low shore line of Upnor Hard then the buildings ceased. They were out upon a flat seascape bordered by a flat landscape. Sailing out of the Medway was not unlike sailing out of Amsterdam or any other Dutch port. Alex decided that Admiral de Ruyter must have felt very much at home, when in 1667 he had sailed up the same river with the famous broom at his masthead.

'You're lucky,' said the Lieutenant Commander, indicating the black bowl of the sky studded with stars. 'The weather couldn't have been better. Tide and weather together, that's a good omen. I wouldn't have been so happy if we'd had to delay it.'

Alex was amused and touched by the captain's interest and concern. 'Do you do this often?'

The Lieutenant Commander shook his head. 'Once is enough.'

They were brought sheepskin coats and told that the submarine wouldn't dive until they were well out into the Thames estuary. They passed a destroyer that signalled 'Good hunting!' The Lieutenant Commander laughed and said that it was meant for them and not his boat. They were looking up at the stars, wondering what the dawn would bring, when the bridge suddenly burst into life.

'All hands at diving stations!'

'Clear the bridge!'

They were waved towards the hatch. They clattered down the steel ladder followed by the watch. The Lieutenant Commander slammed shut the hatch, clipped it and followed them down.

'Clutches out!'

The Engineer Petty Officer disengaged the diesels.

'Both full ahead!'

The ammeter needles of the electric motors swung into the red discharge area.

'All clear for diving!' called the First Lieutenant.

'Dive! Dive! Dive!'

'Open main vents!'

Two petty officers spun the wheels that controlled the vents, the ballast tanks filled with sea water, the forward hydroplanes drove the bow under, the rear hydroplanes brought the stern up. The submarine slipped below the surface.

'Take her down to sixty feet! Steer zero-seven-five! Check all compartments!'

They felt the slope. They opened their legs and braced their muscles. The noise was different. The thump of the diesels had gone; they were back to the hum of the electric motors.

'Steady on zero-seven-five, sir, at sixty feet.'

'All compartments checked. No leaks,' said a voice from the gloom of the control room.

They were to run silent. No one was to talk or make any noise. The First Lieutenant took them through the bowels of the vessel to the tiny wardroom. He offered them a drink which they all refused. Then he told them to try and get some sleep and left them.

They sat with their thoughts and laid their heads back. The submarine was a new world. None of them had been in one before. In a way it was a gentle transition. Far more gentle than jumping out of an aeroplane into the night. With the weather good, paddling ashore should not be difficult. They all had implicit faith in the Royal Navy. Now they were in its hands, it never occurred to them that anything could go wrong or that the Lieutenant Commander should miss his landfall. It seemed inconceivable that the womb they were travelling in could be anything but safe. Alex had never felt safe when he had gone aloft in the balloon at Ringway or made his final jump from the old Whitley bomber. He was glad he was on the water, or under it. For that he had to thank Chidson. He glanced at his watch. There were at least five hours to go. Somewhere in England the Colonel would be having his last whisky. Alex hoped he slept well.

None of them believed they could sleep. Indeed, the First Lieutenant's words exhorting them to sleep or try to had seemed almost foolish. With so much on their minds, sleep had seemed impossible, as remote as the Himalayas. But they needed sleep. The next day could be long and difficult. It was the gentle motion of the submarine that did it. Alex watched first Meisner then Grosman loll their heads on to their shoulders, open their mouths and change their breathing. Then he too drifted into nothing. Unconsciousness seemed to last for a fraction of a second and was broken by a rating shaking him by the arm.

'Captain's compliments, sir, would you come to the control room?'

Alex awoke disorientated. The sleep had been dreamless but not deep. The sailor seemed strange, so did the wardroom. But even with that understanding there was something else. At first he couldn't make it out, then he realized. He had been lulled to sleep by the motion of the submarine and the gentle hum of the electric motors. All that was gone. There was a silence he had never known before. They were in a soundless world. Then he heard the gentle drip of a tiny drop of water. He was under the sea and the boat had stopped. The job he had trained for for the last five months was about to begin.

Alex woke the others and the sailor took them to the control room.

'We are at periscope depth,' announced the Lieutenant Commander. 'I'm about to take a look on top.' He looked questioningly at the First Lieutenant.

'Asdic reports all quiet, sir, nothing about,' whispered the First Lieutenant.

'Say a prayer,' said the Lieutenant Commander softly, then indicated 'Periscope up!' with his thumb. He twisted his cap around so that the peak should not be in the way, bent his knees, gripped the handles of the periscope, and rose to his full height as the lens broke the surface overhead. He turned the periscope slowly round, his feet and legs moving sideways as he scanned the complete horizon. Then he centred on the direction straight ahead, to where the Dutch coast should be.

'Still quiet, Number One?'

'Quiet, sir. Asdic making a full sweep.'

There was a long silence. The Lieutenant Commander swung the periscope for twenty degrees either side of the bow. Very quietly, he whispered: 'Can't see a bloody thing. It's too dark and there's a mist.' Then he glanced at Alex. 'Ideal for you. Just what the doctor ordered.' He snapped the periscope handles shut and stepped back.

'Down periscope! Stand by to surface! Bridge party stand by! Hold her down on the planes as long as you can, Number One.'

'Aye, aye, sir.'

'Blow tanks!'

The submarine shuddered. They felt the surge upwards.

'Hatch open! Bridge party take station.' The Lieutenant Commander's orders barely rose above a whisper but they were heard and instantly obeyed. The SIS men were ushered to the forward hatch. They watched their rubber dinghy being manhandled up through the hull. They heard the hiss of compressed air as the dinghy inflated. There were whispers above then they were waved up on deck. The cool, crisp air took their breath away. Alex was handed a pair of night glasses. The Lieutenant Commander indicated. 'Straight ahead. We're exactly where we should be.'

Alex scanned over the bows. Through the mist and darkness he could just make out a thin coastline. The land was flat, the sea calm. He passed the glasses to Grosman and grunted: 'Holland.' Grosman surveyed the coastline and thought he could see Bergen aan Zee. They handed the glasses back and the Lieutenant Commander glanced up at the sky. He was anxious to go. His boat was particularly vulnerable five hundred yards off the enemy-held coast. The three agents looked at the tiny rubber dinghy, a darker blot upon a dark sea. Two ratings were already in the boat, their oars in position. They saw their suitcases loaded into the well between the canvas seats.

The Lieutenant Commander shook hands. To each he whispered, 'Good luck.' It was the moment of rupture. 'Will it be *you* who picks us up?' asked Alex anxiously, peering into the barely visible face. The Lieutenant Commander nodded. 'We brought you, we'll take you back. You've got a return ticket. This is just *au revoir*.'

They scrambled off the edge of the steel hull into the dinghy. The dinghy was fended off. The sailors pulled on the oars. The submarine melted into the darkness and there was nothing but the slopping of the oars. No one spoke. They just stared ahead, each cocooned within his own thoughts. The journey seemed ludicrously short, yet infinitely long. When they heard the gentle lap of the sea upon the shore it was as if they had been rowed across a very small lake. But in the mind it was as great a gulf as any ocean.

One of the sailors shipped his oars and jumped into the water. They felt the jar and heard the grinding of the rubber on the sand. One by one they climbed out. The sailors handed them their suitcases, gave a half-wave, half-salute and pushed the dinghy back into the sea.

They walked a few paces up the sand and stopped. They suddenly realized that they had been put ashore dry. They were deeply thankful. They had been spared the problems of wet trouser bottoms in the daylight. They turned and looked at the sea. The dinghy had vanished. There wasn't even the sound of the oars.

16

In their training and during their time with Chidson, one point had been instilled into them. Whether they landed by sea or air, they were to move away from their point of arrival immediately. Without a second glance at the water, they picked up their luggage and tramped up to the comparative safety of the dunes. They found a spot where a dune rose steeply and clumps of coarse grass grew in defiance of nature. There they sat and waited. It was 4 a.m., Thursday, 13 December 1941. It was cold and dark and the atmosphere had all the misery and wretchedness of any midwinter night. At that moment as they sat in the black, soundless wilderness, only one thing seemed to be in their favour. It wasn't raining.

Alex was not yet twenty years old. In normal times he would still be a student commuting daily between his home in Amsterdam and his technical college in Delft. Now he was sitting in total darkness with two equally young companions upon the coast of Occupied Europe. He was in a homeland that was now alien, dressed in the uniform of an SS officer. Were he to be caught he would most certainly be tortured before being shot. The same applied to Grosman and Meisner. Alex felt a hollow, sickening pain in his stomach. In spite of the cold, his hands were clammy. He knew the pain was fear and wondered if his companions felt as he did.

'Do you feel sick, Abe?' he whispered.

Grosman nodded in the darkness. His mouth was too dry to speak.

'It's seasickness . . .' muttered Meisner.

For an instant the joke broke the tension. Automatically all three looked at the sea. The very gentle, almost imperceptible lapping emphasized how calm it was.

With the silence, the strangeness and the hour, Alex became more and more conscious of the only humans he knew to be near him. His companions. He had chosen them in the summer, trained with them throughout the autumn and now, six months after first meeting them, he was alone with them in a position of extreme danger. He knew them yet he didn't know them. They were young men, united with the depth of understanding of young men. They had none of the doubts and cynicism of older men. Except in the relative safety of training they had never been tested together. Now, with the first step upon the beach, all that had changed.

Alex couldn't see their faces, only their presence, but that was enough. He was glad that Chidson had insisted that he must not go alone. He had once considered himself a loner but not now. Now he needed Grosman and Meisner and thanked God that they were here. However scared they might be, at this moment they seemed like rocks. They gave him confidence; in return he gave them all his faith and trust. There was no room for doubt. In the darkness they were three against a whole world. Their single common enemy, the Nazis, bound them like brothers.

'Roll on the dawn,' whispered Alex. 'I bet you wish you were back in that camp in Wales . . .'

Grosman grunted. Meisner sunk his head deeper into the collar of his greatcoat and shivered.

'The night's always the worst,' said Alex.

'Except when you're courting,' murmured Meisner.

The joke fell as flat as the coastline. They lapsed back into the silence that seemed to be part of them.

As they waited for the first light, and the cold from the ground seeped upwards into their bodies, it seemed that time too was frozen. There was nothing to do but watch and listen. Nothing to see but the everlasting darkness and, on those rare moments when the starglow broke through the low clouds, the faint glitter of the distant sea. Their minds and bodies were tired with the time of the night. Their nerves were tense, their anxieties deep. Stray sounds startled them. A creature of darkness scratching in the sand, the eerie cry of a sea bird, made them clench their fists and brought beads of sweat to the backs of their necks.

With the first strip of pale yellow from the eastern horizon, before the ground around them had a trace of colour, they struggled to their feet. Carrying their suitcases, feeling slightly ludicrous, they stumbled towards the dawn. Movement helped them. Once again the blood surged through their veins. Cramped legs warmed. Dulled brains began to work. None of them knew the district in which they had landed, but they had studied every inch of it in air photos. They saw the outline of a wood and knew that just beyond was the small town of Bergen. They had the luck that Menzies said they would need. No one saw them enter the town, they were just there with the early morning. They found the bus station without difficulty and caught the first bus for Alkmaar. The first hurdle, in some ways the most difficult, was over. They were in their new environment; henceforth they would be part of the Occupied landscape.

Alkmaar was a cheese town. In peacetime, every Friday during the summer, cheeses were piled high upon the cobbles of the square and the carillon in the Weigh House tower would drown the surrounding countryside in Dutch folk music. Now it was a wartime winter, dour and grey. They walked across the cobbles and made for the outskirts of the town. Again from the air photos they had no difficulty in finding the safe-house. The moment they set eyes on it they realized how excellent it was for their purposes. Not only was it on the edge of the town but it was surrounded by a large garden. There seemed to be no close neighbours: they could come and go without causing attention.

Slightly surreptitiously, for he had not yet got used to his new alias, Alex took the key of the house from his pocket and put it in the lock. Although unused for a long time, the lock worked and the key turned sweetly. With a sense of enormous relief they let themselves into the house and locked and bolted the door behind them.

But for the dust they were in luxury. The dust had settled everywhere. It lay thick upon the tables, chairs and floors and in places it graced the threads of enormous spider webs. There was something eerie about entering and moving within a house that had been unused for so many months and yet had been left in such immaculate condition. Every door had been carefully shut, every room tidied ready for the return of the owner.

To all three, as they explored the interior, it seemed as if behind one or other of the closed doors the man or woman of the house must be sitting, quietly reading. But the house was empty. Hauntingly empty.

There were four bedrooms so they had a bedroom each with one to spare. They unpacked, hid the contents of their suitcases as best they could and washed. Together they went downstairs and stood self-consciously in the kitchen.

'Nice furniture,' whispered Grosman, running his finger along the edge of the table. 'Expensive, too.'

'You don't have to whisper now,' said Alex, grinning. 'We're in a safe-house, remember?'

Grosman nodded and grinned.

'You know what I could do with?' said Meisner, and began to open the cupboards. There were empty tins, maggot-ridden flour, herbs and condiments but nothing to eat.

They all had the same thought. They were in a safe-house. Safe. But they were hungry. Very hungry. They had eaten the little chocolate they had landed with and hidden the wrapping in the dunes. To assuage their hunger they would have to go outside into the alien world.

'I'll go out,' said Alex. 'I've got the ration cards.'

Grosman offered, but Alex turned him down.

Alex went back upstairs and changed into his civilian clothes. Watched by the others, he let himself out of the door and walked steadily and sedately back into the town and the shops. He bought bread, butter, cheese and ersatz coffee. Then he walked slowly and sedately back to the safe-house. It had all been astonishingly easy. So easy he was amazed. When he put the goods down on the kitchen table he wasn't even sweating. It boded well for his next expedition.

'God, I feel better.' Grosman blew out his lips with satisfaction. 'I could have eaten a horse, hooves and all. I didn't know this sort of thing made you so hungry.'

'You've burned up the calories,' said Meisner. 'All that nervous energy. I reckoned it reached a peak when we saw that group of German soldiers.'

'Artillerymen,' said Alex, remembering the red flashes on the tunics.

'Coastal defence,' said Grosman.

Alex shrugged. Grosman might or might not be right but he had reminded them all of the reason why they were there. The relief they felt at having got into Holland was heavily tempered by the thought of the task that still faced them. Set in the reality of their new surroundings it suddenly assumed almost impossible proportions.

Alex studied the faces in front of him. Grosman had a slight smile as if he was challenging the gods, defying those fates who looked after the Germans – particularly those who guarded the naval base at Den Helder. His fine, thin face and blue eyes had the appearance of a warrior on the eve of his vigil. There was something clean and honest about him that for an instant made Alex regret what he was about to say. He glanced at Meisner. Meisner wasn't smiling, he was frowning. There was nothing the least bit challenging about his dark eyes. He looked worried and kept moving his fingers through his thick black hair. Alex was surprised by the evident Jewishness in Meisner's face. The long nose reminded him of another long nose. On Meisner the nose was ugly, on Rachel it had been beautiful.

'I'm going out.'

Alex had spoken softly. The other two swung their heads and stared at him. The smile had gone from Grosman, the worried look from Meisner. Both were alert. Both were about to get up.

'I thought you'd be wanting to make a recce soon,' said Grosman. 'But oughtn't we to wait for the evening?'

'I'm going on my own.'

Meisner raised his eyebrows. 'On your own . . .? Surely one of us should follow you, that's only common sense?'

Alex got up. 'I have to be on my own.'

Neither Grosman nor Meisner understood. The feeling of relaxation, of well-being from the food, vanished. Doubt and suspicion clouded their faces. They had considered themselves an interdependent team, invincible so long as they stayed together. Now one of the team, the most important member, was going off on his own. They couldn't understand. Then darker thoughts crowded in upon them. They even wondered if they were about to be betrayed.

'Why do you have to be on your own?' asked Grosman suspiciously. 'Anyway, where *are* you going?'

Alex said nothing. He just stared at them, then he got up and put on his coat.

'Don't move from the house,' he said curtly. 'Whatever you do, don't go outside. I shall be away a few hours.'

They no longer felt betrayed, just cheated. They had thought there was no secret between them. Although they accepted Alex as their leader, they had been briefed together. They thought they knew everything that was to happen. They could see no reason why Alex should have to go off on his own so early in the day, so soon after landing. It had already been agreed that they wouldn't begin their reconnaissance of the bars until it was dark. Alex saw the looks upon their faces and was sad. He could never tell them what he had to do, but he hated to see their dismay.

'I'll be back, I promise.' It was a promise he knew he might never be able to keep. Intentions were one thing; events might override them. But with that final remark he went out of the house and shut the door behind him.

He walked to the station, bought a ticket to Amsterdam, and waited half an hour for a train. A German soldier asked him the time and he answered in Dutch. When the soldier seemed not to understand, Alex spoke in broken German. Satisfied, the soldier went off down the platform. The train was slow, stopping at every station. The journey to Amsterdam seemed unending. Two more Germans got into the carriage and it appeared to Alex that they had nothing to look at but him. When he eventually got out at the Central Station, in spite of the cold, he was sweating.

The square seemed smaller and dirtier than he remembered it. There were fewer people about than usual and a fair proportion of those were Germans. A Wehrmacht lorry was parked outside the station and drawn up in front of it was a small Volkswagen Type 82 and a larger Luftwaffe radio vehicle, both of which Alex identified from his training.

He walked to the spot where just over two years ago he had

been arrested by Bearends. A number 25 tram stood exactly where one had stood that night. Then he had been seized as he was about to board the tram. Now he considered it with interest and a considerable degree of temptation for it was bound for the Daniel Willinkplein where his mother still lived. Then he moved away from the tram. His resolve was absolute. Since arriving in England, he had regularly corresponded with his mother through the International Red Cross in Geneva. Chidson had warned him against visiting her in case he might be recognized by a neighbour and betrayed. He had a lot to do and little time to do it in. There was no time for family sentiment even had he thought of defying Chidson.

Alex walked to the Dam where the Queen's Palace stood empty, through the Kalverstraat to the Leidsestraat and down to the Leidseplein. There he stood for a moment staring at a section of dark wall. It was a glimpse of the prison where he had spent the worst six months of his life. He didn't go close to the prison for that seemed to be taking a foolish chance, to be courting disaster. Instead, he walked on to the Museumplein, passed the Concertgebouw and so into Van Breestraat. In Van Breestraat he rang the bell of number 118, a number and a house he knew well. The door was opened from upstairs. Just inside was a long staircase that led to the first floor.

'Who's there?'

Alex knew the voice well. He smiled at the sound of it. He had last heard it in the visiting room in the House of Custody.

'Cornelis Verloop . . .'

There was a moment's silence, then the voice said, '*Who?*'

Alex raised his voice. 'Can you come down a minute, Paul?'

There was the sound of feet on the stairs, then a young man appeared.

'Hullo,' said Alex blandly, fighting his emotions.

Paul Wilking stared at Alex in utter amazement. He looked him up and down, from the toes of his shoes to his hair. He shook his head and his mouth fell open. 'My God!' he said, at last. 'It's *you*! *Alex!* I thought I recognized your voice, but it didn't make sense. You're supposed to be in England. That's what your mother said.'

'I was in England. I was in England yesterday afternoon.'
Alex had to say the words to believe them.

Wilking waved Alex into the house. 'Come in, for God's
sake! You can't stand out there. Not these days.'

'Is your mother at home?'

Wilking shook his head.

Alex walked into the house. He looked around at the familiar
hallway, then indicated. 'Let's go upstairs to your room. We
can be private there.'

Wilking led the way upstairs. Wilking sat on the bed, Alex
sat in the chair. Wilking continued to stare at Alex as if he had
just risen from the dead. 'What's it all about?' he said at last.
'And who the hell is Cornelis Verloop?'

Alex produced his identity card and held it up. 'My cover,
or one of them. At the moment I'm Cornelis Verloop. And
don't forget it.'

Wilking grinned. It was the grin that Alex knew so well.
The one that, in the old days, Wilking had seemed to live with.
The one that bisected his freckled face and gave him his
permanent, impish joyousness. The grin that had so cheered
Alex when Wilking had been brought into the House of
Custody as his cousin. Yet now, when Alex looked more
closely, when Wilking moved his head slightly so that the light
from the single window fell across his eyes, the grin couldn't
conceal the shadows. There was now a strain in the joyousness;
life under the Occupation was taking its toll.

Alone together after so long apart, they were like strangers,
unsure what to say, where to begin. Two lives that had once
been so close had been abruptly separated. Yet beneath the
strangeness their friendship remained, warm and honest as it
had always been. Alex felt a sudden surge of comradeship.
'What's it like here now?'

Wilking shrugged. 'Depends what you make of it.' He
hesitated, then added, '*Awful! Bloody awful!* It's a matter of
existing as best you can.' His face suddenly lightened. 'Of
course, there's fun to be had fooling the Germans. Stealing
from them. Little things like that and, of course, sometimes
big things.'

Alex was satisfied. That was what he wanted to hear from

Wilking. He knew his friend well. He could never have conceived of him being anything but anti-Nazi, but he had to make sure.

'Anyway, enough of that,' said Wilking, his grin back again, his dark eyes laughing. 'What the hell are you doing here?'

'A job. I'm on a job.' Alex would have liked to say more, but he couldn't.

'A secret mission?' asked Wilking eagerly.

They were the same age. They were boys again. For a second it was as if they were playing together as they had played in the past. Then Wilking saw Alex's face. 'Shut your foolish mouth, Wilking,' said Wilking, laughing. 'You can't tell me, of course you can't.'

'No one must know I'm here, Paul. No one, not even my mother.'

Wilking's grin vanished. He nodded.

'There is also a private matter. Something I have to do. For that I need your help.'

'You've got it,' said Wilking eagerly. 'Of course you've got it. You know you have.'

Alex shook his head. 'It could be dangerous, damned dangerous.'

Wilking shrugged.

'Seriously, Paul, this isn't a game. When I said it could be dangerous, it could be . . .' Alex stopped.

Wilking leaned forward on the bed. 'Listen, Alex, I've lived with the Germans in Amsterdam for a year and a half. We're at war here in Holland just like you are. We're fighting the Germans too, in our own way. That's dangerous enough. I've grown up, you know, just like you.' He paused, then said, 'So what do you want me to do?'

For a moment Alex was silent. He had told no one of his own private plan. He had carried it around with him for the last six months, ever since the day he had told Chidson he was prepared to go back to Holland. Now he was to share it. Or at least unveil a little of it. There was pleasure mixed with anxiety.

'Do you remember Fatesma, the Public Prosecutor who handled the court case against me?'

145

'That rotten bastard! Of course I remember him. Everyone knows him. His name really stinks around here.' Wilking grimaced. 'He got promoted by the Germans. He's Attorney-General now.'

'He was always a Nazi,' said Alex quietly, and became aware that his hands were so clenched, he was digging his nails into his own thighs. 'No doubt his promotion was the reward for killing Rachel.'

Wilking looked puzzled. Alex suddenly realized that what he had lived with and brooded over for so long and taken to be common knowledge was still known to only a few. He told Wilking what he now knew of events on the night of 9 November, two years ago.

'The bastards!' said Wilking grimly. 'The real bastards, but I can believe it. Any Dutchman who works with the Germans is capable of strangling his own mother.' He looked up into Alex's face. 'Knowing you, I'm beginning to scent something . . .'

Alex ignored the remark. 'Do you know Detective Sergeant Bearends and Detective Constable Deepground?'

'I've never met them but I know of them. In the Underground we've got a black list, people who we believe are working with the Gestapo. I seem to remember their names on it.'

Alex nodded. Wilking was as useful as he had hoped he would be. 'Listen carefully, Paul. I want to know where Fatesma, Bearends and Deepground work. What time they arrive at their place of work in the morning, what time they leave in the evening. Do you reckon you can do that?'

'Sure,' said Wilking with his usual grin, 'of course I can do it, no problem at all. The main thing is how much time have I got?' He looked at Alex's suit and overcoat. 'I mean, how long are you over here?'

Alex didn't answer the question. Instead he said, 'I'll come back in about three days. I'll come back here. Is that all right?'

Wilking hesitated.

'Three days,' repeated Alex. 'I can't give you more.'

Wilking suddenly nodded. 'Fine. Three days is fine. By Monday I'll have everything you want to know.'

Alex got up. Wilking got up. Alex put his hand on Wilking's back. 'It's a bit different from being a student, isn't it?'

Wilking laughed. 'In Holland we do the two things together. Perhaps you should stay and find out.'

They let him into the house, watched him, stared at him, but said nothing. They didn't ask him where he'd been or how he'd got on. They didn't even bark out a joyous reception like dogs would have done. They remained mute and acted as if Alex had never left the house. Alex was thankful. If there was a shade of resentment and hostility, he brushed it aside.

'As soon as it's dark, we'll go out,' he said breezily. 'And what have you two been doing?' Then he saw the open books on the table and nodded. 'Good idea. Take your mind off things.'

There was a big, well-filled bookcase in the sitting room. Alex examined the shelves and picked a book for himself. Grosman gave him a cup of coffee. He sat down with the book and the coffee and began to read. In ten minutes he had nodded off to sleep. He had a short, dreamless sleep and it revived him. When he awoke he felt fresh and ready for anything. His confidence was high. He had already walked about Amsterdam, watched German soldiers and even travelled with them in the train. He had no doubt that in a few days he would be photographing the map in the safe in the Admiral's office in Den Helder. He had no doubt either that once again he would see Fatesma, Bearends and Deepground. He was astonished at his own optimism. It seemed to him then, in the safe-house at Alkmaar, that after all he had been through, he was now invulnerable. Suddenly the Germans held no menace for him.

'We'll wear civvies,' said Alex thoughtfully, 'but we'll take SS identity cards. If we are stopped, they should be helpful.'

They left the house soon after dark. They had supper in a small restaurant near the railway station and then took the train to Den Helder. On the train they caught their first sight of the men of the Kriegsmarine. Two sailors were already in the carriage when they boarded it. When they got out at Den Helder it was drizzling. The town was small, a little like a miniature Chatham but not so old. Everything revolved around the harbour and dockyard. It was around those walls that the bars and cafés were to be found.

The blackout was strict, the few lights dim, but they had been well briefed and knew exactly what they were looking for. They visited several bars and cafés and although the bars in particular had their quota of Germans, both sailors and soldiers, there were no naval officers. They decided that the reconnaissance had been a good start but that they must go back on the next train to Alkmaar otherwise they would be too late to signal London.

The return journey was as uneventful as the outward journey. By ten o'clock they were back in the safe-house, congratulating themselves upon their first foray. Meisner unpacked the wireless and from an upstairs bedroom transmitted the agreed message indicating that they had arrived and were ready to start operations. Alex watched Meisner's hand on the morse key. He thought of the Luftwaffe wireless truck outside the Central Station, then put the thought from him. This was their first message, so there could be no chance of a German wireless interception vehicle appearing this night.

After transmitting the message, Meisner retuned the receiver and sat with the earphones on, listening. Suddenly he gave the thumbs up signal. London had acknowledged. The message was received and understood.

The next three evenings Alex, Grosman and Meisner continued their visits to the pubs and cafés of Den Helder. By Sunday night they had an intimate knowledge of the off-duty drinking habits of all the Kriegsmarine stationed at the naval base. They also knew that in one café in particular, with its long bar against one wall, the naval officers loved to gather. Indeed, when they had gone in, there were so many Kriegsmarine officers they had felt quite conspicuous. However, they need not have worried. The Germans were happy and enjoying themselves. They had had no time for three very ordinary-looking Dutchmen.

17

On Monday morning, giving no more information to his colleagues than he had before, Alex got ready to set out a second time on his own. Grosman and Meisner watched him put on his overcoat and check his identity cards. Alex was at the door when Grosman said, 'Would you mind letting us know when to expect you back and whether we're supposed to do anything particular in the meantime?'

There was sarcasm in the voice but Alex ignored it. Grosman glanced at Meisner for confirmation. Meisner nodded.

'I'll be back this afternoon,' said Alex quietly. 'I shouldn't be away long this time. As for what you do . . .' He glanced at the books lying about. 'Read. Keep your heads down and get ready for tonight. Tonight we go into action.'

'You mean, move to Den Helder?' asked Grosman.

Alex nodded.

'Get on with what we're here for?'

'Exactly.'

For the moment there was silence as Alex stood with his back to the door buttoning up his coat. The other two continued to watch. 'Anyone would think you had a girl here the way you go out,' said Grosman. The remark was meant to be funny, but the barb was far too pointed, too near the mark to be humorous to Alex. He scowled.

'Not funny,' said Meisner, shaking his head, 'not funny at all.'

'Sorry,' said Grosman. 'Good luck, whatever it is. But if only you'd tell us what these mysterious outings are about, we might be able to help.'

'I'll be back this afternoon,' said Alex, and went out of the door closing it carefully behind him.

At 118 Van Breestraat, Paul Wilking was waiting. The moment Alex rang the bell, the door opened and Wilking, wrapped in an overcoat, the collar up around his neck, was outside on the pavement taking Alex's arm and steering him away from the house.

'My mother's at home. We'd do better to get out of the place.'

They walked westwards towards the Vondel Park. Alex was impatient and asked Wilking if he had the information. Wilking grinned and said he never broke a promise. 'Of course I've got it. But it's no good talking here.' He indicated the houses. 'In this place now it's not just a matter of who's listening, it's also who's watching. Wait till we're in the park.'

They walked through the open gates and on to the grass. It was a cold, misty morning. The skeletons of the trees were pale and shadowy, human forms loomed up at them and disappeared, voices came softly out of the opaqueness, their own feet moved silently over the dampness. They stood by a strip of water, dark and grey beneath the leaden air, and Wilking picked up a stone and threw it far out into the middle where the water widened into a small lake.

'Fatesma has an office in the Court Building on the Prinsengracht,' said Wilking quietly. 'It's in the front of the building on the first floor. So far as I can gather he's a punctual creature with a pretty exact schedule. He gets there dead on the dot of eight-thirty and leaves at five-thirty.'

'He leaves at five-thirty *every* evening?'

Wilking shrugged. 'That's what I'm told.'

'He doesn't have one special day when he leaves early or late?'

'Not so far as I know.'

Alex said nothing. Wilking picked up another stone and threw it even further into the lake. Then he started to walk again.

'So we can reckon that Monday to Friday, Fatesma comes down the steps of that building at five-thirty,' said Alex, thinking aloud.

'It's a good bet, I'd put my shirt on it. The informant is reliable.'

Alex had his thoughts and his heart was beating fast. He felt his hands and realized that they were clammy. He remembered the Court Building in the Prinsengracht. It was a large, imposing building with a wide flight of stone steps leading up to the door. Already he could imagine Fatesma walking down those steps muffled in his black overcoat and carrying his briefcase.

'And Bearends?'

'Bearends is a different story,' said Wilking apologetically. 'He's just disappeared. He hasn't been seen for months.' Wilking saw the look of disappointment on Alex's face. 'I'm sorry, Alex, I've made a hell of a lot of enquiries and got nowhere. Nobody seems to know what's happened to him.'

Alex shook his head. It was a sad little shake. 'Never mind, he was a nasty bugger, but he wasn't the worst of the bunch. Fatesma told him what to do and he got Deepground to do it.' Alex glanced at Wilking. 'I hope you had better luck with Deepground?'

Wilking grinned. 'Up-to-the-minute information. He's left the police force and been promoted by the Germans. He's now in charge of a concentration camp.'

'That should suit him perfectly,' said Alex. 'Where is this camp?'

'Near a village called Westerbork in Drente.'

Alex felt a deep sinking feeling. His private war too depended on an element of luck and good fortune. It had to be fitted inside his other, more public war. It was essential that the characters in his private war were not too widely dispersed. Ideally he would have liked to have them all still in Amsterdam.

'*Drente!* That's a hell of a long way away! It's right up by the German border.'

'I didn't send him there,' said Wilking.

'Does he live in the camp?'

'He lives nearby in a house that belongs to the camp. He walks to work in the morning at eight and goes home in the evening at six.'

'And is he as meticulous in his timekeeping as you say Fatesma is?'

'As far as I know. Aren't all policemen and ex-policemen meticulous in their timing? That's what makes them so predictable.'

Alex grabbed Wilking's arm and squeezed it. 'You've said

it, Paul, you've said it all,' he said excitedly. 'That's how we shall get them, by their very predictability.'

Wilking looked into Alex's face. 'Would you mind telling me exactly what this is all about? I mean, I know you want to know about Fatesma, Bearends and Deepground, and I know *why* you want to know about them, but I don't know what you want to do about them.'

'Pay them back for what they did to Rachel,' said Alex, with astonishing simplicity.

'Kill them?'

Alex nodded.

'Knowing you, I thought as much.' Then the humour went from Wilking's voice. 'But it's a hell of a job, Alex, a hell of a job. It's hard enough staying alive here now without going out actually looking for trouble.'

'It won't be difficult with your help,' said Alex without turning his head.

They walked on in silence. They were on a gravel path; Wilking scuffed the small stones with the toe of his shoe. 'Got it all worked out?' he asked at last.

'I thought I had,' said Alex thoughtfully. 'I was pretty sure I had, until you told me that Deepground was miles away up in Drente. That must be a couple of hundred kilometres even as the crow flies. Four hundred, four hundred and fifty kilometres there and back.' He paused, then said, 'Can you get hold of a car, Paul? An SS car?'

'For God's sake, Alex . . .'

'There's no other way. It would take too long by train.'

Wilking again looked into Alex's face. 'You really are a single-minded bugger, aren't you? I've never met one like you before. If someone told me about you, I wouldn't bloody well believe them!'

'Can you get hold of an SS car?'

Wilking said nothing.

'I owe it to Rachel . . .'

After a while Wilking said, 'A German army car isn't all that difficult. I know where we can lay our hands on one of those, but an SS car . . .' He shook his head. 'That's a different matter. Quite a different matter.'

'All right, get hold of a German army car and change the number plates for SS plates. How about that?'

Wilking grinned. 'Now you're talking. An army car's no problem, no problem at all. We can forge the plates, there's quite a little industry here now in forgery.' He paused, then said, 'When do you need the car? And for God's sake don't tell me it's tomorrow.'

'In three days' time. We shall need the car for two days.'

'*We?*'

'Whoever heard of an SS officer, a Hauptsturmführer from the Sicherheitshauptamt, without a driver?'

They walked to the gates of the park and stood staring up at the watery sun slowly emerging from the haze.

'Can I give you a bit of really good advice?' asked Wilking.

'What?'

'I take it you're based in England?'

Alex gave a half-shrug, half-nod.

'Then may I advise you to go straight back there?'

'I will in five or six days' time.'

'I meant earlier.'

Alex laughed. 'I know you did. But you don't expect me to go back earlier, do you?'

Wilking shook his head.

They walked out of the park into the Huygenstraat. A tram rattled by. They crossed the road and made for the Rijksmuseum. 'In three days' time, I want that car,' said Alex. 'I'm relying on you, Paul. I can't go back to England without doing this.' He stopped, then very quietly added, 'Repaying them for what they did to Rachel is really what I came over for.'

'You're mad, quite mad. Completely crazy. You'll be the death of us both.' Behind the seriousness of Wilking's words, there was a certain jocularity.

'The car . . .'

'You'll have the car, don't worry. And the driver. Everything will be ready, you know it will.' As an afterthought Wilking winked and said, 'And the tank will be full. I wouldn't like to run out of petrol half-way to Westerbork and have to sit and watch you grinding your teeth.'

153

'I'll be wearing SS uniform,' said Alex, talking to the sky. 'Don't get too much of a fright.'

'I'm used to the buggers. Not that I've ever actually walked out with one.'

Outside the Rijksmuseum, as the winter sun began to throw thin shafts of light on to the street and illuminate the tops of the buildings, they parted.

They started to change before it was dark. Alex and Grosman put on their Luftwaffe uniforms and packed their civilian clothes into their suitcases. Their SS uniforms they hid next to the water tanks in the attic. Meisner stayed in his civilian clothes but packed his SS uniform in his suitcase. Carefully they checked each other and their identity papers. They peered anxiously into the mirror. Alex considered his grey Luftwaffe uniform very becoming. The bright yellow collar flashes with their oak leaves, wings and silver piping were particularly smart. When he put on the high peaked cap with its flying eagle echoing the large one on his right breast, he felt every inch the successful Luftwaffe fighter pilot. Adding the Iron Cross First Class completed the illusion.

Once again they checked everything they had on them and the contents of their suitcases. Alex and Grosman checked the clothes they would need when they got inside the naval barracks, the cream with which they would black their faces, the camera with which they would take the photographs and the key to the safe. Grosman and Meisner normally talked together in German for it was their native tongue. Now Alex joined them. Satisfied with every detail, the two Luftwaffe men went to the door. Meisner wished them good luck and said he'd give them ten minutes' start.

'Mind you lock up properly,' said Alex. 'And don't lose the house key!'

Meisner grinned, shook back his mop of hair and gave the thumbs up.

They walked to the railway station and took a train for Den Helder. Alex and Grosman sat together and tried to chat as if this evening was as normal as any other evening in their lives.

They found it impossible to be relaxed but hoped they looked it. At least they had one another for support. Meisner had no one. He was alone in another carriage. They got off at Den Helder and noticed Meisner also getting down on to the platform. They had picked the hotel, a small boarding house near the station, on a previous visit. Now Alex and Grosman together and Meisner separately checked in. They had supper in the hotel, the two Luftwaffe officers again keeping away from the single civilian, and after supper made for the café which they knew to be the haunt of the naval officers from the base.

The blackout was effective. Such lights as there were on to the street were exceedingly dim. They heard the noise from the café twenty yards away.

'Our moment of truth,' whispered Grosman.

'Here goes!' said Alex. 'If we really are Luftwaffe fighter pilots from Russia, we may as well behave like them.' He took a deep breath, pushed open the door and threw aside the heavy blackout curtain.

The heat of the room after the cold December night air hit them like an open oven. They stood by the bar, gathered their wits and looked at the tables. The café was full, every table was occupied.

'We're either in luck or out of luck,' whispered Alex and pointed.

Two Kriegsmarine officers sat slightly apart from the others at a table where there were two empty chairs. One officer had on his cuffs the three rings and star of a Kapitänleutnant, the other, the two rings and star of an Oberleutnant zur See. Alex walked over to the table followed by Grosman. His heart was pounding, his mouth was dry but he managed to sound nonchalant as he indicated the two empty chairs and addressed the senior of the two officers: 'Herr Kapitänleutnant, do you mind if we sit there? If we share your table?'

The Kapitänleutnant took in the grey of their uniform, the yellow collar patches and the large flying eagle over the right breast pocket and muttered: 'Luftwaffe . . . make yourselves at home.' Then he sat very upright and introduced himself as

Kapitänleutnant Heinrichs and his companions as Oberleutnant Bachmann.

'I am Hauptmann Baader,' said Alex, clicking his heels
together, then indicated Grosman. 'My friend is Oberleutnant
Wiegand.'

Alex and Grosman sat and a Dutch waiter took their order
for drinks.

'Are you stationed around here?' enquired Heinrichs.

Alex shook his head. 'No such luck, but we used to be near
here. We were here earlier this year. In fact we were here until
April when we moved east.'

Heinrichs raised his eyebrows and looked from Alex
to Grosman and back to Alex. 'You're on the Russian
Front?'

Alex nodded.

'Then what the hell are you doing here?'

'We're on leave . . .'

'I thought people went home for their leave,' said Bachmann
pointedly.

Alex grinned at Grosman. 'Kurt and I had a pretty good
time here. The Dutch girls can be very accommodating.' Alex
touched his collar patches. 'They used to like the Luftwaffe
uniform.'

'Ah, you've come back to look up some old girlfriends!'
cried Heinrichs. 'Cement German–Dutch relations in the best
possible way.'

'That's the idea,' said Alex, his grin even wider.

Good-humouredly, Heinrichs shook his head. 'Six months
is a long time to be away from a woman. Especially in wartime.
There have been new squadrons here since your day. New
army units, not to mention the Navy. If those women were
nice enough for you to have come all the way back from the
Russian Front after so long, you can reckon someone else
thinks the same.'

'They were beautiful,' said Grosman, his eyes filled with
yearning.

'Show me a beautiful Dutch woman!' cried Bachmann. 'I
tell you, there's no such creature!'

'Ours were exquisite, quite exquisite,' said Grosman, keeping a very straight face. 'Nor were our relationships fly-by-night affairs.' He looked at Alex. 'In both our cases it was true, everlasting love.'

Alex nodded. The two Kriegsmarine officers rocked in their chairs with laughter. Bachmann beat his glass on the table. Heinrichs bought more drinks, the Luftwaffe returned the compliment. The drinks began to take their effect. The Kapitänleutnant grew mellow, the Oberleutnant grew maudlin. They talked of their war experiences and then went back to women. When they returned to women, the Oberleutnant had a new lease of life. He asked about the women that Alex and Grosman had come back to find. Alex described his girl, Grosman described his. Alex grew concerned when the Oberleutnant persisted in asking questions about the two mythical ladies, but fortunately a new round of drinks and a suggestion from his senior officer that there were other things to talk about took his mind off the matter.

It soon became evident that Heinrichs in particular admired and somewhat envied the two Luftwaffe officers. People from the Russian Front were not all that common. When the bantering, lighthearted conversation flagged the Kapitänleutnant, looking most studious, asked about conditions in the east and in particular about air fighting.

'We're particularly lucky,' said Alex. 'We have the new 109 G. They're a bit heavy, a touch difficult to land, but they're well worth it.'

'Good armament,' said Grosman. 'Two MG 17s and an MG 151. And plenty of power.'

Heinrichs nodded. His balding head caught the light. He was short, almost gnome-like, but he had a kind, welcoming face. 'Oh, to be young again,' he said and waved his hands, childlike, in the air. He was only thirty-three.

'I thought the Russian Air Force was destroyed on the ground,' said Bachmann surlily. 'I thought we caught them with their trousers down at the very beginning?'

'They send up fighters like they send on men,' said Alex. 'They seem to come out of the forests.'

Heinrichs glanced at his junior. It was a glance of reproval. 'We hear a lot about the Sturmovik,' he said quietly. 'Reading between the lines it seems to be an effective ground attack aircraft.'

Alex was truly thankful for the thoroughness of his briefing. 'Well constructed, good armour and in the hands of a good pilot not bad at tank busting. But it's heavy, difficult to manoeuvre and quite nice to shoot down.'

Heinrichs laughed, even Bachmann smiled. Alex decided that the ice had been sufficiently broken, the conversation sufficiently warmed for him to make the next move.

'We've talked about us a lot,' he said, holding his glass up in an act of salutation, 'but what about you? Even we pilots don't think that the whole world revolves around the Luft- waffe. We don't see any Kriegsmarine where we are, but we remember the sea.' He nodded towards the harbour. 'After all we were here for the best part of a year. We've looked down on the waves often enough.'

'And nearly ditched in them,' said Grosman.

'I have a corvette,' said the Kapitänleutnant and indicated Bachmann, 'and Bachmann is my First Officer. It's a cold, dirty life and there's none of the glamour of the big ships or, of course, of the U-boats. On the other hand, I suppose we're lucky. We have a reasonable base and we come back here after patrols. We get regular letters from home.' He raised his glass. 'And there are worse places to be in than Holland.'

Alex felt the sweat running down his back. He prayed that he looked calmer than he felt. He was about to put everything to the touch and he hoped that at that moment his stars were as propitious as they ever would be.

'I'm a pilot, but I've always been interested in ships. When I was a kid we used to have holidays on the north coast. I remember seeing the *Bremen* and the *Europa* coming out of Bremerhaven. Marvellous-looking ships, wonderful.'

Heinrichs chuckled. 'I'm afraid our old corvette isn't much like the *Bremen*.'

'There were warships too. We weren't far from Wil- helmshaven.'

Heinrichs glanced at Bachmann with a glance full of mean- ing. Alex was not sure of the meaning but he prayed it was a preliminary to the invitation he was seeking. Bachmann was lying right back, tilting his chair so that the front legs were off the ground. He had his eyes half closed as he muttered: 'Why not, skipper? It'll cure him for ever. Evaporate all that silly romantic rubbish about the deep blue sea.'

Bachmann was no longer sober, but the meaning of his words was quite clear. Alex's heart was pounding so hard he was certain the Germans would hear it.

'Your friend is a bloody masochist,' said Bachmann addressing Grosman. 'What about you?'

'I like the sea even though I'm not a very good sailor.'

'There's something wonderfully enigmatic about the sea,' said Alex quickly, 'like no other element. You can't see what's beneath you when you're on the sea. Just hundreds and thousands of feet of pure mystery.'

'We go out on patrol every day . . .' said Heinrichs, and stopped.

Alex waited a moment then blurted out: 'Would you take us?' The moment he had spoken he wondered if he had messed the whole thing up. He should have waited just a little longer. If he had waited, the Kapitänleutnant would have suggested it himself. He was obviously about to.

'You want to spend a whole day of your precious leave in the North Sea?' said Heinrichs teasingly.

Alex nodded.

'Of course if you're that mad . . .'

Bachmann laughed and clattered back on his chair towards the table. Alex waited. They were there, yet not quite there. 'Tomorrow,' said Buchmann, shaking his head. 'We go out on anti-submarine patrol tomorrow. Come with us and get the whole wretched experience over.'

'You really mean it?' asked Alex, addressed Heinrichs, then indicated Grosman. 'You'll take us both?'

'Tomorrow at nine,' said the Kapitänleutnant, smiling.

The first of their prayers had been answered. Their stars really were in the best of all configurations. 'That's great, terrific,' said Alex with all the feeling he was capable of. 'It's a great honour, we'd love to come.'

'If you're as enthusiastic as that I shall begin to think you have an ulterior motive,' said the Kapitänleutnant, laughing.

Alex swallowed hard and bit his lip. He had one more hurdle to leap. 'You said you were going out at nine,' he said, a little doubtfully, and waited.

'Nine or perhaps a little earlier.' Heinrichs paused then said, 'Where are you staying?'

Alex indicated with a nod. 'In a hotel in town . . .'

'Far away?'

'Near the station.'

There was a long pause. Even the café noises seemed to be stilled. Alex fought to keep calm. He was sure his excitement would betray him. Everything now rested upon what Chidson believed to be the innate gregariousness of the German character. Would they or would they not be invited to stay in the barracks?

Slowly Heinrichs shook his head. 'It's no good, young fellow, it won't do. It won't do at all. There are no decent hotels in this town. None. There are good bars, good cafés . . .' He raised his glass and squinted into the amber liquid. 'There are decent drinks, damned decent drinks, and decent women . . .' He stopped a second time and stared at Alex. The look was so penetrating, Alex felt his heart miss a beat. 'By the way, what about the ladies? Those two lovely girls you fliers came to see? Have you forgotten them?'

'They can wait . . .' said Alex. 'One day isn't going to make all that difference.'

Bachmann sniggered. Heinrichs nodded, a thoughtful, understanding nod. 'As I was saying, there are decent drinks and decent women in this town but *no* decent hotels.' He looked up at Alex. 'So what are you two doing staying in a third-rate, crummy boarding house and paying for it?'

Alex shrugged. 'We have nowhere else. Not in this part of the country.'

'The flying field down the road?'

'We live with fliers. We see them day and night.'

Grosman nodded.

'What about sailors?' asked Bachmann.

'They're quite different. Sailors are a different race.'

Heinrichs put out his hand and grasped Alex's arm. 'Good! Excellent! Sailors it is then. You can stay with us at the barracks. We've got masses of room and it's *free*.' He waved towards the door. 'Go and get your baggage, we'll wait for you here.'

They finished their drinks, thanked the Germans a second time, then they set out for the hotel. At the bar, Meisner watched them go. He gave them five minutes' start then followed.

'It worked!' said Meisner excitedly, seeing the open suitcases on the beds.

'Like a charm,' said Alex, 'like a beautiful, exotic scarab beetle or a handful of horseshoes. Chidson was right. They may have their faults, but those Germans really are hospitable.'

'We're not only getting free lodgings for the night but a boat trip tomorrow!' said Grosman.

'You do realize, don't you,' said Alex sombrely, 'that everything, absolutely everything, depended on that invitation. This whole bloody escapade rested on the Germans asking us into their barracks. Without that we might as well have gone home.'

'And the key,' said Grosman. 'That's the other ingredient, the key.'

'The key,' said Alex and nodded.

'So it's tonight or tomorrow night . . .' said Meisner, slowly, as the implications sank in.

'Tonight we get the feel of the place, tomorrow we act,' said Alex. 'The day after that we should be out of there back on our search for those girls.'

'In the meantime . . .?' asked Meisner.

'Keep clear of us, but keep a watch out for us.'

'The very best,' said Meisner and there were tears in his eyes.

They shook hands. Meisner went to his room in the hotel, Alex and Grosman walked back to the café with their luggage. They rejoined the Kapitänleutnant and had two more drinks then, although the journey was less than a quarter of a mile, they all got into the Kapitänleutnant's car and drove into the barracks. It was dark, but they took in every black shape as it loomed out of the night. As they crossed the cobbles they remembered the hours with the air photos. They recognized the guardroom, the main blocks, the low, long sheds that contained the stores, and two of the smaller basins. They stopped outside the officers' mess. The Officer of the Day allocated them an empty room, they said goodnight to their hosts and went up to bed.

Behind the shut door of their bedroom they went through a mime of congratulations.

'We've made it! We've made it!' They mouthed the words silently, waved their hands with excitement and tiptoed about the floor like two ballet dancers. Alex pointed towards the blackout panels of the windows. *'It's over there!'*

Grosman nodded. Such was the excitement, emotion and nervous tension, he had a job not to collapse on the bed in a fit of hysterical laughter. 'We're right in *front of it*! They couldn't have given us a better place. It's almost as if they *knew*!'

They stopped. A cold horror gripped them. They crept to the door and tried to stop their own breathing while they listened. There was nothing. No sound. The whole barracks was enveloped in silence.

'You idiot, Abe,' whispered Alex.

Grosman giggled with relief then indicated the blackout panels. 'Do we take them down and have a look?'

Alex shook his head. 'Not tonight. We need all the sleep we can get. Tomorrow's early enough for that. Wait till it's light.'

They got into their beds and lay staring up at the ceiling. They pinched themselves to see if it was real. At last, after all the planning and training, they were inside the Den Helder naval base. In spite of their desperate need for sleep it was hours before sleep came. They not only thought of what they had to do tomorrow, they worried about Meisner on his own in the hotel and even the safe-house they had left. They hoped no one had seen them come in or go out nor gone snooping around the building.

For Alex, there were other things on his mind. When all was over here in the barracks, he had yet more to do. He would like to have shared those thoughts with someone else, but it wasn't the moment to tell Grosman. As the night dragged on and they whispered to one another, he had the strength of mind to put his private war away. Everything was concentrated on sleep and the map in the safe.

18

They took the blackout down and saw the building that housed the Admiral's office. To the eye, there was no evident change since the latest air photos. Everything was as it had been upon the screen in London. They had no doubt it was the right building and they couldn't have been luckier. It was directly in front of them, not more than twenty yards away across the cobbles. 'Admiral Furstner's old office,' breathed Alex, taking in the dark red brick and white wood windows as if they were the golden stones and mullioned apertures of Camelot. 'They've parked us within spitting distance. Let's hope to God that the inside is as unchanged as the outside.'

'And that no one's moved the safe,' said Grosman.

Alex closed his eyes and murmured, 'Amen.'

At breakfast, Heinrichs introduced them to the base commander, a Kriegsmarine Kapitän. When the Kapitän learned that Heinrichs was planning to take the two Luftwaffe officers out on patrol, he suggested that, as a matter of courtesy, the Admiral should be asked for his permission. Heinrichs agreed that it was the right thing to do. 'Luckily the Admiral's an early bird,' said Heinrichs to Alex and Grosman, 'so he'll be there now.'

They had sat and listened to the conversation between Heinrichs and the base commander, mesmerized. Now Alex wanted to leap up and shout, *'My God, are you, the Kriegsmarine, going to take us into the Admiral's office?* Conduct us into the inner sanctum? Are you, the Germans, going to give us a free, close-up view of that wonderful safe?' Instead, with only the most cursory glance at Grosman he said, as casually as he could, 'We are to meet the Admiral?'

Heinrichs indicated. 'He's right opposite. Just across the road. He lives a bit in the past, but don't take any notice of that. As admirals go, he's not a bad sort.'

They had never expected to enter the building until they broke into it. Now the Germans themselves were to take them on the reconnaissance they most wanted to make. The building they had first seen in the air photos in the quiet of the Broadway office in London, then looming through the blackness of the night, and this morning through their own window, they were to be taken into as honoured guests. They would know in a few minutes whether the interior was as unchanged as the exterior and whether the safe had been moved. Had they tried to contrive the visit, they would never have succeeded. Dame Fortune, Lady Luck, their special star, whatever it was, was not just close to them, but a step ahead.

They finished breakfast, drank their last cup of coffee and left the mess. The twenty yards across the road seemed a mile. Each had his own individual struggle to keep calm and smother his excitement. The big Mercedes car with the admiral's pennant was parked outside the building exactly as in the air photos. Even the doorway gave them a sense of *déjà vu*. Then they were in the building and taking in everything around them. The number of steps across the small lobby, the flight of stairs to their left, the exact position of the door to the adjutant's room and the number of paces from that room to the door of the Admiral's office. Then they were there. In the holy of holies.

They stood before the Admiral, saluted but had a struggle to concentrate upon him. Beside the desk, hard against the wall, was the large, deep green object, the focus of their odyssey. It was exactly where Chidson said it would be and it fitted the description. Alex was certain it was the same safe. He had no doubt whatsoever. So far, at every turn, luck was keeping up with them.

The Admiral was saying that he had no objection whatsoever to their going out on patrol. In fact, it was an excellent idea. The more the various arms of the services got to know each other, the better it would be for the Reich. Alex only had the vaguest idea of the words. He heard them and they made sense in his mind, but even when he was looking at the Admiral, all he seemed to see was the safe.

The Admiral got up from behind his desk and held out his hand. Alex and Grosman shook the hand and gave the correct smile to the smile of the grey-haired man in front of them. Then they saluted again, smartly about-turned and made for the door.

'You must dine with me tonight.'

Alex and Grosman halted and looked back. The Admiral was still standing behind his desk, one hand out towards them.

'Of course, you must. It isn't every day one meets two young men from the Eastern Front. There's a lot I want to ask you. A very great deal. I read reports and listen to the wireless but there's nothing like getting it straight from the horse's mouth.'

'Thank you, sir,' said Alex, hoping he hadn't blanched too much. 'Thank you very much. We shall look forward to that.'

'Seven-thirty,' said the Admiral, 'and have a good day.' He looked at Heinrichs. 'Perhaps we can show our guests some real action?'

'Let's hope so, sir,' said Heinrichs.

The Admiral turned back to Alex and Grosman. 'It's not only the Luftwaffe that sees action, you know. We got an English submarine out there not so long ago.'

Alex grinned with feigned pleasure. They saluted the Admiral a second time and went out on to the cobbles. Half an hour later they boarded the corvette. The day was cold with low, scudding clouds and a sharp breeze that blew from the north-east. They shared the bridge with Heinrichs, a young Leutnant, the bosun and a signaller. Alex and Grosman were brought fur-lined, reed green anoraks and but for the lighter blue of their headwear and trousers were indistinguishable from the ship's company.

They slipped their moorings a few minutes before nine and headed out of the harbour into a choppy sea that grew decidedly rough as they turned west and steered through the narrows of the Marsdiep that separated Den Helder and the mainland of Holland from the island of Texel. In the open sea, two miles out from the coast, they steered south. With the wind and sea abeam, the corvette rolled alarmingly. As they had asked for the journey, Alex and Grosman did their best to appear to be enjoying it. Alex managed to keep a grin and listen to the explanations Heinrichs gave, but Grosman had to clutch the rail and suffer silently. They turned about, just south of Bergen. Heinrichs picked out the landmarks for them. Alex went close to Grosman and whispered, 'Never thought we'd be out here like this four days ago.'

'Let's hope, for all our sakes, that that damned submarine's not hanging about,' groaned Grosman.

They looked at the sea expecting to see a periscope or the track of a torpedo. But the sea seemed too wild for anything else to live on it or under it.

'And that when we go back, this bloody boat's tied up in harbour,' added Grosman, between his teeth.

Alex laughed.

When they steered north into the wind and waves, the corvette pitched alarmingly. On the bridge they were constantly being drenched in spray. It was when they were out of sight of land, just turning east to begin the journey home, that the alarm bells sounded with their harsh, shrill clatter. Heinrichs called, 'Hard to port!' and the corvette heeled like a motor cyclist on a ninety-degree bend. The horizon that had been rising and falling so frighteningly now suddenly stayed somewhere above them and they were staring down into the green depths of an angry sea. The next moment Heinrichs was calling, 'Hard to starboard!' and the horizon was beneath them and they were staring into the grey sky. In the midst of this wild zigzagging, a plane flew out of the clouds and passing directly overhead dropped a stick of bombs. They flung themselves into the shelter of the bulkhead and watched the bombs come slowly down and the flak go up. The plane disappeared back into the clouds and the bombs burst harmlessly into the sea.

'The bloody RAF!' whispered Alex under his breath and the Kapitänleutnant laughed and talked about 'a bit of action especially for them'. Two hours later they were back in Den Helder tying up in their berth. They thanked Heinrichs profusely and, with the great stones of the quay seeming to sway beneath them, staggered back to the mess.

*   *   *

As they washed and got ready, both realized just how nervous they were about having dinner with the Admiral. The fact that they would have to be on their best behaviour, that the Admiral was unlikely to get merry like Heinrichs in the café or more or less drunk like Bachmann and that as a mature and senior officer he might be expected to ask deep and penetrating questions, particularly about the war in Russia, sent shivers through them. In the event they need not have worried. Like so many senior officers in late middle age, the Admiral liked to talk himself. And tonight he had a most polite captive audience. An audience that unlike his own officers had heard none of his stories, nor experiences.

The Admiral was fifty. He was a handsome man with grey hair cropped close in the Prussian style, a round, cheerful face and pale blue eyes that seemed to convey nothing but friendliness. In the 1914-18 war he had been a Leutnant on the big battle-cruisers of Admiral von Hipper squadron. He had been at Jutland in the *Derfflinger* and seen the English battle-cruisers, *Queen Mary* and *Invincible*, blow up. To his everlasting shame he had been one of the officers at Scapa Flow and witnessed the scuttling of the High Seas Fleet. Now, although in something of a backwater in naval terms in that he had no real fleet nor any of his beloved capital ships, he did have an extremely responsible job. 'Coast defences,' he muttered. 'That's my task now. To keep the Englishmen out. We are turning Europe into one, massive, impregnable fortress.'

By the time they got to the main course, a fine loin of Dutch pork, Alex and Grosman knew that the Admiral had been in Chinese waters, East African waters and throughout the Mediterranean. For one horrific moment Alex was about to ask the Admiral whether he had ever been to Java, but he managed to stop himself in time. However, the fact that Alex had begun to speak reminded the Admiral that, in the interest of good manners, his guests must be allowed to say something. In addition, the excellent moselle, of which he was drinking far more than usual, was making him sleepy.

167

'Now, young fellows,' he said, looking from Alex to Grosman and back to Alex, 'tell me about *your* war. Exactly what is going on on the Eastern Front? I have a brother out there. I hear from him that people as respected as General Guderian have expressed astonishment at the quality of the Russian tanks?'

Alex dug into the depths of his memory and imagination and again thanked God and Chidson for his briefing. He was thankful too that he was with sailors and not airmen. He said that as a fighter pilot he hadn't seen all that much of events on the ground. His job had mostly been interception. But he had certainly seen a good few Russian tanks burning.

'I have heard', said the Admiral, 'that there were times where the swiftness of our advance and the lack of suitable airfields left our fighter bases too far back to give proper cover to the soldiers?'

Alex agreed. That had certainly been true in the early days, but it only proved how fast the advance had been.

'Who is your commanding officer?' asked the Admiral suddenly.

'For most of the time we have been operating with the Second Panzer Group, sir,' said Alex, 'first on the Minsk and Smolensk Fronts and then more recently nearer to Orel. Colonel Mölders is our commanding officer.'

'I hear from my brother that Smolensk was taken almost intact and that it has a very beautiful cathedral that the Bolsheviks had turned into an anti-Christ museum?'

'We never actually went into Smolensk, sir. We were a little way south operating from an airfield at Shatalovka not far from the town of Prudki.'

The Admiral was satisfied. The strange Russian names were evidently too much for him. He called for brandy and observed that as it was now winter he supposed little was happening and that little would happen until the spring. 'You're absolutely right, sir,' said Alex, with all the confidence of an Eastern Front veteran. 'The weather now is quite appalling. Hard to imagine. Conditions for the soldiers terrible. In our section of the Front there isn't a single decent road. Everything was a quagmire in the autumn, we had our first snow as early as the sixth of October and now there's nothing but frost.'

'Frostbite?' asked the Admiral vaguely.

'It's like an epidemic,' said Alex, 'and when we left, the temperatures were so low, the oil was freezing in the engines.' Alex looked to Grosman for confirmation.

'Thirty-one degrees below, sir,' said Grosman.

The Admiral sighed, and said how glad he'd been to hear Dr Goebbels announce on the wireless that every man on the Russian Front was now well fitted out with thick winter clothing. With that observation, he shut his eyes. The dinner formally ended just after ten with the Admiral jerking awake and saying that he must go to bed. He asked them where they were sleeping and whether they were comfortable.

'We're upstairs in the mess,' said Alex, indicating, 'and we've got an excellent room.'

Jocularly the base commander pointed out that the Admiral didn't live in the mess. It wasn't good enough for him.

The Admiral beamed. 'I must admit, I'm even more fortunate. Those Dutch sailors certainly knew how to look after themselves. I have the old Admiral's rooms. Everything I could want.' He lowered his voice in mock confidence. 'Bath . . . double bed, real springs and a feather mattress. None of your old horsehair.' He pointed across the road. 'Better than being on board ship in the winter.'

The Admiral thanked them for their company, observed that he wasn't as young as he used to be and left. They had a few more drinks then went back to their room. Once inside, they locked the door and took down the blackout. The sky was broken cloud and there was no moon, but they had little difficulty in making out the black bulk of the building opposite. The longer they looked the more their eyes grew accustomed to the darkness. They watched the front of the building and listened for the patrols. They saw someone come out of the building and he appeared to shut the front door without locking it. Later he returned and came out a second time. Neither upon entering nor leaving did he appear to take the time to unlock or lock the door.

'Looks like he's not locking it,' whispered Grosman, in relief. 'We won't have to pick it.'

'Let's hope he's not going to make a practice of going in and out,' said Alex, grimly.

They heard the patrol marching along the cobbles and timed it as it went past. 'Nineteen and a half minutes,' said Grosman when they heard the sound of the boots again.

'We'll give them another two or three goes. Make sure there's no variation.'

Again they timed the patrol. Now they could not only hear it, they could see it. It consisted of four men, helmeted, armed and wearing greatcoats. The first gap was just over twenty-one minutes, the second close to twenty. They decided that twenty minutes was the regulation time. Whatever they had to do when they crossed the road, they should either try and get it done within the twenty minutes or remember to lie low at that critical period.

At midnight they took off their Luftwaffe uniforms and put on the black trousers of their civilian suits and dark blue sweaters. They blackened their faces with the cream Chidson had given them, put on black plimsolls and black, cotton gloves and completed the camouflage by pulling black, woollen caps over their heads. They checked the tools they might need and stuffed them into their pockets. Alex flashed the torch. It worked.

'The key!' whispered Grosman.

Alex grinned, took the key of the safe out of his suitcase and put it in his pocket. Grosman checked that the key was there. They went on watching from the window of their room until two in the morning. The patrols were regular at twenty-minute intervals and no one had entered or left the building for the last three hours. The base slumbered, two in the morning is the nadir of the twenty-four hours. They decided it was time to move.

The moment the patrol passed, they unlocked their door, shook hands, in soft whispers wished each other good luck, then slipped out into the corridor. They crept down the stairs and opened the front door of the mess. They glanced quickly to left and right then ran across the road to the dark building that Alex had first seen in the air photos and Chidson had called 'the pearl in the oyster'.

They reckoned that the front door should be unlocked and it was. They had been inside the building and now knew what to expect. They were prepared to pick the lock to the Admiral's office, but that too was unlocked. They went into the room and checked that the blackout completely obscured the windows. Alex shaded his torch and flashed it on the safe. He took the key from his pocket and inserted it into the lock. He tried to turn the key to the left, but it would not go. He tried again using more pressure. There was no movement.

'It's an old lock,' whispered Grosman. 'Maybe it turns the other way?'

Alex tried to turn the key clockwise but again there was no movement. He took the key out and stared at it. It was a big key, apparently unbroken nor distorted in any way. He put the key back in the lock and tried a second time. The key was jammed tight and refused to turn. Alex indicated to Grosman that he should have a go. Grosman tried turning the key in both directions without success. Shaking, the sweat running down his cheeks, Alex took the key out and tried to insert it upside down. In that position he couldn't even get the key into the lock.

Alex looked at Grosman. The sweat was now making lines through the blacking on his face. His hands were shaking, he was moving his head from side to side in a gesture of deep and hopeless despair. 'It doesn't work. *It won't work!*'

Alex fought back the tears. After all the strain of the months of training, the journey, the visits to the Den Helder bars, the entrance into the barracks, culminating with the dinner at the Admiral's table, his nerves were near breaking point. The good luck that had followed them so closely right up to this moment had suddenly vanished. Alex could not believe it nor could he understand the change. He felt bitterly cheated.

'*The buggers have changed the lock.*'

'There could be a key in one of the drawers.'

At great speed, but with all the silence they had been taught, they searched the drawers of the desk but there was no key. They looked into the shelves of manuals and under the carpet by the desk and found nothing. Then they stopped and stared at each other.

'What the hell do we do now?' whispered Grosman.

Alex glanced at his watch but said nothing. Five minutes of their precious time had gone. He went back to the safe, crouched down and examined the lock. He had no plan, no idea, but he hoped that by staring at the lock, something would materialize.

'It's an ordinary lock,' whispered Alex, 'a very ordinary lock. I mean, it hasn't got anything fancy on it. They must have just taken out the old lock and put in a new one.'

'Where do you keep the key to a safe?' whispered Grosman, almost to himself.

'In your pocket . . .'

Alex's mouth fell open. He stood up. He looked about the room, then clasped Grosman's arm. 'Wait here. Stay exactly where you are.' Alex made towards the door. 'I'll be back in one minute.' He held up one finger. 'One minute.'

He went out of the door, into the lobby. When they had been brought in yesterday to see the Admiral, Alex had noticed the flight of stairs. He had never expected to use them but he had made a mental note of their location along with everything else. Now he crossed the lobby, found the banister and began to climb the stairs. He climbed carefully and silently, testing each tread before putting his weight upon it. At the top was a small landing. He shaded his torch and flashed it. He saw a door, crept to it and stood outside listening. He heard snores from within. The snores were steady and evenly undulating. Whoever was asleep was well asleep.

The Admiral had told them that he occupied the Dutch Admiral's old rooms. He had indicated towards the building where his office was. It was extremely unlikely that he was the sole occupant of the building; at the same time it was a certainty that he had the best room. The door Alex stood against belonged to a central room that looked out over the front of the building. So far as Alex could make out from the configuration of the first floor, that room should be the best room. He could only conclude that the snores he heard came from the Admiral. Gently he turned the handle and pushed open the door.

There was no blackout at the window. Evidently, when

going to bed, the occupant of the room had taken the panels down. Alex made out the vague shape of a bed and tiptoed towards it. The occupant made no move but went on snoring. As he drew closer, Alex could just make out a head upon the pillow. He could see none of the man's features, but he was certain that the hair was grey and close-cropped. When he was standing very close he decided that the man in the bed could be none other than the Admiral and thanked his lucky stars that he had drunk so heavily of the excellent moselle and brandy they had had at dinner.

With his hands in front of him, Alex felt the back of a chair. The chair was close up to the bed. Moving stealthily, his fingers spread out, Alex felt the clothes hanging over the back of the chair. He identified a shirt and beneath it a pair of braces. Beneath the braces was a pair of trousers. Carefully Alex slipped his right hand into the pocket. At the bottom, amongst a handkerchief and a few coins, was a bunch of keys. He took a deep and silent breath. He gave a little prayer of thanks and, closing his hand around the keys so that they could make no noise, he gently withdrew the bunch from the pocket. He left the room as silently as he had entered and two minutes later was back downstairs in the Admiral's office.

'What the hell . . .?' murmured Grosman, staring at the keys in Alex's hands.

Alex put his finger to his lips and shook his head. Grosman was still staring at the keys in astonishment when Alex selected the largest and inserted it into the lock of the safe.

'Pray . . .'

Alex and Grosman shut their eyes. Alex turned the key anti-clockwise. It turned easily and sweetly. They heard the tumblers of the lock move, then Alex swung the heavy door open. Inside, occupying the bulk of the space on the top shelf, was a thick, two-foot roll of paper. They pulled it out and laid it on the desk. Gently they unrolled it and saw the line of the Dutch coast running south-east from the mouth of the Ems River. Alex glanced at his watch. Nine minutes of their precious time had gone.

Grosman switched on the desk light and took out his subminiature camera. While Alex moved the map, carefully unrolling it and sliding new portions under the light, Grosman photographed it. It was as Chidson had said, a massive sheet of paper, ten feet by two feet. Coping with the sheer size, manoeuvring the plan silently, was an exceedingly difficult task. Indeed, they had to work so fast, and were so occupied, they hardly noticed what was on the plan. It was only in the last few minutes, when nearly all of the twenty square feet had been under the desk light and before the lens of the camera, that they began to appreciate the staggering amount of information in front of them. The map showed what the Atlantic Wall would eventually be like. Most evident were the big fortifications, gun emplacements and blockhouses. But also marked were minefields, flame-throwers, ammunition dumps, anti-aircraft batteries and command posts. By each site the technical data had been religiously recorded. There were the calibre, range and firing angles of each artillery battery, and schematic diagrams of signals communications and radars. Engineers' stores and supply dumps were marked, as were the specifications of each fortification including the thickness of the protecting concrete.

They worked silently, saying nothing, moving the map and taking photos. The only noises were the rustle of the paper and the click of the camera shutter. When they had been there eighteen minutes, Alex signalled. They turned the desk light out and stood silently behind the blackout panels. They waited for the patrol to pass and gave them a minute and a half to clear the area. After the last photo, of projected blockhouses around Biarritz and north of the Spanish border, they rolled the map up exactly as they had found it, put it back into the safe in its original position, closed the safe and locked it. As they left the office and shut the door, Alex told Grosman to wait. He crept back up the stairs into the Admiral's bedroom and, reversing his original procedure, returned the keys to the Admiral's trouser pocket. Then he left the room, shut the door and crept back down the stairs. They had taken exactly half an hour. They had ten minutes to get back into the mess before the patrol passed again.

★   ★   ★

174

They ran across the road, into the mess, and crept up to their room on the first floor. They shut the door and the moment they were safely inside, Grosman whispered the question that he had had such difficulty in containing: 'Where the hell did you get those keys?'

'From the Admiral's trousers.'

Grosman was speechless. His mouth was open, his eyes were shining with success and he was shaking his head.

'If you remember, after dinner the Admiral very kindly told us where he slept and how nice it was. Well, he wasn't lying. It is nice. He has a lovely big bed and a well-upholstered chair beside the bed. It's on that chair that he thoughtfully laid his trousers.'

'Good God! You really *did go* into his bedroom!'

'When that damned key that Chidson gave us didn't fit and I squatted by that safe, we asked ourselves where the hell would the owner of the safe keep the key? I said, "In his pocket." The only problems were, was it in the Admiral's pocket or his adjutant's and which was the Admiral's bedroom?'

Grosman gave a deep sigh and collapsed on to the bed. Alex began to take the black off his face. 'Anyway, he was fast asleep and never even stirred. Thank God for that dinner and all the old man drank.'

'I'm glad you didn't tell me what you were up to,' said Grosman. 'I'd have had a heart attack waiting for you to come back.'

'That's exactly why I didn't.'

They grinned at one another. Only now was the success of their efforts beginning to sink in. They clenched their fists and shook their arms to express their excitement. They shook hands with grasps like iron. They were filled with emotions they had no proper way of releasing. They were still in an area of extreme danger. They couldn't leap upwards, shout 'Hurray!' or tell anyone. They would have to go on suppressing their joy until they were out of the barracks and away from Holland.

'Time we got all this stuff off,' said Alex, indicating the black streaks still on Grosman's face, 'and then we'd better get into bed like decent, law-abiding pilots.'

They cleaned their faces, undressed and hid their black clothes in their suitcases. They got into bed but they couldn't sleep. Excitement vied with anxieties. Grosman wondered whether he had worked the camera properly. He even wondered whether there might have been anything wrong with the film. They hoped Meisner was all right in the hotel. They talked a little about their training and how far away tonight was from the camp near Cardiff.

'You made yourself a real bloody nuisance that day,' said Alex.

'All for this,' said Grosman contentedly. Suddenly he sat up in bed. 'Hey, did you see what was *on* that map? *Everything*. Everything but the kitchen stove!'

'Go to sleep . . .'

Grosman was quiet for a while, then his thoughts were too much. 'What's so wonderful is to have done something *useful*. All that time while I was a kid in Berlin, we used to watch the Brownshirts strutting about. God, how we hated them! I was just twelve when they brought in the boycott of Jewish businesses. That was when they started dismissing Jewish officials, doctors and lawyers. That was when my father really began to suffer. I remember one hot summer's day when we went to a swimming pool and they wouldn't let us in. They stopped my grandfather going to his favourite concerts.' Grosman stopped and turned his head so that he was looking at the dark form of Alex in the next bed. 'Where were you in 1933?'

'In Java.'

'That was a bad year in Germany. I remember seeing Jews beaten up on the Kurfürstendamm, placards everywhere saying "Jews not wanted here". I remember that one evening in May, just before midnight, there was a massive torchlight parade that ended opposite the University on the Unter den Linden. That's where they burned the books. Hundreds of thousands of them. Good authors like Thomas Mann and Erich Remarque. With the Nuremberg Laws, 1935 was a bad year, an awful year, but that's when we got out.'

'Don't worry,' said Alex quietly. 'I may not have been in Germany, but I've seen them at work.'

176

'That's what's so wonderful, doing something to get our own back. Do you know, Alex, but for you coming to that godawful camp, the most I would ever have done against the Nazis would have been to fill a thousand sandbags.'

'We've still got to get back . . .' said Alex quietly.

'It's over,' whispered Grosman, shutting his eyes tight. 'It's over. We've paid them back, Alex, we've paid them back.'

Alex said nothing. For Grosman it might be over, he might even feel that he had paid them back, but for Alex there was more to be done. Much more had to be put into the scales before he could consider the balance level.

The next morning they had breakfast with Kapitänleutnant Heinrichs, thanked him for his hospitality and left the barracks. They contacted Meisner at the hotel then, still acting separately, returned to the safe-house at Alkmaar. From there, during the evening schedule, Meisner radioed to London that the mission had been accomplished. On the following evening they should hear when the submarine would return to pick them up.

19

For twenty-four hours, while they were not making up on lost sleep, they had talked and remembered. Alex and Grosman had recounted every second of their stay in the barracks. With repetition the story tended to become embellished. Already it was heading toward myth. To talk about it was not just to relive it, it was also a way of getting out the last of the tensions, the residue of the fear that had accompanied every step. Meisner, with little to recount of his own, was avid for details. He found it hard to believe the episode of the key and for a while thought Alex and Grosman were pulling his leg.

'You couldn't have done it, Alex,' he said, shaking his head. 'It's just not possible. Now, sitting here, it sounds almost damned stupid. How did you know which was his room?'

'He more or less told us at dinner,' said Alex. 'So far as I remember, there were only three doors on that landing and I took the middle one. If you'd seen the moselle and brandy he drank you'd have realized that an elephant could have walked in without waking him.' Alex paused, then added, 'It wasn't so much foolhardiness as sheer bloody desperation. We couldn't have come all this way and got that far and gone home empty-handed.'

'What about the key? The one that didn't fit.'

Alex indicated. 'It's upstairs.'

'You'll take it back?' asked Meisner.

'Of course. It belongs to Admiral Furstner. It's only on loan to Chidson.' Alex smiled. 'After the war, Furstner can throw it away.'

In some ways, Meisner's lot had been even harder. He had had to stay alone in the dingy little hotel ignorant of all that was happening, just praying that everything was going well and living with the constant, sickening knowledge that if things should go wrong, not only would he lose his companions, but the real Gestapo might bang upon his door at any moment.

'If I'd known what was going on I wouldn't have slept a wink that night.'

'If I hadn't been there,' said Alex thoughtfully, 'and it had just been you and Abe, one or other of you would have done the same. There was no other way.'

For the most part, their feelings at what they had done coincided, but in one important aspect they differed. Alex was Anglo-Dutch. He had no conflict. He hated the Nazis and the Germans. His personal vendetta over the fate of Rachel Blum spurred him along. After seventeen months, the sight of Rachel upon that bed with the marks around her neck had not dimmed. The return to Holland had merely sharpened that memory. Grosman and Meisner were German-born. Germany had been their country. They were Jewish, but they were also German. They hated what was happening in Germany, but they had had good times there. It hadn't always been bad. There was a great, underlying sense of sorrow for the country

178

that had fallen under the devil's spell. They had hit back at the Germans and were pleased, but in their minds they had hit back in particular at the marching feet, the black uniforms, the death's head, the runic flashes and the black swastika on its white circle set in blood red.

There was a lot to talk about and a lot to think about, events that with hindsight seemed like miracles, but even such drama as picking the pocket of a sleeping German admiral couldn't be recounted forever. Gradually the talk became sterile. Their thoughts became their own and they drifted into silence. They went back to their bookshelves and sank themselves into other people's, less exciting, stories. For Grosman and Meisner, but for getting back to the submarine, it was all over. All they were waiting for now was the evening contact with London. Then they would know just how much longer they had to hibernate in the safe-house. For Alex, the action was still in its infancy.

He held the book in his hands but was not concentrating upon it. He had been thinking and mentally preparing himself. Planning the details helped. Timing was extremely important. He had no wish to get there too early and become conspicuous, too late and miss his quarry. Every fifteen minutes he glanced at his watch. At last he decided it was the right moment. The other two were reading and neither took any notice of him, not even raising their heads as he went out of the room. He climbed up into the attic, took his SS uniform out of its hiding place and brought it down to his bedroom. He shook the dust off and then very carefully began to dress.

He was an SS-Hauptsturmführer in the SD, the Sicherheitsdienst, the SS Security Service. His uniform wasn't the notorious all-black service dress, so popular with senior SS officers in Berlin, but the now much more common olive jacket and pale blue trousers of the field units. He put on the white shirt and black tie and then the trousers and boots. He brushed his jacket again, put it on and clipped the black leather belt, with the pistol holster, around his waist. He checked himself in the mirror. On his left lapel were his insignia of rank, unique to the SS: two silver bars and three silver stars on a black patch.

On his left sleeve below the Nazi eagle was a black diamond with the letters SD in white. They were the most feared letters amongst all the German forces and in the Occupied Territories. Today Alex was happy with them for they had an almost paralysing effect on all those who set eyes on them and should certainly help see him through. Finally he put on the high olive cap with its black band, black peak, silver braid and silver death's head. With a grim expression into the mirror, Alex was satisfied. This was the uniform he had landed in, and first seen Occupied Holland in. It had sufficed then; it would suffice today. He took the two rolls of film with the photos of the map out of his suitcase and put them in his pocket. He took the Luger out of its holster and checked it. He slipped the magazine out of the butt and counted the eight 9 mm bullets. Satisfied, he clipped the magazine back in and returned the pistol to the holster. With his SS greatcoat over his arm he went downstairs and into the sitting room.

Grosman looked up from his book. In the winter light he saw the SS uniform before he saw the face. For an instant his heart stopped beating, the goose pimples rose on his back, his breath choked in his throat. Then he saw who was in the uniform and a different fear took over. The sickening fear that *he had* been betrayed. There was no rationality in his thoughts. For that instant he didn't question why someone should have come all the way to Wales to find him, train with him, merely to betray him. All he could see was Alex in his SS uniform, a grim expression on his face and, as his right hand went into his tunic pocket, it brought out the most incriminating evidence, the two rolls of film.

'For God's sake, Alex!'

Alex had no idea of the apprehension he had caused. He had only two thoughts in his head: the job ahead and the safety of the films. Now he held the films out towards Grosman. 'Look after these, Abe . . .'

'Is this some sort of joke?'

Alex looked bewildered. 'Joke?'

Grosman, his face white, got up and pointed at the SS uniform. 'What the hell are you wearing that for?'

'I have to go out.'

Meisner, who had followed Grosman's glance and also had his moment of terror, nodded. 'So we can see.'

'You might have warned us,' said Grosman, still not quite sure what was happening. 'Springing that uniform on a chap out of the blue could give the poor sod a heart attack.'

'We thought we'd finished everything,' said Meisner, then eyed the uniform. 'Evidently we were wrong.'

It was Grosman's turn again. 'Why dress up in that garb?'

Alex said nothing.

'We've got used to you going out in civvies. Why the sudden change?'

Grosman wanted to add something about a woman liking her man in uniform, but refrained. Alex looked down and saw the rolls of film in his hand. Again he proffered them to Grosman. 'Look after the films, Abe, that's the important thing.'

Grosman looked bewildered. 'Are you staying in Holland or something?'

'They're very precious.'

'I'll say they're precious. They could easily have cost us our lives.'

Alex put the films into Grosman's hand. 'If I don't come back, don't wait for me. Listen to the radio tonight and get your instructions on the submarine. Then beat it to London and *take those with you*.' Alex indicated the two rolls of film.

'For God's sake don't talk like that,' said Meisner. 'Just tell us what's happening.'

Alex took a deep breath. 'I can't tell you. It's something between me and . . .' He stopped and shrugged.

'Can't we help?' asked Grosman, 'Wouldn't you like one of us to shadow you?'

Alex wanted to say that he had help, but if Grosman and Meisner knew that, and were to be caught and made to talk, Wilking could be in jeopardy.

'I've got to do this on my own.'

'Then, for heaven's sake don't talk about *not* coming back,' cried Meisner.

Alex suddenly grinned and patted the SD badge on his sleeve. 'This'll help, don't worry.'

'It certainly frightened me,' said Grosman.

181

Once more they offered to help, the offer turning into a plea. Alex thanked them and refused any aid. He put on his greatcoat, patted the SD badge that was also on the greatcoat sleeve, gave a cheerful salute together with a smart click of the heels and went to the door.

'Whatever it is, Alex,' said Grosman anxiously, 'don't do anything stupid will you? Be careful.'

'I'll be as careful as we were careful in the barracks,' replied Alex, grinning.

Grosman shook his head. Alex opened the door and let himself out into the winter afternoon.

At a quarter to five, when it was already virtually dark, Alex walked slowly along Van Breestraat. He rang the bell of number 118, walked a little further and waited. Wilking opened the door and slipped out into the street. They strode along side by side.

'Have you got the car?'

Wilking nodded. 'No problem. Exactly what you asked for. A Wehrmacht car with SS number plates.'

Alex looked at his watch. If they were to be at the Court Building in the Prinsengracht ten minutes before Fatesma normally came out, they had exactly thirty-three minutes.

'Where is it?'

Wilking indicated. 'In the garage round the corner.' He paused, then said, 'You might as well tell me now exactly what you want me to do.'

'Drive me to the Court Building, keep the engine running, sit in the car and wait.'

'Nothing else?'

'Just drive away like hell afterwards.'

The car was one of the ubiquitous little Volkswagen Type 82, painted drab olive green and having its normal Wehrmacht number plates replaced by SS ones. In the shadows of the garage, a man gave Wilking the ignition key. No word was spoken but Alex knew that both he and his uniform had been carefully noted. They got in the car and Wilking drove out into the street.

'Straight to the Prinsengracht? We could be a little early and you said you didn't want to hang about.'

Alex looked at his watch. 'Go by the Leidseplein. It's as short a way as any.'

'Renewing an old acquaintanceship or getting a touch of inspiration?' asked Wilking, grinning.

'A bit of each.'

They drove north; Wilking knew exactly where Alex wanted to go in the Leidseplein. He took the car into the street beside the square and slowed in front of the grim outline of the prison. Alex saw the three arches of the entrance, the large central arch, and the two smaller arches on either side. Above the left arch was the word '*Portier*'. It was through that doorway that Chidson had charged with the marine sergeant just over a year and a half ago. Alex saw the date of the building, carved upon two stones, one above each of the smaller arches: 'ANNO 1891'. Alex decided that 1891 had been a bad year.

'OK, let's drive on.'

'You don't want to call in at the Achterburgwal too?'

'The Court Building on the Prinsengracht,' said Alex grimly.

They drove north again into the Leidsestraat and then into the Prinsengracht. They drove slowly along beside the canal until Alex told Wilking to pull into the side by the railings. They were twenty-five yards from the building and could see the bulk of its four storeys in the darkness. There were blackouts at all the windows, but a dull light shone from the foyer on to the three long stone steps that rose from the pavement.

Alex took off his belt with the holster and Luger and put it on again over his greatcoat, then he told Wilking to drive right up to the front of the building, but still to stay on the far side of the road by the canal. Wilking drove to the stop Alex indicated. Alex checked his watch. It was five-eighteen. Wilking looked at the pistol and said, 'You don't want to miss him.' Alex nodded and got out of the car.

The Court Building had three arched doorways ten feet apart. Alex stood at the bottom of the steps nearest to the left-hand doorway but able to cover the other two. It was an exceedingly cold day, the wind blew from the east and came

183

cutting down the street. Inside his heavy SS greatcoat Alex shivered. His hands inside his gloves were soon icy. But it wasn't just the weather that was making him shiver. It was the wait, the anticipation and the danger.

Men and women suddenly started coming out of the building, mostly using the doorway nearest to Alex. He scanned the men's faces eagerly, but Fatesma was not amongst them. He wondered if Fatesma hadn't come to his office that day. Perhaps he had a case elsewhere, or was sick. Then he looked up at the windows. In spite of the blackout, there were chinks of light from several of the first floor offices. Wilking had told him that Fatesma's office was in the front on the first floor. All the central offices still had lights on. Alex decided that his quarry had not left. All he had to do was to have patience and wait.

To steel himself he began to think again of Rachel. He saw the building on the Achterburgwal, tall and narrow with its five floors, large casement windows and small squat roof. The canal beside which they had walked when coming back from the pictures. The sparsely yet prettily furnished room he had grown to love and in which he had found such happiness. And Rachel herself, so elegant and beautiful. He saw her and heard her. He remembered her words about the Nazis, but at the time, in his innocent youthfulness, they had meant little. Now the words were real and the horror in them, the horror of her memory, was real. He remembered too Rachel telling him that she was safe in Holland. He heard her words again and gave a silent, sardonic laugh. On that cold pavement on that cold winter evening, he saw her face and heard her voice. The big dark eyes and the black flowing hair were there in the darkness. The calm quiet voice that had given him such pleasure haunted him. With Rachel clear in his mind, he knew that what he was about to do was right.

Alex moved into the soft glow from the foyer lights and checked his watch. It was a quarter to six. The fear that Fatesma had already left the building returned. He glanced up at the windows of the first floor and was relieved to see that there were still chinks of light at the edges of the blackout. He looked back at the car and Wilking, but in the darkness

Wilking was invisible. He went back to thinking about Rachel and cursed Fatesma for keeping him waiting.

It was five minutes to six when a lone man came out of the Court Building. The man was wrapped in his overcoat and had a hat pulled tight on to his head. He was broad-shouldered and looked even broader wrapped up against the cold. Alex smothered a gasp and held his breath. He knew instantly that the figure was the man he remembered as the Public Prosecutor. He watched the man approaching. Each step Fatesma took seemed to be infinitely slow. Alex wasn't on the steps of the Court Building, he was watching a slow motion film in the cinema. Then beneath the rim of the hat, he saw the face. It was the same heavy, lugubrious face he had remembered so clearly and hated so much.

Fatesma was tired and irritable for he had had a long and wearisome day. He was beginning to loathe the winter and the evening journey in the blackout, and liked to get away from his office promptly at five-thirty. Tonight he was late, and that always put him in an ill mood. Then he saw the SS uniform in front of him and thrust his personal feelings aside. He knew many of the SS and considered them his friends. Now he raised his arm in the Hitler salute. Alex ignored it.

'Fatesma, now Attorney-General, once Public Prosecutor?' Alex had found his mouth almost too dry to speak, his tongue had actually hurt. He hoped his voice had sounded sufficiently firm.

Fatesma stopped and nodded. 'That's me.' He noted the black collar patch with the two silver bars and three silver stars and the silver epaulets with the gold stars. 'What can I do for you, Herr Hauptsturmführer?'

'Do you remember Rachel Blum?'

Fatesma frowned and looked puzzled. 'A lot of people go through my hands every year, Herr Hauptsturmführer, a very great number.'

'Rachel Blum was the Jewish girl who lived in the Walletjes.'

Fatesma saw the black diamond with the letters SD in white on Alex's left sleeve and it triggered his memory. 'Of course,

I remember her. She was the bitch that worked for British Intelligence. We sorted her out all right. Did exactly what you wanted.'

'You served the Reich well, Fatesma,' said Alex, gritting his teeth, 'very well indeed.'

'Thank you,' said Fatesma, and made as if to pass Alex.

'Do you remember me?'

Fatesma peered into Alex's face. Alex was no longer sweating nor shivering, he was deadly calm. He was actually enjoying Fatesma searching his face, seeking some clue to the identity of the SS officer who had so abruptly stopped him on his way home.

'You look familiar . . .' said Fatesma, shaking his head. 'But I am very sorry, Herr Hauptsturmführer, as much as I should be able to remember you, I can't exactly recall who you are.'

Alex unbuttoned his holster and put his hand around the butt of the Luger.

'I am Alex Richards, the man you framed for the murder. The murder of Rachel Blum.'

Fatesma took a step back. His eyes went down to Alex's right hand. He saw the barrel of the Luger as it came up towards him.

'Alex Richards . . .' he said stupidly, staring up at the silver death's head on the band of Alex's cap.

Alex saw the curled lips that had so infuriated him during his trial and which had reminded him of a wolf. He remembered the black beetle, the shaggy he-devil and the cross between a giant and a toad. He remembered Fatesma raving at him in the Prosecutor's office and sneering at him in court. But above all he remembered Rachel lying still on the bed, her black dress hardly ruffled, her hair across the pillow, the red weals around her neck and the blue tinge upon her lips. He remembered the handcuffs biting into his wrists as he tried to reach out to her, and the chill when he laid his head upon her breast.

He took a step forward, cocked the Luger then brought it up towards Fatesma's chest and pressed the muzzle into the overcoat exactly over the Prosecutor's heart.

'I have a present for you from Rachel Blum . . .'

Fatesma's eyes, wide with horror, went down towards the pistol. He had begun to say, 'No . . .' when Alex pressed the trigger.

Alex watched the black bundle collapse at his feet and wondered whether to fire again, but Fatesma lay sprawled, face downwards, one knee under him, and there was nothing to aim at but the arched back. In any case, there was no sign of life. The bullet must have gone through the man's heart and blown it apart. Alex stood staring down for what seemed an eternity, then he turned and ran down the steps. Wilking had brought the car across the road, the engine was running, the near side door open. Alex jumped in and slammed shut the door. He was conscious of someone coming out of the Court Building, moving towards the heap on the steps that had once been the Public Prosecutor and looking towards the Volkswagen. Then Wilking let in the clutch and they were racing along the Prinsengracht.

'Anyone behind us?' shouted Wilking.

Alex turned his head but could see no one. They drove at high speed towards the Concertgebouw, Alex constantly looking back to see whether they were being followed. With no other car behind them, Wilking drove back to the garage. They left the Volkswagen and walked out into the road.

Alex took out his handkerchief, tipped back his cap and wiped his forehead. 'Thanks, Paul, thanks very much. I couldn't have done it on my own. I needed you there.'

'One gone and one to go,' said Wilking quietly. 'And one more after the war.' He glanced at Alex. 'I hope the gentleman tomorrow won't be any more difficult.'

'It's a long drive,' said Alex thoughtfully. 'It will give us time to talk.'

They watched him come into the safe-house, take off his SS greatcoat and make a big, strong cup of coffee. They asked no questions, just showed their relief in their eyes and faces. Alex sat, put his feet up and drank the coffee. He watched his companions watching him and gave a faint smile. He was grateful for their silence for at that moment his thoughts were too complex for words.

Rachel was dead; now Fatesma, the man who had instigated her murder, was also dead. And yet Fatesma had not been the prime mover of the crime. That had been the Gestapo. One day Alex hoped to learn their names. One day . . . Gently he shook his head. How high, how far back could he go? Ultimately all trails led to Hitler and that conclusion was ludicrous. Fatesma he had met. The Public Prosecutor had hated and tormented him. Within Alex's vision, Fatesma was the pinnacle. The knowledge that Fatesma was dead had left him strangely flat when he had expected to be elated. He put the flatness down to tiredness and the fact that he had one more awesome day in front of him. He realized too just how lucky he had been on the steps of the Court Building. He had grown angry at Fatesma for keeping him waiting for so long, but in the end the man had come out of the building on his own. There had been no police witness, no German military, no one to pursue the car. Indeed, good fortune had been his companion ever since he had stepped out of the dinghy upon the beach six days ago.

'We've been lucky . . .' said Alex, almost to himself. 'Do you think it will go on?' He looked up into Grosman's and Meisner's faces. 'Do you think luck will always stay with us?'

'We weren't lucky over the key,' said Grosman.

'That was bad luck turned to good luck,' said Alex.

Meisner indicated Alex's SS uniform. 'You're not talking about the key are you? Or the map? You're talking about what *you're* doing. What you're *doing on your own.*'

'It's the same luck,' said Alex.

For a while they were silent, then Grosman said, 'Have you more to do or was today the end?'

'One more day. Tomorrow afternoon and evening. But I'll do my best to get back here tomorrow night.'

Alex went upstairs and changed out of his uniform into his civilian clothes. He cleaned his Luger and checked it. He had seven bullets left. They should be enough, even for a giant like Deepground.

That night, in the safe-house at Alkmaar, they heard on the radio that the submarine would pick them up in two days' time. Alex breathed a sigh of relief. He had worked his own schedule out perfectly.

20

Again dressed in his SS uniform, Alex left the safe-house at a quarter to ten in the morning and caught the train to Amsterdam. Soon after eleven, with Wilking driving, they were in the Volkswagen, heading north-east towards Zwolle, the first town on their long journey to Drente. The low clouds of early morning had given way to patches of pale blue sky. But the air was cold and, in the semi-open Volkswagen, both men had their overcoat collars pulled up and their caps well down.

'Did you sleep well last night?' asked Wilking. 'That is, if you have a decent bed, wherever you are.'

'I've got an excellent bed and I did sleep well. Very well.'

'No ugly mugs looking at you from out of the darkness? No nightmares?'

Alex was silent for a moment, then he said, 'I had to do it, Paul, you know I did. I told you, I came over here to do this. I'd sworn to do it long ago, but I never knew how it would happen. They have to be made to pay for what they did to Rachel.'

Wilking gave Alex a glance. 'Are you sure it is *all* for Rachel? You're not by any chance doing any of this for yourself are you?'

Alex said nothing.

'After all, they did treat you pretty bloody badly.'

'That had an effect,' conceded Alex.

Wilking nodded. 'I bet it did.' He hesitated then said, 'But I don't blame you. Fatesma, Deepground, Bearends, all those Nazis are real bastards, but you're taking a terrific risk.'

For some miles they drove in silence, then Alex said, 'What do you think about luck?'

'Luck?'

Alex nodded. 'Yes, good luck and bad luck. Everything going right for you?'

'You have to believe in good luck in Holland these days. You'd give up if you didn't.'

'Do you believe that if you're in the right, good fortune will favour you? If you set out to do something, something that should be done, luck would be on your side?' Alex glanced across at Wilking. 'The British talk a lot about fortune favouring the brave.'

' "*Fortis fortuna adjuvat*", Terence,' said Wilking laconically. 'Virgil puts it, "*Audentis fortuna adjuvat*". It's been around a long time. Anyway, why shouldn't luck be on the other side? The German side?'

'Because they're in the wrong,' said Alex simply.

Wilking was not disposed to argue. He wasn't quite certain of the logic of anything, but he had to agree that the Germans were in the wrong.

'Luck was certainly on your side yesterday. Come to think of it, it seemed to be on your side all the time. I don't know what else you're doing over here but I assume that also needs a bit of luck?'

'That's just what I mean, Paul. It worries me, how lucky we've been. I can't tell you what's been happening, but now I come to think about it, we've certainly had our ration of luck.'

'And you're worried it might run out?'

'It's a thought. A little nagging doubt.'

'You mean we might find a road block round the next corner and they might start taking you to pieces.'

'They'd also start taking you to pieces,' said Alex, laughing.

The conversation was too tempting of fate to continue. They lapsed into silence. After a while Wilking said, 'Have you worked out what to do with Deepground? There are bound to be sentries at the gate of that camp. It won't be like the Court Building. You can't shoot him on the doorstep like you shot Fatesma.'

'We'll have to entice him away.'

'I can't say I altogether like the idea. You told me he was a bit of a gorilla.'

'Oh, he's the heavyweight all right, the one who does the ultimate dirty work, but I never thought he had much brain. Bearends was a miserable little horror but he had ten times the brain of Deepground.'

'Where do we entice him to?'

Alex shrugged. 'We'll tell him we're going to take him to see someone. Someone important. That'll make him come, he's not just a stupid bastard, he's a vain one too.'

'Put him in the car?' cried Wilking in horror.

'I'll sit in the back with him. I've got the Luger if he turns awkward.'

Wilking grunted. They drove on into the afternoon, not stopping until they reached Hoogeveen where they went into a café and had coffee. They now had less than twenty kilometres to cover and from Hoogeveen took a cross-country route to Westerbork. They arrived at Westerbork at 4 p.m. just as it began to get dark. They found the concentration camp, a small one set near the town and surrounded by pine forests. They drove slowly past the gate and, as Wilking had suspected, there were sentries there as well as others stationed on two towers near the road. Three hundred yards beyond the barbed wire of the camp, Wilking pulled into the side of the road and stopped.

'Where now?'

Alex glanced at his watch. 'Let's drive around a bit. Take any of the lanes into the forest. Let's find a particularly lonely one.'

They toured the immediate area, exploring every lane and side road within four kilometres of the camp gate. Some of the lanes had houses, others seemed too open, but they found one deep in the pine trees and particularly isolated. Alex decided it would do. They turned the car round and waited. They said nothing and just sat, staring into the darkness. At twenty minutes to six, Wilking drove back to the camp and parked a few yards from the gate.

Alex sat in the car, his hand on the butt of the Luger, his

mind filled with memories similar to those he had had the day before while waiting upon the steps outside the Court Building, only now it wasn't Fatesma sharing with Rachel in his mind but Deepground. He had no more difficulty remembering Deepground's face than he had remembering Fatesma's. The etching in his memory had not dimmed. The cold grey eyes, the big mouth, the massive shoulders were as clear this evening as they had been in the courtroom, but now it wasn't so much Deepground's face and shoulders that haunted Alex, as his hands. They were the hands that had beaten him, the hands that had strangled.

'Did you ever see Deepground?'

'I don't think I ever had the pleasure.'

'When Bearends was doing the interrogation, Deepground used to stand just behind me. He used to shout in my ear. If I turned or said anything, he clouted me. He had a hell of a punch. He beat me up in the cell once – luckily, I passed out.' Alex turned his head slightly. 'He was the one who strangled Rachel . . .'

Wilking knew, he'd been told. But he knew that Alex had to say it again, that Alex was reliving it all. 'You be careful of him in the car. I shall be in the driver's seat, remember. The last thing I want to feel are his hands on *my* neck.'

'He won't do anything with an SS uniform beside him.'

Alex glanced at his watch. It was after six. 'When we go to get them, they're always late.'

'I can't say I blame them,' said Wilking drily. 'If they haven't got luck on their side, if you've got it all, then maybe they have a bit of sixth sense. Perhaps last year when they were beating you up, tormenting you, they decided that you were such a resilient bugger, you'd be back. Perhaps they knew then that once you had the bit between your teeth you'd never let go. After all, they never managed to break you down, did they?'

Alex smiled. Wilking was trying to help, keeping their spirits and morale up.

They watched the gate but there was none of the exodus from the camp that there had been from the Court Building. Between ten to six and ten past, only three men came out and

192

none was Deepground. Alex began to tap his fingers on his thigh with impatience.

'You actually get angry with them for keeping you waiting, don't you?'

'Very. We've got a long drive back and I've got a train to catch.'

Wilking began to laugh. Alex could see nothing to laugh at. 'It *is* funny,' said Wilking, 'damned funny. I can't explain it, but it's damned funny. You waiting to shoot a man and that man keeping you waiting. If that's not funny, I'd like to know what is.'

Again Alex glanced at his watch. 'A quarter past six. The bastard went home early. Or he's on leave. We've come all this way for nothing.'

Wilking pointed through the windscreen. The camp gate had been opened and a giant of a man had come out into the road. Now he was walking slowly towards them. Alex took a deep breath and stepped out of the car. Like Fatesma, Deepground saw the SS uniform, the silver death's head on the cap and the badges of rank on the collar and shoulders. He threw up his hand in the Nazi salute. 'Heil Hitler!'

This time Alex returned the salute. 'You are Herr Deepground?' Alex asked in German.

'Yes, Herr Hauptsturmführer, I am Deepground.'

Alex felt his mouth going dry, all the tensions were back in his stomach. The sight of the man, the sound of his voice were reminders of the most terrible days of his life. He wanted to shoot Deepground there and then and forget the plan he had worked out. Then, over Deepground's shoulder, he saw the sentry. Alex indicated the car. 'Will you please come with me. I have something very important to discuss. Something that cannot wait.'

'Something special, Herr Hauptsturmführer?'

'Very special. Very important and very urgent.'

Without the slightest hesitation, indeed with an air that, in spite of being tired after a hard day's work at the concentration camp, he was only too delighted to be of use to an SD officer, Deepground got into the car. As he settled his great frame in the back seat, as Alex got in beside him and Wilking let in the clutch and the car began to move away, Deepground appeared completely contented. The SS uniform and the SS number plates had been as reassuring as a lifebelt to a drowning man.

'Where are we going, Herr Hauptsturmführer?'

'Not far. There is someone I want you to meet. Please be patient.'

'Is it a job you want me to do, Herr Hauptsturmführer?'

'A sort of job . . . yes.'

Deepground nodded. Alex gave him a glance, but it was too dark inside the Volkswagen to make out anything more than the barest outline of his face. 'Do you like your job at the concentration camp?' asked Alex a little stiffly.

'Very much.'

'I understand you are the commander there.'

'I am indeed, Herr Hauptsturmführer.'

'Have you many prisoners?'

'We're quite a small camp, however we do have a lot of Jews.' Deepground paused, then added rather sadly, 'We don't keep them for long. After a while we send them away.'

Alex said nothing. Wilking turned the wheel sharply and swung the car off the road into the lane. Deepground was surprised and looked out of the car and then towards Alex. Wilking brought the car to a halt and Alex at once jumped out, drawing his Luger and standing a little way from the car.

'The person I want you to meet, Herr Deepground.'

Deepground got out of the car and looked into the darkness as if seeking someone. He turned slightly, back towards Alex, and saw the barrel of the Luger. 'What the hell's going on . . .?' he said gruffly then, nothing about him making sense, again looked into the darkness. 'Where's the man you said you wanted me to meet?'

'I am that man.'

Deepground turned back to Alex. He saw the pistol and shook his head. The man in the SS uniform was watching him intently, but he couldn't understand why.

'Who are you?' asked Deepground, his voice still gruff but now filled with suspicion and alarm.

'Don't you remember me?'

'I thought you were an SS officer. I thought . . .'

'I'm Alex Richards, the friend of Rachel Blum. You must remember Rachel Blum. You killed her, you strangled her. Then you, with Bearends and Fatesma, framed me for the murder. You used to beat me up, Deepground. Kick me.'

Deepground peered at Alex, trying to see his face in the darkness.

'*Where the devil have you come from?*'

'Never mind about that.' Alex's voice was cold with hate. 'I'm here to pay you back for what you did to Rachel Blum.'

Deepground stared at the barrel of the pistol. 'I only did what I was told! Bearends, Fatesma, they ordered me to do it!'

'You killed Rachel Blum, Deepground. You murdered her.'

Deepground's voice was cracked with fear. 'Give me a chance! *Go on, give me a chance!*'

'Did you give Rachel Blum a chance?'

'*I only did what I was told! Give me a chance!*'

Alex said nothing. He had said all he had to say. He had made sure Deepground knew what was happening, why he had to die. Suddenly Deepground lunged forward, his long arms outstretched, his hands trying to grab the Luger. Alex was ready. As the giant came towards him he fired three times. The man stopped, his arms and hands recoiled back towards his body, he clasped himself and began to bend. He said something that was indecipherable, stood swaying for a moment, then crashed to the ground like a felled tree. He lay face downwards as Fatesma had lain, made a few choked sounds, then suddenly throughout the forest there was a strange, lingering silence.

Alex stared at the body, his mind blank, his own body suddenly very tired. Slowly he put the Luger back into the holster. He was still staring at the dark heap sprawled beneath his feet when he became aware of Wilking struggling to turn the body over. Automatically Alex helped. In death Deepground seemed a prodigious weight. They had to heave with all their strength to turn him face upwards. Then Wilking ran his hands down the trunk until he found Deepground's pistol. With a flourish and the words, 'This will come in handy,' he put the pistol in his own pocket. Then he pushed Alex into the Volkswagen and drove quickly out of the lane into the road.

They drove south. For a long time neither spoke, both cradled within their own thoughts. For Alex, what had been tiredness while standing over the body of Deepground was now exhaustion. He laid his head back and closed his eyes. It had been an astonishing week. Everything he had set out to do he had accomplished. Looking back on it now, it was like a dream. It was even more like a dream because of the separation and secrecy of the two events. Only a tiny few knew about the safe and the map, only Wilking knew of the killing of Fatesma and Deepground. Then he opened his eyes and saw the reality. He was wearing SS uniform and in the magazine of his Luger there were now only four bullets.

Wilking too had his thoughts. He had been swept into something highly dramatic, had had a few days of tense and dangerous activity, and no doubt the person sitting next to him in the Volkswagen would disappear as suddenly and abruptly as he had arrived. There was always a sense of anti-climax when a short intense visitation came to an end, the more so when the visitor was an old and close friend. Now it would be back to his studies and the work in the Underground: the latter, although dangerous, was often tedious.

'When are you going back?'

'Soon. Very soon.'

'Do you think you'll come back to Holland?'

Alex thought for a long time. He was conscious again of the good fortune that had accompanied him so closely. Indeed, the feeling of luck now began to haunt him.

'I don't know. I suppose it's possible. It depends if they want me to come back.'

Wilking gave Alex a glance. 'It wouldn't be the same for you next time, would it? I mean, with Fatesma and Deepground dead, there wouldn't be the same sort of driving force.'

Wilking's words triggered two themes in Alex's mind. Fatesma and Deepground had been Dutch, but they had taken their orders from the Germans. Now Alex separated the Dutch from the Germans. In the English language, the word

196

'Dutch' was often used in a derogatory sense: 'Dutch courage', 'Double Dutch', 'Dutch comfort'. Now he thought of 'Dutch justice'. The justice he had received in Holland was 'Dutch justice' in the English sense of the word. He had repaid the 'Dutch justice' but the Germans still remained. 'There are still the Germans . . .' he said quietly. 'They started it all.'

Wilking drove fast, for Alex had said he had the last train to catch. Even so, it was almost midnight when they got back to Amsterdam. They abandoned the car behind the Central Station. Alex grasped Wilking's hand and gave it a hard, warm shake. 'Thanks, thanks a hell of a lot.' He paused, then added, 'It's tomorrow. I go back tomorrow. Look after yourself and I'll see you after the war.'

'Any more of these jobs, let me know,' said Wilking, grinning. 'Good luck and a happy landing in England.'

They parted in the night and each went in his own direction, Wilking back to his home in Van Breestraat and Alex into the station and on to the last train for Alkmaar and the safehouse.

Grosman and Meisner were still up. They were sitting at the kitchen table, dirty coffee cups in front of them and open books beside them. They looked at the door when it opened and stared at the tired figure in the SS uniform.

'Thank God,' said Grosman, and his voice and face betrayed the anxiety he had suffered and the relief he now felt, 'We'd given you up. We didn't know what the hell had happened.'

'I said I'd be late . . .' said Alex and threw off his overcoat. He went to the sink and started making coffee. The others watched, waiting for an explanation. At last Meisner said, 'Are you going to tell us?'

Alex made three cups of coffee and took them to the table. He sat and laid his arms out in front of him. 'I never told you about my own experiences in Holland, did I?'

'Not really,' said Grosman. 'You said you were in prison here. That the Dutch Nazis set you up in some way.'

'I knew a girl in Amsterdam called Rachel Blum.' Alex looked from Grosman to Meisner. 'Like you she was German

197

and Jewish. In her case however both her parents were Jewish. Her family got put in Dachau, she fled the country. She was working for British Intelligence in Holland and that's where I met her. To cut a long story short I fell in love with her.'

Alex stopped.

'And?' asked Grosman.

'You can't stop at that point,' said Meisner.

Slowly, fighting his tiredness and the sense of anti-climax that had begun to envelop him, Alex told them the full story of Rachel Blum, her murder, his own imprisonment and finally his own actions in retribution.

'You mean you've gone out *shooting the buggers!*' cried Grosman, in horror. 'While we've been sitting here, wondering what the hell's been happening, even to thinking that you might be about to give us the chop in some way, you've been running around Occupied Holland paying off an old private score!'

Alex was surprised at Grosman's reaction. 'I had to do it. I owed it to Rachel.'

'You could have told us, for God's sake. After all, there were *our* lives to consider too.'

'I couldn't involve you . . .'

'You could have been picked up,' said Meisner accusingly.

'Or trailed back here . . .' said Grosman.

'I knew I could do it,' said Alex quietly. 'I knew it would go off all right.'

'You do know, don't you, Alex,' said Grosman, 'that in spite of your cocksure attitude, you could have buggered up the whole thing. You could have buggered up all we came over here to do.'

Alex got up and made more coffee. He knew that his companions were right, he knew that he could have jeopardized them all, but it was a case of compulsion. He had acted as if he had no will of his own, as if that will had been taken over. As if someone else had been driving him. He sat down again at the table.

'I'm sorry if I've caused you worry . . .'

'You shot them both,' said Meisner, 'just like that? The

198

Public Prosecutor and the detective? You shot them in cold blood?'

'It wasn't cold blood . . .'

'Are you sure they're both dead?'

'Certain.'

There was a long silence, then Meisner said, 'I'm not saying they shouldn't be dead, I'm sure they should, I'm sure they were real bastards, it's just that to do it the way you did it must have taken a hell of a lot of something.'

'And the one that got away?' asked Grosman. 'Bearends or whatever his name was, are you saving him up until after the war?'

'If someone else doesn't get him in the meantime.'

Suddenly Grosman put his hand across the table and clasped Alex's forearm. 'If only you'd told us all this before. If only we'd known why you kept going out. If only we'd known what had happened to you the last time you were in Holland, it would all have made sense.'

'We'd have understood,' said Meisner.

'You'd have stopped me going out,' said Alex flatly. 'Or tried to have done. You'd have told me it was crazy.'

They were silent again, then Grosman said, 'You still should have told us.'

'I couldn't tell you. I couldn't tell anyone. I just had to get even with those bastards and that's what I've done.'

'You must have told someone,' said Grosman. 'You couldn't have done all that on your own. You said you drove to the north of Holland in a Wehrmacht car? Where did you get the car from?'

Alex said nothing.

Grosman suddenly shook his head. 'All right, enough said, I understand. Tell us when we're all back in England.'

'You took a godalmighty risk,' said Meisner.

'I know I did. But I've explained all that. I just had to do it.'

'You could still have told us. We'd both have helped.'

Alex shook his head. 'That just wasn't possible. Anyway, if anything had happened to me you two would have had to take the films back to England.'

'Ah, the films! The films of the map we came over for. I'd nearly forgotten them.' Grosman put his hand in his pocket, took out the two rolls and laid them on the table, 'Now you're back in one piece you might as well take charge of them again.'

'I'm really sorry . . .' said Alex. 'If it could have been managed, I would have liked you two to be there. I sort of missed you. You'd have enjoyed seeing those two bastards hitting the ground.'

He picked up the films and put them in his pocket.

The following night, dressed in their SS uniforms, they locked the safe-house, took the last bus from Alkmaar to Bergen and walked north-east. A little way up from the shore, sheltered by the dunes, they settled down to watch the sea. Alex put on a pair of special goggles and they waited for the signal. It came soon after midnight in the form of infra-red morse. Alex replied with the agreed code, flashing his own small infra-red torch. Fifteen minutes later they heard the grating of the rubber dinghy as it beached upon the sand. They handed their cases to the sailors and were rowed out to the submarine.

It was the same submarine with the same ginger-bearded Lieutenant Commander. In the wardroom they were given a stiff drink and changed into their civilian clothes. As they whispered to one another, the magnitude of what they had done began to dawn upon them. They had been in Holland, behind enemy lines, for *eight* days. They had accomplished all they had set out to do and they were *alive*. In Alex's case the wonder was even greater. His revenge had been sweet and Rachel Blum's spirit could rest in peace. In the womb of the wardroom the realization came slowly and patchily for the excitement had gone, the anti-climax had set in. They struggled to remember each of those eight stupendous days and convince themselves that they had really existed, but nervous exhaustion, the warmth, the gentle motion of the boat and the hum of the electric motors dulled their minds and made them drowsy.

They were two hours out from the Dutch coast when Alex, half asleep, half awake, had a chilling dream. Fatesma and

Deepground, dressed like clowns, were rolling over and over on the ground in front of him. As they rolled, they crept closer and clutched out towards him. They mouthed words he couldn't understand and laughed demented laughs. He awoke in a sweat with no idea where he was. Then he heard the drip of a single drop of water and knew he was sixty feet below the sea. The chilling dream turned into a chilling fantasy. Heinrichs' corvette, the one they had been on only four days ago, the one they had been taken out on as guests, was above them, hunting them.

Alex opened an eye to quell the panic and comfort himself. The wardroom had not changed, a bottle of gin stood on the small table, and both Grosman and Meisner, their heads back against the hard leather padding of the bench, were smiling in their sleep.

21

It was a cold but bright morning and the sun exactly matched their mood. Seaweed glistened on the wooden piles of the jetty, sparrows hopped in the dust of the roadway, gulls bobbed gently on the water. As they came up the gangway, still carrying the suitcases they had landed with, Chidson was standing by his car. His eyes were wide and shining and the joy that the mission he had thought almost impossible had ended so successfully and that his three agents had returned safely made his normally phlegmatic face glow.

Keeping his emotions in check, he offered his congratulations, gave each his firm handshake, then ushered them like chicks into the car. When they were out of the dockyard and on the main road to Dartford and London, he let his excitement and curiosity take over.

'We were damned relieved to get your signal, I can tell you.' He beamed at each one in turn. 'Of course, you'll get debriefed properly, but I must hear the bones of it. It sounds as if it all went astonishingly well?'

'Not all the time, sir,' said Alex, with a touch of humour in his voice. 'The RAF tried to bomb us and the key you gave us, the famous key of the safe, didn't fit the lock.'

Horror clouded Chidson's face. It was as if he had seen some hideous spectre. *'It didn't fit!'*

'They'd kept the safe but changed the lock.'

All the excitement drained from Chidson. He felt a chill within him. 'But you photographed the map?' he asked anxiously, paused, then added, 'You signalled that you had. Or are you telling me . . .?'

'We filmed the map, sir, we did that all right.'

'You . . . you filmed the map?'

'Every square inch of it.'

Chidson looked puzzled, he was frowning. 'If the key didn't fit, and that's what you've just said, how on earth did you get the safe open? You couldn't have blown it and I doubt very much if you could have picked it . . .'

'We got the right key,' said Alex simply.

Very quietly Chidson said, 'I think you'd better explain. Take your time and start at the beginning. The very beginning.'

Alex recounted all that had happened from the moment of their first visit to Den Helder to their departure from the base. As he talked, so Chidson began to frown. By the time Alex finished, Chidson's face was set hard. It was not the reaction that Alex and his companions had expected.

In Chidson's mind a world had snapped. His sense of well-being had vanished. He had just heard recounted in a matter-of-fact, almost blasé way a quite astonishing story. But for the key not fitting, everything had worked so perfectly, too perfectly, for Chidson to consider the story plausible. That after all the good fortune of getting into the barracks and being accepted there, the Admiral should be sleeping upstairs, right above the safe, his trousers hanging over the chair begging to have their pockets picked, seemed to Chidson's suspicious and intelligence-orientated mind too good to be true. Chidson's problem was further compounded by the fact that, were the story true, the courage to pick the pockets seemed to be almost superhuman.

202

When he had sent them out, as well trained and prepared as it was possible to be, in his mind Chidson had given them less than a fifty-fifty chance of success. When he had seen them on to the submarine he had had to admit to himself that that could well be the last time he would ever see them. Now they had come back having accomplished well nigh the impossible. It didn't fit, it was *too* easy. One thought kept pounding in his head. *He was dealing with double agents, they had been 'turned'.*

He glanced at Alex. 'Are you sure all that happened? Certain? You didn't by any chance dream it?'

'It happened all right, sir. Every bit of it. Ask Grosman, he was there.'

'The Admiral sleeping right above you, and *you took the keys from his pocket!*'

'He'd had a lot to drink. Wine and brandy. A whole troop of soldiers could have gone into his bedroom without waking him.'

'How did you know where he slept?'

'He told us at dinner . . .'

Chidson looked straight into Alex's face. 'He told you which room was *his*?'

'He indicated the building. I just crept up the stairs and went to what looked like the main room.'

Chidson looked at Grosman. 'You didn't go with him?'

'No, sir, I stayed in the office.'

Again Chidson looked into Alex's face. 'So you were on your own?'

'It only took two minutes, sir. The whole thing was a chance, an idea, it seemed mad not to try it.'

Chidson shook his head. He wanted to believe but it was exceedingly difficult.

After all he had done, all he had gone through, Alex felt cheated. 'It *worked*, sir, it worked perfectly, so I don't see why . . .' He stopped.

After a while Chidson shook his head a second time and said, 'All I can say is that if that's what you really did, it must have taken a lot of guts. A hell of a lot. I'm glad I didn't have to do it.'

'It was desperation, Colonel, sheer desperation. I didn't

203

really think about it. We were right in the place, we had the safe in front of us and we couldn't get the map out. It would have been impossible to come back empty-handed after getting so close.'

Alex put his hand in his pocket and took out the two rolls of film. He looked at them for a moment, then handed them to Chidson. 'It would be better if you had them now, sir. I like to think of them in safe keeping.'

Chidson took the film but went on staring straight ahead into the winter morning. Had the Germans worked all this out? Was some Gestapo officer, even now, sitting in his office in the Prinz-Albrecht-Strasse visualizing this very moment? Laughing his head off at the thought of British Intelligence taking possession of photographs made with the SD's blessing? In the face of the difficulties, the mission had been too successful. Espionage missions never worked that way.

Again Chidson glanced at the three men in the car. They were evidently surprised and disappointed by his reaction to their story, for that surprise and disappointment showed on their faces. But there was another expression, innocence. He reminded himself that he had met innocent-looking people before who were not what they appeared to be. He hated his suspicions but they were professional and correct. He particularly hated his suspicions of Alex and felt ashamed of them. Then he remembered Menzies' words about fortune favouring the brave. He relaxed a little, even allowed himself a slight smile. Indeed, for a while he did even more, he tried to persuade himself that his agents were spotlessly 'clean' and let his mind wander a little into the future.

As they were entering the grey suburbs of London, without turning his head Chidson suddenly said, 'I suppose now all this is over you'll want to go back to your old units?' He glanced at Alex. 'Back to the RAF, back to Manston?'

'After this,' said Alex thoughtfully, 'I don't see life ever being quite the same.'

Chidson looked at Grosman and Meisner. 'What about you two?'

'Filling sandbags was never really exciting, sir,' said Grosman, 'or very rewarding.'

'Anyway, going back to the Pioneer Corps would be a waste of our training, sir, wouldn't it?' added Meisner.

'One thing, sir,' said Alex. 'If we do ever go back, if you ever have another job for us, next time please make sure the key fits.'

Chidson smiled. He had spoken lightly, he had tested out their feelings for the future, but even with all his experience he was still not sure. This area of doubt, always a part of his job, was something he particularly disliked. All agents were brave. In the world of espionage, every traitor was a patriot. He sighed. The debriefing would tell. The debriefing was the great stripping that brought everything to light. Then he would know for certain.

'*Fortis fortuna adjuvat*,' he murmured to himself, unaware just how fortunate the brave really had been.

Epilogue

They were debriefed separately at the Royal Victoria Patriotic School in Wandsworth. In the course of the debriefing, each one had to account for every minute of his time in Holland. Inevitably, Alex's pursuit and killing of Fatesma and Deepground were discovered. When Chidson heard, he was furious and felt he'd been betrayed. He lambasted Alex on his stupidity and selfishness and even Menzies delivered a formal reprimand. For Chidson, however, there was more. The further he delved into the expedition, the more details he learned, the more concerned he became at the apparent ease with which the whole operation had been carried out. The luck and good fortune that had accompanied them, and in particular had accompanied Alex, rekindled all Chidson's suspicions. Once more he debated whether Alex Richards might not be a double agent, 'turned' by the Germans during his stay in Holland.

In the end, it was the shortness of the stay, only eight days, that made Chidson rule out anyone being 'turned'. Nevertheless, it wasn't until the end of a further lengthy period of interrogation that the Colonel became fully convinced of Alex's complete integrity.

After a short period in England, all three, Alex, Grosman and Meisner, returned to Holland and served there as agents during the Occupation for a further two and a half years.

The object of the mission, the photographs of the map, turned out to be of good quality. From them the original map was reconstructed and was to prove invaluable in Combined Operations planning.

Of the persons in the story, Mark Klisiak, the Polish foreman in the armaments factory near Dortmund who had copied the blueprints, and the lorry driver who had carried the envelopes to Rachel Blum in Amsterdam were both arrested by the Gestapo, tried for espionage and sentenced to death. Both were beheaded. The wrath of the Gestapo even descended upon

Klisiak's wife. She was arrested for not informing the authorities of her husband's treasonable activities and sent to a concentration camp.

Major Stevens and Captain Best, kidnapped at Venlo, were both subjected to many months of interrogation. That the interrogation was partly successful was evident from documents captured at the end of the war. In the *Informationsheft Grossbritannien*, an intelligence summary compiled by the Reich Security Agency early in 1940, there was a section on British Intelligence. The details of MI6 were particularly thorough and accurate, including its location and head, and in many cases the sources were named – most damning to them – as 'Captain Best' and 'Major Stevens'. Thanks to Schellenberg's influence, neither Best nor Stevens was badly treated and both survived to be released at the end of the war.

Walter Schellenberg survived the war, ending up with the rank of SS-Brigadeführer. He was interrogated by one of his victims, Alex Richards, and later wrote his memoirs. SS-Hauptsturmführer Joseph Schreieder also survived the war and he, too, was interrogated by Alex Richards. As for Bearends, the third of the Dutch Nazis, he really did disappear. He was never traced, and to this day the police in Holland have no knowledge of whether he is dead or alive.

To the Dutch penal system, so repressive in 1939, the war brought radical changes. The rules and regulations were relaxed and new and modern prisons built. The authorities realized that long sentences did not deter crime and now sentences in Holland are milder than anywhere in Europe. During the Occupation the Germans did lock up several judges and senior civil servants who found the prisons to be hell on earth, but even the Germans baulked at the idea of making their prisoners wear the hideous masks. The mask that Alex Richards had to wear, so much the trademark of his suffering, was the last of a long line.